THE ULVERSCROFT FOUNDATION
(registered UK charity number 264873)
was established in 1972 to provide funds for
research, diagnosis and treatment of eye diseases.
Examples of major projects funded by
the Ulverscroft Foundation are:-

- The Children's Eye Unit at Moorfields Eye Hospital, London
- The Ulverscroft Children's Eye Unit at Great Ormond Street Hospital for Sick Children
- Funding research into eye diseases and treatment at the Department of Ophthalmology, University of Leicester
- The Ulverscroft Vision Research Group, Institute of Child Health
- Twin operating theatres at the Western Ophthalmic Hospital, London
- The Chair of Ophthalmology at the Royal Australian College of Ophthalmologists

You can help further the work of the Foundation
by making a donation or leaving a legacy.
Every contribution is gratefully received. If you
would like to help support the Foundation or
require further information, please contact:

THE ULVERSCROFT FOUNDATION
**The Green, Bradgate Road, Anstey
Leicester LE7 7FU, England
Tel: (0116) 236 4325**

website: www. ~~SWANSEA LIBRARIES~~ rscroft.com

A daughter of the artist Cyril Hamersma, Theresa Le Flem was raised in London and married at nineteen. After having three children in quick succession, she trained as a hairdresser, then took up pottery, but ended up working in a factory to pay the bills. After her eventual divorce, she married again in 2006. Finally, having the support of friends and family, and with her children settled in New York and Kent, Theresa is able to follow her passion for writing and express her strong views about social injustice. She is an avid listener of Radio 4 and a keen gardener, growing all of her own vegetables.

THE FORGIVING SAND

With the fishing industry in crisis, it is becoming increasingly difficult to make ends meet in a small Cornish town. Christina's quiet beach café is losing money and her ruthless brother-in-law is determined to close it down. Disabled since childhood, Christina is determined to maintain her family business, though neither her mother nor her sister is interested in helping her. But when John Madison, a widowed and lonely local skipper, desperately seeks Christina's help with his young daughter, she is both disturbed by, and drawn to, him. Who can save Christina's beloved Sea Café? And when John asks her to take a risk, will her heart be torn in two?

THERESA LE FLEM

◆

THE
FORGIVING
SAND

Complete and Unabridged

ULVERSCROFT
Leicester

First published in Great Britain in 2013 by
Robert Hale Limited
London

First Large Print Edition
published 2014
by arrangement with
Robert Hale Limited
London

A catalogue record for this book is available
from the British Library.

ISBN 978–1–4448–1931–1

Published by
F. A. Thorpe (Publishing)
Anstey, Leicestershire

Set by Words & Graphics Ltd.
Anstey, Leicestershire
Printed and bound in Great Britain by
T. J. International Ltd., Padstow, Cornwall

This book is printed on acid-free paper

I would like to thank my daughter, Ursula Edgington, for reading and advising on the first draft. Thank you also to my friend, the actress and writer Madalyn Morgan, for her encouragement and down-to-earth critique of my work.

Finally and most importantly, I am immensely grateful to my husband Graham, for his kindness and patience, and for always being with me on my journey to write and complete *The Forgiving Sand*.

1

1994

Taking her usual route along the coastal path, Christina soon felt she needed to rest. Still early, the beach was deserted. Before her, the blue expanse of the Atlantic Ocean spun like a top. She sat down on a bench and watched the waves measure her breath. It calmed her and her pulse slowed. The high tide was turning and in its ebb, the tension that had remained with her from home blissfully slipped away. Rising, she stepped forward eagerly and soon caught sight of her café nestling below at the furthermost point of the beach at Crystal Barr. A smile played around her lips; she felt proud of herself. In spite of her physical disability she had managed to keep the Sea Café going singlehandedly ever since her father had lost heart and left. Her customers were fishermen, beach-combers, holiday-makers, and domestic staff who worked in the numerous hotels and guest houses in St. Ives. All of them were her friends.

If her childhood accident had held her back in any way, it was more in temperament, giving her character a certain reticence behind those watchful and thoughtful eyes. Accustomed to a certain amount of pain, she had an artistic, almost equine, spirit. If she'd been a horse, she could have galloped wildly along the sand at that moment, joyously embracing the blank canvas of the beach. The sun glittered on the sea, the seagulls circled overhead and the salt wind bathed her olive complexion to a russet gold.

As she whistled her Jack Russell and began to descend the path she picked some wild flowers for the tables. But the echoes of her brother-in-law's threatening voice broke through her search for peace and mingled with the raucous cries of the herring gulls. Like him, they were greedy creatures. Nothing and no-one, not even René, she resolved, would take the café away from her. It was her sanctuary. It provided her with a livelihood, however meagre, and it gave her a sense of identity. But more than that, it had become her true home since her other home — the terraced house where she lived — was like a battle-ground.

A figure appeared on the beach with her long hair flying and skirt wrapped around her legs. It was her dear friend, Teagan.

'Hey! Tig!' she shouted, but her voice was snatched away by the wind. 'Go on, Ginger — find her!' The dog raced ahead barking, causing the girl to swing round and squeal in surprise.

When Christina caught up, she greeted Teagan with a hug. 'Sorry if he made you jump!'

'I didn't see you there, Chris,' cried Teagan. 'I was miles away!'

'I've got some thinking of my own to do,' replied Christina. 'René's home and he's in a right mood. He's already had a go at me this morning and he couldn't have chosen a worse time to ask about the café's turnover.'

'Things no better then?'

Christina shook her head. 'I'm only just covering my expenses.'

The girls came to the small jetty where several boats were moored up. Further along, a fishing-boat was stranded on the beach.

'See that boat over there?' said Teagan, pointing. 'It's been stuck there for weeks.'

Christina shielded her eyes. 'Looks like Theo's 'Isabelle'. I don't think he's been out to sea for months,' she said. They picked their way among crab and lobster pots, glistening wet in the sunlight, and soon came upon the small craft. The peeling paint betrayed the age of the boat. On the underside, rust was seeping from steel rivets onto the shingle, staining it amber.

'Shame he hasn't had her repaired,' said Christina.

'Perhaps Theo's getting too old?' suggested Teagan. 'It's so dangerous these days.'

Christina knew Teagan was often afraid that her husband Connor might not return home one day. On stormy nights, when distress rockets shoot into the sky, when the lifeboat is launched and women stand on the harbour waiting anxiously — this is when Teagan is at her most vulnerable. It's hard riding the broad back of the sea day after day, clinging to the rigging while waves pound. Mothers, wives and girlfriends know how easily their men could succumb to the danger. For a second, Christina caught the eye of a passing seagull as it hovered overhead. It was a look of recognition and it gave her a sudden chill. It seemed to cry:

'*I've seen over the horizon, girl. I've been there and I've seen what's coming to you and it's not good.*' The gull turned, leaning its smooth marble body into the wind and changed direction. It gave an unexpected deafening scream as it took lift on an air current, flapping its steel-grey wings. It made height and left them alone with their thoughts.

'Those flipping gulls!' Christina complained. 'They haunt me! They almost seem to know something!'

'They're spiritual, Chris, that's all,' Teagan

said simply. 'They do speak sometimes but not everyone can hear them like you and me.'

'I don't see how anyone can miss them, shrieking away like that all the time!'

'You know what I mean,' Teagan replied. 'Not everyone can understand what they're saying.'

'I wish I could understand,' replied Christina, thinking of René and how his very presence back in St. Ives filled her with dread.

'You can if you try,' replied Teagan, looking at her keenly.

Casting a quizzical eye at her friend, Christina looked around for a distraction. 'Look Tig!' she said, shielding her eyes. 'Isn't that your dad over there on the headland?'

Teagan turned and smiled in delight. 'Oh! Look at him battling against the gale. See him trying to hold his easel up! He's mad!' Quinn was painting with his easel propped right on the cliff's edge where the wind cut across unhindered. Giggling, Teagan gathered her skirt around her legs and began to run. Christina couldn't run, and remembering this, Teagan stopped and waited for her. They left the beach together and began to climb the hill. Ginger bounded on ahead.

'Those seagulls will drive me insane one day,' shouted Quinn as soon as they were within earshot. The artist had oil-paint streaked down the thighs of his jeans, and his donkey jacket was flapping open exposing what looked like a pyjama jacket underneath. As the girls approached, he didn't take his eyes from his subject, squinting and holding his brush out before him horizontally, and using his thumb to measure the distance between sand and breakwater. 'Why did I ever come to this Godforsaken place, eh? Those bloomin' gulls — I swear they're lost souls crying out for vengeance! The ghosts of sailors and smugglers — victims of this damned sea! Dear Lord, will I ever get that sound out of my head?'

'They're only seagulls, Dad,' laughed Teagan. But when Quinn's face turned towards them they saw he wasn't laughing. Christina glanced at her friend in concern. Was it really getting to him? He was painting feverishly, expressing his restless spirit in blocks of vivid colour. They stood watching him as they had done ever since they were children. It occurred to Christina that anxiety must flow through a parent's veins into their child, and that Teagan seemed to carry her father's arterial, artistic and genetic pain. With a few haphazard sweeps of the brush, Quinn began sketching in imaginary people playing among the rock pools dressed in brilliant primary colours, and dangling their pale legs into the turquoise mineral sea. They brought sunshine, life and vigour to the picture. For all his complaining, he held the key to summer in his fingertips. He could create his own world on that empty windswept beach.

'I must get away from this place before I go mad,' he sighed.

'But it's beautiful here, Dad, you know it is! You wouldn't want to move back up country now would you? Mum wouldn't either.'

'No, I suppose not. It's true your mother loves the place. Beautiful here you say?' He snorted and lifted his eyebrows. 'Yes, like a beautiful woman — seductive!' He held his brush suspended, like a kingfisher about to strike, before stabbing his canvas with brilliant spots of cobalt. 'Cornwall! She's dangerous and evil with it,' he cautioned. 'Be the death of me she will!' And with these words he turned and looked directly at the girls as though he had made a solemn promise.

'Dad!' laughed his daughter, 'don't be so melodramatic!' She tossed her long hair. 'He's impossible, isn't he, Chris!'

Christina didn't reply. Instead she looked out across the sea, wishing she could shake off the growing sense of foreboding she felt.

Glancing back, she saw Quinn's life-worn face, haggard under his beard; his frayed scarf; his boots laced with string. Time and again she saw him thrust his brush into the jam-jar of turpentine, dig it into an old rag that hung from his belt and wipe it carelessly on the thigh of his jeans. She marvelled at his intensity. What makes a man wrestle with life so, trying to capture and tame it, as though it was a wild animal?

'Chris?' Teagan prompted. 'Now look, Dad, you've upset her. You shouldn't say such things!'

'Take no notice of me, Christina — crazy old fool that I am! Are you going to open up the café then? I'm workin' myself up to a nice cup of coffee and sandwich. You can't get any peace around here with women interfering all the while!' He winked at them and started to paint in earnest.

'Yes!' said Christina. 'I'd better get going. Are you coming, Tig?' Whistling her dog, they both set off again. People were arriving on the beach now: a couple digging for bait and some children playing with a bat and ball. She was impatient to get there and be on familiar ground again; to fall into the routine that she had followed ever since she was a child. It was home to her, and she felt secure in her own space.

'I'll pop in to see you and Mum later,' Teagan called and waved.

'Yes, bye, my darling,' Quinn shouted. 'Bye Chris, I'll be up at the café soon.' He hadn't taken his eyes from his work, but as they descended the hill again, they heard him roar:

'Get out of it!' Looking back, they saw him raising an arm to shield his head. The gulls were swooping down over his easel, mocking him mercilessly.

* * *

Christina's dog ran here and there exploring the shining surface of sand newly exposed by the receding tide. Out at sea, a gannet hovered in mid-flight and, in a split-second, dived vertically into the water. Moments later it surfaced again, brandishing a fish like a silver sword.

Small and practical in manner, Christina never wore make-up. Her black hair was cut into a fringe to obscure a small scar on her forehead and she was wearing a checked-shirt, fitted at the waist, tapering jeans and leather ankle boots. These boots were specially made for her: one was stacked to counter the effect of one leg being shorter than the other — the result of an accident when she was three years old. This disability caused her to walk with a pronounced limp, but it was an improvement on the steel calliper she had had to wear on her left leg until the age of seven.

Reaching the café door, she paused. Her friend was halfway down the beach throwing stones for Ginger to chase. Suddenly a recollection of her father's voice came back to her with such vividness she stopped in her tracks. It was the last morning. The morning he went away.

'Josie, love?' said her father. 'What d'you say to coming back to work with me an' Chrissy in the café again? Give up this sewing lark!' His ears twitched in anticipation.

Her mother was hunched over the sewing-machine as usual, doing her out-work. She flicked a piece of material under the buzzing needle, gave a snip of the scissors and slipped it out skilfully, like filleting a fish. The machine stopped abruptly. 'Have you taken leave of your senses, Charlie Tobermory? Tell me it's successful then and we've got money in the bank.' She stared at him. 'No, I thought not! If you'd have put in half the effort into that café that I put into this out-work then maybe we'd have seen some profit by now.'

'Come on, love!' he urged. 'We'll get some paint and give the old place a face-lift, shall we? It'll be a family business again! I can't bear to see you hunched over that machine any longer. It's not good for you, and the noise! It's enough to drive a man mad!'

But Josie ignored him. Finally, he turned to Christina. 'Chrissy love,' he said. 'Open up for me today, will you? I've got a few things to do here.' And he handed her the keys.

The note he left propped against the kettle that day often ran through her mind.

By the time you read this I'll be on the train to London. I won't be coming back. I know I've failed you, Josie love. I can't support you, buy you the nice things you deserve — you'll be better off without me. I want you to take over the house and the lease on the café. I'll get a solicitor to draw up the paperwork, so it's all legal like, but I want you to have it. Chrissy is used to running the café and she's a good girl. Between you, you're bound to make a better success of the place than I could. Sorry, I tried me best and I can't do no more.

Love you always, Charlie

★   ★   ★

That had all happened six years ago, and she hadn't heard from him since. Shaking off her

11

memories, Christina took the keys and, opening the door, she whistled to Ginger as Teagan came up the slipway and joined her, her face flushed by the wind. 'Ooh, he thinks I've got time to play all day!' she cried.

Once inside, Christina felt the shiver of excitement that a new day brings. The café had been her refuge ever since she could remember. She threw open the windows, and let fresh air in to drive out the stale cooking smells of the day before. Then she went to unlock the front-door which was actually at the back of the premises. Entering from the beach, customers to the café were spared the sight of the dustbins, and the shabby frontage, where van deliveries were made. Christina's bakery order was waiting on the step: two boxes emitted the delicious aroma of freshly baked pasties, cream cakes and doughnuts.

When she came back bearing the first box, Teagan exclaimed: 'You are lucky having this café, Chris! Being your own boss and coming up here every day! I wish I had something like this — a purpose in life — something to get up for in the morning.'

Christina glanced at her. 'I do love it, Tig, it's true,' she said, opening the box with her penknife. 'It would be all right if balancing the books didn't matter.'

'You do make enough though, don't you?'

'No. Between you and me I need to attract more customers somehow. It's no good putting the prices up, people just can't afford it.'

Soon the coffee filter machine sent the fragrance of fresh coffee wafting through the building and Christina began sweeping sand from the veranda. Next she hauled two pots of flowering geraniums into position, propping open the French-doors with them before bringing out the folding canvas chairs and the small white tables. Casually, effortlessly, she lifted them — her disability didn't hinder her at all — she had been doing this task for years. Ginger trotted about, examining every inch of the deck and covering his shiny black nostrils with sand. Christina spoke affectionately to him:

'All those greedy seagulls, eh, Ginger, just waiting to gobble you up!' Completing his inspection of the decking area, the Jack Russell gave it his sign of approval by cocking his leg up against one of the large plant pots. 'Hey!' she scolded, but already he had trotted back inside.

Putting two teacakes under the grill to toast, and carrying two cups of coffee, she went to sit down by her friend.

'I wish I could help you,' said Teagan. 'Aren't there loans and things you can turn to?'

'I've already been down that road. The bank manager was looking rather irritable last time I went to see him. '*Miss Tobermory*,' he said. '*We're not a charity here, you know!*''

Teagan chuckled at her impersonation. 'But it's only a small place. You can't expect to make a fortune! That's what's so nice about it; it's always so quiet and peaceful here.'

'Yes, a bit too quiet for people like René. Oh, the teacakes!' Christina rushed to save them from burning.

'Tell him to mind his own business!' called Teagan. 'You know what you're doing. I wish I had your independence, Chris, I do envy you sometimes.'

Christina came and sat down again, bearing the tray. 'I'd like to show him one day that you can't judge everywhere by London standards. Life's slower here, it's different in Cornwall. The trouble with René is, he sees everything in commercial terms, and I mean everything! I'm not sure he's got a heart at all under his shirt, only a big fat wallet!'

★ ★ ★

Teagan buttered her teacake thoughtfully. She almost envied Christina's dilemma; she so desperately wanted something to happen! It just felt that her life had been put on hold.

14

Everyone else was experiencing change. She was always left waiting, it seemed: waiting for her husband to come home, waiting for money to spend, and waiting for a baby to come. In her life there always seemed to be something missing! She always felt such a sense of sadness and loss. It was like a ghost that seemed to haunt the Cornish air and it hung around her like an echo. Slowly she drew a letter from her pocket.

'René's not the only one without a heart,' she said. 'I heard from my brother, Peter, yesterday. I can't understand it, Chris. He says Nicola's met someone else and she's just told him to get out.'

'What? Just like that?'

'It seems so. Look, I'll read a bit: he says, *I can't go on living here. There's such an atmosphere and it's not good for the boys. Mind if I come down to stay till I get myself sorted?*' The letter came to rest in her lap. 'How can she do that?'

'It might be just a fling,' suggested Christina. 'If he comes down here for a while, she might come to her senses. What's she like anyway, this Nicola?'

'I always thought she was a bit too sophisticated for our Peter, but he's devoted to her. She's tall and elegant and quite fashion-conscious; a city girl really. And

15

Peter's just a big clumsy oaf, bless him!'

'It might all blow over, Tig.'

'But look at the size of our cottage! Peter's a big chap, over six foot tall and huge feet! I love him dearly, but I can't imagine him fitting into our little house and the only spare room we've got was going to be a — ' She stopped herself suddenly and looked away, biting her lip.

★ ★ ★

'Going to be a what?' Christina glanced at her uncertainly. She was accustomed to her friend's quick changes of mood.

'A nursery, that is if . . . ' She trailed off.

'He'd only stop a short while though, wouldn't he?' asked Christina gently.

'Yes, but . . . ' The mood in the café had become sombre. Teagan got up and walked away to gaze out of the window, her brow darkening. Suddenly she swung back. 'Why does something always stop us, Chris?' she exclaimed, her eyes flooding with distress.

'Stop you? Why? What do you mean?'

'From having a baby!' cried Teagan, choking back her tears. 'Connor keeps saying we should wait, but . . . '

'Look, if Peter does come down, it won't change anything, will it? It won't stop you

16

trying for a baby! Come on now! Cheer up, I'd better get on and make some sandwiches. Then I'll fetch us some more coffee!'

Christina stood up and gave her friend a hug. Perhaps after all she was worrying unnecessarily herself — at least her problems were only about money — and what was money? Not worth the paper it was printed on, that's what her dad used to say.

⋆ ⋆ ⋆

Teagan busied herself removing the vases and re-filling them with fresh flowers. She replaced them on the tables and settled herself down under the window to write her diary while Christina was busy unpacking the cakes and buttering bread. She looked seaward, waiting for the tide to turn and for sight of her husband's trawler heading homeward on the horizon. How she wished Connor would come home! How she longed to reach out and feel his warm body against hers, enveloping her in his sighing sleepiness and dissolving away all her tears. His strong arms would draw her to him, breathing his warmth into her, their flesh becoming like a moving tide. He would hold her in a strong current, raising her up through terrible waters to breathe and gasp and be born. Such love! She could see him now, stretched out like a magnificent animal; how she longed to lie close to him, feeling sleepy and loved. How could she ever get used to being a fisherman's wife?

★   ★   ★

A group of pensioners approached the café, picking their way on the soft sand. Christina heard them before she saw them, coming up the slip-way and climbing the steps; they were complaining with aged, girlish voices.

'Mind these steps, Doris!' one cried, clinging to a gentleman's arm, and reaching out a claw-like hand for the rail.

'Good morning! Would you like to sit outside?' called Christina cheerfully.

The gentleman looked up, surveying some on-coming clouds suspiciously. 'Thank you, it's a bit breezy. I think we'll take our coffee inside — what do you say, ladies?' The three chorused their approval in sing-song unison and when they were all inside he helped each one to a seat. 'Have you any fresh crab in?' he asked, reading the menu with his spectacles balanced on the end of his nose.

'No, I'm afraid not,' replied Christina. 'Salmon or tuna all right?'

'No thank you; don't you have any local seafood?'

Christina apologized again, 'No, I'm sorry.'

'Oh, then I think scones and fresh Cornish cream will fit the bill. You have local cream, I take it?' he asked.

Reluctantly, Christina admitted that the cream was neither fresh nor local. As she saw the gentleman's cheerful smile fade, she made a mental note to tell her mother. It couldn't be that much more expensive to buy Cornish cream — the mass-produced emulsion that passed for double cream which they bought from the Cash 'n' Carry was becoming an embarrassment. While she busied herself brewing the coffee, she listened with amusement to the pensioners' excitable chatter about the cakes. But the gentleman, she noticed, had retreated behind his newspaper and showed no further interest in the menu at all. She must do something about it, she decided, whatever the cost.

Teagan put her diary away and smiled at the pensioners before paying her bill. Leaving Christina to her customers, with a few brief words, she left and turned towards the town.

★ ★ ★

Pausing outside, Theo, the skipper of 'Isabelle', docked his cap to Teagan as she passed him. Knocking out his pipe on the edge of the decking, he coughed and hitched up his trousers.

'Storm brewing,' he growled as he stepped inside. Replacing the pipe in his mouth, he wedged himself into a chair beside the counter and proceeded to study the menu with immense concentration. After several minutes he looked up to catch Christina's eye.

'Tuna sandwich an' tea, please, my flower.'

'Coming up!' she called. He always ordered the same. As she prepared it the sky darkened rapidly. A chill wind cast a silver sheen across the sea and soon, wafting in from outside, the scent of rain. She shut the windows and switched on some lights.

'Have you been out fishing lately, Theo?' she asked.

He looked steadily at the noisy pensioners' party for a moment before replying. 'No, my hip's playin' me up. Anyway she's got a bit needs doing.'

'Didn't you give 'Isabelle' an overhaul last winter though? I heard you spent a fortune on her.'

'Aye, I did that, but she's a fickle one. I'll have to get Jack to take a look at her again.' Accepting the moist pink tuna sandwiches gratefully, he began to eat, his eyes taking on a vacant far-away stare like a baby suckling milk. Christina watched him thoughtfully. She could remember seeing 'Isabelle' sailing out of St. Ives' harbour when she was still at junior school. Suddenly there was a loud crack of thunder, and lightning lit up the sky, causing the ladies to squeal like children. Theo just gave them a cool stare. 'More tea, love, when you're ready,' he said flatly.

She filled a teapot from the boiling urn and took it over to his table. Checking that her other customers had all they wanted, she went back to him. 'Theo, mind if I ask you something?'

'Fire away, girl, there ain't much I don't know about fishin' but if it's somethin' about women, well, there you've got me!' He sighed, poured a large amount of milk into his cup, took a long draught of tea and smacked his lips.

Christina leant closer. 'You remember my father, Charlie, don't you?'

He looked at her in astonishment. 'Fancy you askin' me that! Sit yourself down here, girl, by me. That's it.' She obeyed, looking keenly into his face.

'Your father was a good man — loyal — worked his fingers to the bone to keep this here caffy runnin'. He had half a mind to jack it in, several times, I don't mind tellin' yer. He was only just keepin' his head above water

21

but he wouldn't give in, see, didn't want to let your dear mother down, no, he wouldn't ever do that.'

'But he went away,' she sighed. 'Why did he leave us then, Theo? Mum won't ever talk about him, you know. It's like he doesn't exist!'

'She's a strong-minded woman, your mother, an' you takes after her, I can see that,' replied Theo, glancing at her in earnest. She watched his face eagerly and saw the spider-veins travelling across his eyelids and the stubble on his jaw like the barnacles on an old boat. Theo sucked in his lips and stared into his tea for a moment before taking a deep breath and letting the air escape loudly from the deep barrel of his chest.

'There's only so much a man can take, Chris, and he took more than most. Your mother, with due respect, she wouldn't bend, wouldn't give him a chance. Charlie wanted her to help run this here caffy with him, he begged her. He came to me one night an' he said, '*Lor, if that woman won't give up that damn sewing machine soon I think it'll drive me insane. I've a mind to get hold o' the blessed thing an' chuck it in the bloody sea — either that or myself.*'' Theo looked up and saw Christina's troubled face. 'Don't think hard on him. He loved you, y'know, loved you two girls more than I could ever tell yer. He cared for your mother too, I don't doubt it, but she wouldn't give an inch. Folks say, if Charlie hadn't upped an' gone he'd have chucked himself off Smeaton's Pier an' be lying dead at the bottom o' the sea before the year were out.'

'Do you know if he's still alive?' she asked, fighting back tears and watching the old man's eyes roam across his memories.

'Child! He's as alive as you an' me, the old codger! Sure as I'm sat here, he's alive an' well. He's livin' up Plymouth way; saw him I did only last month!'

'You saw him last month?' she gasped. It was as though the image of her father, which had been locked away in her mind like some faded photograph, had suddenly taken breath and sprung to life before her eyes. Physical memories of him enveloped her; she could almost smell his rough sweater against her cheek, feel his strong arms around her again.

'I see him regular — had a jar with him only the other day, I did, an' he's doin' all right for hisself, got a job, he has, bakin' bread. Up at four every mornin'. He works hard, mind. But he's got no-one else see, never got over Josie, I guess. Now don't go botherin' your mother, will yer, or I'll be thinkin' I should'na told you. Still, I would

have told you afore if I knew you was pinin'
away for him like.'

'But I thought he was in London somewhere! Does my mum . . . does she know
where he's living?'

'Oh, she knows all right, my flower. He's
written to her on an' off over the years many
a time and she's wrote back a few times.
Don't ask me why she don't write more but
there you are. She's a single-minded woman,
proud too. I wouldn't hold it against her, not
if I were you.'

Christina stood up and, casting an eye at
the pensioners' table, planted a fleeting kiss
on the old man's cheek. 'Tell him next time
you see him, Theo. Tell him I was asking after
him, will you?'

'Aye, I will, lass, I will that.'

2

When Christina came downstairs for breakfast the next morning, she found her brother-in-law, René, sitting in the kitchen. The smell of his after-shave hit her full on. At a glance she saw the untidy breakfast table scattered with Kellogg's Cornflakes, and several dirty bowls and mugs. He was munching toast noisily. Within a year of their daughter Caitlin's birth, her sister Deborah had become increasingly isolated in London. With the intention of picking up her dance-teaching again, she had persuaded René to let her move back home. While he continued with his own career and refused to give up his city apartment, she returned to St. Ives. Only occasionally did René drive down to stay a weekend with his wife and daughter. The family still lived in the old Cornish terraced house in St. Ives which Charlie had fled from six years before. It was built of granite and cob, and was on three storeys. The walls were thick, and the windows small, making the rooms dark and cool, summer and winter alike.

'Morning, René,' she said. He had come in

very late the night before and was presumably nursing a hangover. The hall table had apparently gone flying — and she had had to restrain Ginger when the lumbering fool climbed up the stairs to his wife's bedroom. Her poor sister! She couldn't imagine what Deborah would have felt, woken by a husband who only came home to roost when the mood took him, without warning, and usually drunk.

He didn't answer or even acknowledge her presence. Sitting at the table, wearing a pink shirt carelessly unbuttoned, he was reading. Middle-aged, his greying blond hair half-obscured his usual expression which was feverish and flushed with inexplicable excitement. René, Christina knew, considered himself a bit of an old hand when it came to business. He didn't suffer fools gladly. As he shook the paper irritably, muttering to himself, his gold bracelet rattled.

'I said, *good morning*,' she repeated.

His face twitched into slight recognition. But as she went to make her coffee, he still made no reply. Finally, he folded the newspaper and put it down, staring vacantly ahead of him and snorting phlegm at the back of his throat. He gulped like a toad as she paused before pouring her coffee, holding the jug aloft and waiting for his response.

'Yes, morning Sister-in-law,' he replied finally.

Christina sighed audibly and muttered: 'At last!' Replacing the jug, she carried her mug to the window and stood leaning against the window-sill watching him. His eyes still didn't move to meet hers, but his gaze floated over in her direction and rested nonchalantly on the net curtains behind her, which were yellowed from cooking fumes and age.

'Don't suppose Her Ladyship's up yet?' he drawled. 'No, she wouldn't be.' He gave his humourless twitch of a smile.

She wished he wouldn't hold a conversation with himself like that, as though anyone present was superfluous. But having answered himself satisfactorily, he appeared to hit on a topic of conversation when he suddenly declared:

'Well!' Looking directly at her for the first time, he said, 'I hear the Sea Café's not exactly drawing the crowds in! What do you think the reason for that is, mmm?' He leaned forward to stare straight at her, putting two pink hams of arms on the table in front of him.

Now it was her turn not to answer. She shrugged off his question and turned her back on him, looking out of the window and sipping her coffee. There was nothing to look at, though. The backyard was no more than a dumping ground, with an old steel dustbin used for burning rubbish. The concrete path, cracked in places, had failed to withstand the onslaught of nettles and ragwort. She hated being confronted first thing in the morning.

René pulled himself up into a straighter position, rising to the challenge. 'Mmm?' he mused, prompting a response. She could feel his globular eyes on her back. 'Any particular reason for that, Sister-in-law, do you think, mmm?'

'It's a bit early in the season to be making any judgements, René,' she replied, turning to face him.

'Bit early?' replied René, rather too loudly. 'Don't you mean a bit late? We can't afford to have another failed season like last year, can we! It's all about profit! What you need to get into that thick head of yours is that profit is even more important than the air we breathe, do you realize that? Be positive! Unless you give the punters the impression that business is on the up, you're sending out the wrong message, girl. We can't afford to do that, you know.'

'Give our customers the impression we're raking it in when we're not? Come off it, René, you can't mean that!' She had to smile.

'Yes, that's exactly what I do mean. Flutter

28

some money around! If you haven't got it, borrow it. It doesn't matter in the end how much you owe the bank, or whether you can actually pay it back at the end of the day, the secret is to keep your customers sweet! Give them the impression you know what you're doing.' He burped loudly and shifted his ample body in the chair.

'Even if you don't?' she mused.

'Yes, of course. It's a case of the Emperor's new clothes if you like.' He beamed as though beginning to tell a child a story. 'Impress enough people and they begin to convince each other. Give the appearance of success in the market place and you're halfway there, my girl. Money attracts more money. Trust me.'

'We're only talking about the Sea Café, René, or have you forgotten? It's not one of your London casinos; it's only a small quiet place where people can drop by for a coffee and a sandwich.'

'See! That's just a typical comment coming from you! You're starting to sound like someone else I know — that idiot relative of yours who let the place go right down the pan.'

'Oh?' Christina retaliated. 'And who would that be then? For God's sake, René what the hell are you talking about now?' She knew perfectly well who he was referring to. He meant Charlie, but she couldn't bear to feel his cynicism encroaching on the precious memory of her father. 'Can't I even have a quiet cup of coffee in the morning, René, without you starting on?' A vivid rash of anger broke out on her cheek and she tossed her dark hair back in restless fury.

'Oh, never mind, girl! Forget I mentioned that. He's history anyway.' He backed down, physically withdrawing, sliding his ample frame back into its mould like a snail retreating into its shell. 'Anyway, Sister-in-law,' he said, suddenly drawing on a new angle of attack, 'I presume you've made considerable changes to increase the turnover this year, since last year was so much shit! What new plans do we have in particular?'

'We? What's this sudden cosiness? Since when have you been so interested in the café's turnover anyway? It's not exactly your business, René, so I suggest you wait until Mum and I are ready to discuss it.'

He gave an ugly snort and gulped like a frog swallowing a fly. 'Yes, well, we'll see about that.' Dismissing her, he picked up his new acquisition, a mobile phone, and began thumbing the buttons. She watched the muscles in his jaw flexing as though he was clenching his teeth. His eyes narrowed to slits.

She felt as tense as a taut spring and she just couldn't let it rest there. 'What's that supposed to mean exactly?' she asked. But he ignored her, tapping away at his mobile phone obliviously. If only I had been a bit more adventurous with the café before, she thought. If it was thriving, he wouldn't have the opportunity to criticize, start flexing his muscles and throwing his weight about. All I want from him is a bit of respect.

'René? René!' she repeated impatiently. He made no reply. Slamming her coffee down, she swore and stormed out of the room. He did no more than raise an eyebrow in response.

It wasn't often Christina lamented the fact that she couldn't walk gracefully. But leaving the room just then made her long for elegance. If only she could walk tall. The effect of her injury had given her a permanent limp which she was accustomed to, but just occasionally, at times like these, she cursed her own clumsiness. It was just like René to take advantage of another's misfortune. With increasing frustration she thought of how René always addressed her — not once had he ever called her by her name. It was always that irritating term he used: 'Sister-in-law'. She was, and presumably would remain, nothing more than a legal attachment to a marriage certificate, and nothing more.

Leaving the house immediately to open the Sea Café, with Ginger at her heel, Christina made for the coastal path. It was fresh and cool in the morning air. Wild flowers sprang from banks and hedgerows. She took some deep breaths and tried to throw off the anger and tension which had so quickly built up. The Cornish coastline was her one solace. Throughout her school years nothing could hold her back from flinging off her uniform, donning jeans and T-shirt and going down to the beach. She sought out the sea after school as urgently as any other child would run to the welcoming arms of its mother. The bright sunlight cut sharp as a knife across the surface of the sea; it was as calm and still as a sheet of glass. The tide was just turning, leaving hard wet ripples of corrugated sand.

Christina removed her boots and rolled her jeans up to her knees. Her good leg was bronzed by the sun, while the other, a couple of inches shorter, was slightly deformed, and looked shrivelled and pale in the morning sun. No amount of sunshine seemed to touch it. Her left leg had been that way for as long as she could remember. It never normally worried her. It was only bullies like René who made her feel self-conscious about it. She carried her boots, trailing the laces, and felt the hard, moulded waves of sand pressing into her bare feet. Looking back over her shoulder, she was comforted by the sight of her footprints. They were even, like anyone else's. It was a forgiving sand. The footsteps she left behind showed no trace of her awkward limp. At least she could be thankful for that.

* ★ ★

At the end of the day, Christina was about to lock up when the door flew open and John Madison entered. He was a local fisherman, skipper of the 'Coral Princess'. The strength of the tide surged in with him; the smell of seawater and fish clung to his clothes.

'Hello John!' she called. 'I was just closing but did you want something? I'm not in a hurry.' She had no wish to return home while René was there.

The fisherman smiled, his eyelids were as red-raw as a mountaineer's. 'I've brought you a couple of herrings for your supper, fresh off the boat. You're always busy feeding others — I thought you might like a hot supper yourself tonight.'

'What a lovely thought! Thanks! I'm tempted to cook them right now. Want to join me?'

'I would but I've got Sylvie outside.' He tossed his head towards the figure of his 6 year-old daughter who was chasing seagulls further down the beach.

'She can have some too, if she'd like to — there's enough here.'

He agreed and thanked her. Seeing him stride across the beach shouting to Sylvie, she put a frying-pan on to heat and was beginning to fillet the fish when he returned alone.

'She's happy to keep playing — not hungry apparently. I'm not surprised, after all the sweets Maudie's been giving her.'

He came and stood beside her, watching her quizzically for a moment. 'Here, let me show you,' he said. Taking the knife from her, he moved nearer. His masculine presence momentarily overwhelmed her as she watched his skilful hands divide the silvery skins. The sharp knife sent flashing darts of evening sunlight across the café as he separated the pearly flesh from its backbone and passed her the fillets to fry.

'You'd think I'd be sick of them after fishing all day, Christina, but I always enjoy a fresh herring.' He pronounced her name carefully, she reflected, rolling the syllables around on his tongue. She liked his soft warm voice and the way he used her name. It made her feel special. Soon the café was filled with the delicious aroma of frying herrings. Failing again to entice Sylvie away from the beach, they sat down together under the window. It was dusk and a deep crimson sunset lit up the sky. As they ate their fish with bread and butter, they watched the little girl playing on her own some twenty feet from the café door.

'She looks a lot like her,' he said suddenly, nodding towards the child. Christina glanced at him quickly. 'Like my Kate I mean. It's hard not to be reminded of her every day.'

'Yes, of course — her poor mother!' Christina was taken aback. John was notoriously distant. No-one had been able to get close to him since his wife had drowned when Sylvie was a tiny baby. Kate had been caught up in a strong current while swimming. At least, that's what was surmised although the mystery seemed to hang around in the air afterwards. Fingers were pointed, and by all accounts, the relatives blamed John for not keeping an eye on her. Why had she gone swimming so soon after giving birth? Was it recklessness or a symptom of post-natal depression that had caused her to leave her clothes in a bundle on the beach and take to the dangerous water when there was a spring tide and no-one else around? Her body had been washed up along the coast at St. Just

35

two days later. It had been a dreadful time.

'Does Sylvie ever ask about her mother?'

He shook his head. 'She was too young to remember her,' he replied. 'When it happened, she cried a lot — Kate was breast-feeding — but after a while she adapted. I had to learn how to make up a baby's bottle a bit sharpish. We managed alone somehow, her and me.' He pursed his lips thoughtfully. Christina saw the whites of his eyes flood to pink, and she heard him swallow hard. 'But look at her now!' he continued. 'She's a little madam, full of mischief, and inquisitive about everything. I think she's inherited her mother's independent streak.' He put down his knife and turned to her. 'I've never been able to talk about Kate before.'

'The years are passing, John. It gets easier as time goes by.' She was thinking about her father.

'Yes, I suppose it does. You know, I love that child.' He pointed at Sylvie's distant figure with his fork and shook his head sadly. 'I wouldn't be without her for the world, but I wish to God she had been a boy.'

Christina looked up in surprise. 'Why?'

'I'm a fisherman. I can't keep leaving her at home with Maudie Peacock, not when she gets older. I don't know about girlish things

36

either. A boy I could've taken to sea with me, taught him the trade, broken him in as it were to our ways, making a living out the sea.' He cast his eyes about as though wondering himself where this was leading. Sylvie was in the distance at the water's edge, throwing pebbles for Ginger.

'Girls should be able to go to sea!' she said. 'Why shouldn't they? Sylvie might want to when she's older.'

'Nah!' He dismissed her idea as a joke. Christina, unwilling to enter into an argument, changed the subject. 'The Easter holidays will be over before you know it. You won't have to worry about her once she's at school, will you? Is Maudie still happy to fetch her for you? If I have time, I could meet her myself. I often collect Caitlin for my sister. Mum's too busy and my sister — ' She faltered. It was complicated, and the difficulties within her family were of no concern to him.

'Thanks, but I've been looking at the pros and cons of my work,' John said. 'Nothing's secure in fishing at the moment you know. With all these huge sums of money the government are offering for decommissioning, there's a lot to tempt a man out of sea-fishing these days. But it's been my life up until now. I'm not sure what else I could do.'

'You're not seriously thinking of giving up, are you, John?' she asked, looking into his clear blue eyes. He looked away and stared at his hands. He had long tapering fingers; they were sensitive, she thought, more like a musician's hands. They weren't scarred and calloused like those of other fishermen she knew.

'The EU are always on our backs these days, Christina. Either the government or Europe I mean, saying you can do this, but you can't do that.' He shook his head. 'They'll fall over backwards to please Brussels, but don't give a damn about their own fleet back home. They don't bother to ask us fishermen, the only people who know what needs doing. If only they would stop those French and Spanish beam trawlers tearing the sea-bed to ribbons, that'd be something. Wish the government would stop meddling in things they know nothing about. Bet half of those bureaucrats don't know a hake from a halibut anyway!'

She gathered up the plates and took them to the counter. They would have to be washed up before she left or the place would stink of herrings in the morning. 'It's getting dark, John. Shouldn't you be calling Sylvie back?'

'Yeah, I will in a minute. If only they'd let us get on with the job, instead of policing us all the time. I don't want to see stocks depleted either, but they're going about it all the wrong way. Once those trawlers have got a load of cod in the net and they've only got quota to bring back turbot or Dover sole, what can they do but chuck it back over the side? It's illegal to do anything else. What a waste!' He shrugged, scraping back his chair irritably. 'It's mad. People are starving in this world and they're telling fishermen to tip good wholesome food back over the side. All that hard work gone to waste!' He thumped the table in frustration. 'The way things are going, they'll sell off all our fishing-rights in the end and leave the Cornish fleet with nothing! It don't make any sense to me!' His anger had risen to the surface so quickly it rather alarmed her.

'It does sound crazy,' she said, wondering how she could direct his attention back to the task in hand. 'I can understand why you're worried, having your daughter's future to think of.'

'I'm worried sick,' he replied. 'Sylvie's a good girl, but now she's growing up she needs more spending on her and I'm earning next to nothing these days. She needs more attention too. I'm wondering whether to give up going to sea for good, that's why I'm looking at this lot.' At that, he took a fat brown envelope out of his inside pocket.

'What's that? Are you applying for another job?'

'Nah! It's a decommissioning form. That's what they want us to do — decommission our boats and send them for scrap. And what will they give us? Thirty pieces of silver!' He pushed his chair back restlessly. 'I'm sorry, barging in here and giving you all this grief.' He looked at her, relaxed and smiled sadly. 'You didn't ask for all this tonight, did you, Christina!'

'You're OK, it beats some of the stuff I have to put up with at home. They're always at each other's throats, especially when my brother-in-law's there. So, what will happen? If you go for decommissioning I mean?'

'Oh, I don't know!' he sighed. 'My boat's got years of life in her yet. Maybe I'm being a bit hasty. My crew won't thank me for it, that's for sure. It'll throw them out of a job as well. They'll be hard pushed to find anything else in Cornwall.' He fell into a sombre, brooding silence.

'How many men have you got working for you now?' she asked. It makes a change, she thought, to be talking about another business in trouble.

'Only two, but they're good men. One's getting married soon. He won't thank me if I make him redundant on his wedding night. He's asked me to be his best man as well.'

The air had cooled. It was getting dark and Christina knew Sylvie ought to be called back. John didn't move, however. He seemed lost in thought.

'Have you considered what else you could do then?' she asked, picking up the remaining cakes and scones and putting them into a bag. Teagan, she knew, would be pleased to make use of them.

'I don't want to give up fishing. I can't do much else really and there's nothing out there anyway. Suppose I'll get myself a smaller boat, work on my own and go round the coast fishing for brown crab and lobster. There's money to be made in shellfish, and at least I'll be home at night. Like I was saying, Sylvie needs me at home.'

Washing-up the dishes hastily, the hot soapy water sent steam rising, she left them to drain and wiped down the counter. 'Let's finish up here now and call Sylvie back. Ginger will want his supper too.'

'Sylvie's more aware of what's going on now, though,' he persisted, ignoring her move to leave. 'She needs help with her homework and time to talk. It's only fair and natural. She's bound to want to spend time with her father. And now she wants to know exactly when I'm going to sea and when I'm coming home.'

Christina looked at him, catching his eye: 'She's getting more like a woman you mean!' she teased.

'Suppose you're right, yes,' he smiled, 'but I don't like leaving her behind either. I'd like to be here more. She's growing up so quickly. A girl needs to have her father at home.' Suddenly he sat down again and put his head in his hands. 'Oh, Christina! I don't know why I'm telling you all this!'

She caught her breath. 'Sylvie's OK, John. Look at her now!' she said, watching the small figure skipping across the beach in the half-light. The receding tide was leaving a vast expanse of shining silver sand.

'It's just, life would've been so different if Kate hadn't — ' He almost broke down.

'John, you can't change history.' At the moment she said this, she knew it was true. He turned, caught her gaze and held her in a tragic stare.

'Do you think I don't tell myself that very thing every single day?'

'Of course! I didn't mean — ' Desperately she tried to backtrack. 'Sylvie's growing into a lovely sensible young girl, and you've coped so well. You can be proud of her.'

'Don't you patronize me!' he exclaimed

angrily, flinging his chair back and standing up. 'I know she's a good girl. It's easy for you to dish out praise and sympathy like cream teas, but it's not as simple as that.'

'So, that's what you think is it?' she retaliated. 'You think that's all I do, that's all I'm good for? I was going to say that I'm glad she's made friends with Caitlin, it helps her too. Having a friend like Sylvie brings her out of herself a bit. Caitlin's so shy. If anything, your daughter's more confident than some girls. She's an independent young lady, that's what I meant.'

'I'm sorry, Christina.' He spoke gently again; her name slipped off his tongue as though he was reluctant to part with it. 'I can be an irritable sod at times.'

She stared at him, watching the flash of steel in his eyes, and she felt afraid. 'I hope you don't remind me of that fact too often,' she said.

'I'll try. You got more than you bargained for with those herrings, didn't you,' he said. 'Forgive me?'

She nodded. 'Yes, you're OK. It's time we locked-up and went home though.' Turning off the lights and switches and making a few last minute checks, she picked up the bag of leftover cakes and took her coat. 'Ready?' she asked. The keys were in her hand.

John put on his jacket and was buttoning it up when he said, 'I don't know how much longer I can leave her with Maudie.'

'Maudie's a good, reliable woman, isn't she?' asked Christina, anxious now to be away.

'Yes, she means well. I can't fault her on lots of things but . . . '

'Is Sylvie unhappy there then, when you're at sea?' she probed, opening the door and watching Ginger make his way across the beach towards them with Sylvie chasing after him.

'No, it's not that but . . . '

'What is it, John? Come on, tell me!' she pleaded. 'It can't be that bad!'

'It's Maudie's lifestyle that worries me actually.'

'Her lifestyle?' Christina couldn't help but laugh and then, seeing his serious expression, she asked: 'What's wrong with it then? You mean the cats?'

'Oh, it's not just the cats. You know I'm not a fussy man, but there should be a certain level of hygiene. I shouldn't be talking like this, she's a dear old soul and I don't mean her any harm at all, it's just — '

'It's all right, I know what you mean. She is getting more and more eccentric. Her cats have almost taken over completely. There are cats asleep in boxes all over the house! Her poor husband seems to sleep in a cardboard box too, like the animals!' Seeing she had managed to cheer him up she took her chance. 'Let's see if Sylvie's ready to go home now, shall we?'

John took a step towards her, putting a hand firmly on her shoulder and squeezing it. 'I'm sorry about my outburst. Can we do this again sometime?' he asked, his blue eyes searching hers. 'I'll try not to bore you so much next time.'

'I'd love to,' she replied, feeling a catch in her throat as his physical presence again seemed to overpower her. 'Thanks for the herrings, John. I'll try not to ask so many probing questions.'

'Why? I might have a few questions of my own to ask. I've been talking about myself the whole time. I hardly know anything about you at all.'

'You know one thing, I'm not much good at filleting fish!' she replied.

'Next time I'll show you how. It's easy, Christina,' he said and brushed her cheek gently with his fingers. 'I'll go now, and thanks. See you.'

'Yes, see you.'

At his call, Sylvie came running straight into his arms. 'Gotcha!' he cried; hugging her and swinging her round. Christina stood and watched his lonely figure making off towards the headland, with Sylvie hanging tightly onto his hand. Something of his anxiety had rubbed off on her and her heart went out to them both. She waited for several minutes thinking about their conversation, his gentle touch on her face, his sad eyes and his anger.

★　★　★

Turning away, Christina decided she couldn't face going home quite yet and leaving the beach, began walking along the coastal path towards Bent Cross. Teagan would be glad of the spare cakes, she always enjoyed them. Bent Cross was a small hamlet, inland from St. Ives, where Teagan and Connor shared a two-up two-down fisherman's cottage. It was a walk of about two miles, but Ginger needed the walk after being asleep in his basket in the café most of the day. Overhead, clouds threatened to return, but occasionally a sword of sunlight shot across the sea. The tide was far out, no more than a silver spit of light. The setting sun scattered shards of crystal in the wake of a returning trawler. Herring gulls were circling around the boat, making a raucous din. '*Catch! Catch me if you can!*'

they seemed to say and she laughed at them.

The news from Theo of her father living in Plymouth was occupying her thoughts. A seagull flew close and perched on the gate infront of her. '*What?*' it croaked loudly. '*Why?*' it screamed and took off, wailing mournfully: '*It's too late, it's too late!*' No wonder Teagan's father is spooked by them, she thought. Stupid things!

Leaving behind the steep cliffs, where wild flowers and buddleia sprouted from every crevice, she contemplated the giant landscape around her. The ancient rocks absorb the heat from the sun, glistening with their precious fragments of quartz and mica. They dwarf our humanity, with our pathetic problems, she thought. Their age and silent presence far outshines our poor existence on this earth. The air itself, pungent with the sweet scent of gorse and heather was as heady as a drug. 'I so love it here!' she whispered.

Slipping Ginger's lead on, she left the rough path and passed through the kissing-gate. A hush in the village made her feel conscious of the sound of her own uneven footsteps on the cobbles. Cornish granite stone cottages knelt together along the street. Hyacinths, cyclamen and forget-me-nots, decorated garden borders and stone-walls. It was eerily quiet, and the windows revealed nothing of the folks inside. Teagan's cottage, with its red front door and hanging baskets, looked welcoming. She lifted the Cornish Piskie brass knocker and almost immediately the door opened.

'These cakes were left over and I felt like a walk — hope you don't mind, Tig.'

'Why should I mind?' laughed Teagan. 'Thank you! Come in!'

'Connor not back yet then?' she asked, glancing around. There were no boots by the fireside nor wet oilskins slung across the kitchen to dry.

She shook her head. 'He rang this afternoon. They've drawn a blank off Scilly so they're going further south. Would you like some lamb stew? I've just made it and there's fresh bread too.'

'Smells wonderful! I've just had some herrings, but I can't say no — just a little please?' She sank back into the sofa and snapped her fingers for Ginger to lie at her feet. Night fell as they enjoyed their supper. More bread was fetched from the kitchen, a bowl of stew given to the dog, and the kettle set to boil.

'Did you tell Connor about your brother when he phoned?'

'No, it was such a bad line I . . . ' Teagan looked away, her face flinching against the fears that buffeted her.

'Well, there's time yet. I hardly remember him you know, he was a schoolboy when I last saw him.'

Teagan pointed to a photo of her brother. 'That was taken on the day he and Nicola got married.'

'They look so happy!' said Christina. 'Where did it all go wrong?'

Teagan shrugged and padded into the kitchen in her bare feet. 'Let's have our tea. Tea always helps me think.' Ginger followed her through to the kitchen keenly and Christina heard him eating again, the bowl ringing on the stone floor.

Studying Peter's big friendly face in the photo, with his heavyweight stature and arm swept casually round Nicola's shoulders, she remembered the boy she once knew. By nature he was a soft, good humoured trusting sort of chap — like a Labrador, with his big clumsy hands and trusting brown eyes. She looked at the bride's face. Thin, sharp features, eyes that gave nothing away, and black hair swept tightly back into a veil. Not a wisp of hair out of place.

'When were they married Tig?' she called.

'Eight years ago now; the boys are five and three,' she replied, returning with mugs replenished and sitting down again. 'He's a big man. He needs his home and his tools about; he needs his space. Chris, I don't know, there's just no room for him here!' She looked exasperated.

'I've had some unexpected news too, actually,' ventured Christina. She gazed into her tea thoughtfully before glancing up to see her friend's curious face. 'Theo told me something about my father.'

'Oh! Chris! He hasn't died has he?'

'No! He's living in Plymouth. He's been there all these years. I never knew he was so near and still friends with Theo. It's stupid I never knew before.'

Teagan looked at her dubiously. 'But he's never been in touch?'

Christina looked perplexed. 'That's just it. Theo said he had written, many times, to my mum. She never told me.'

'Families!' Teagan sighed. 'How can people be like that?'

'That's my mum for you. Poor Dad! I think I'll write to him. I'd love to see him again. I can't believe he's — ' She broke off, and shrugged. Teagan, after waiting for several moments, left her to her thoughts and went to do the dishes.

Soon after finishing their supper, Christina began the walk home. It was now dark and the lights in the harbour below twinkled.

Gulls wailed in the distance. The presence of her father was almost tangible.

★   ★   ★

When Christina got home René and her mother were in the sitting room. The atmosphere was tense, in complete contrast to Teagan's quiet cottage. Josie was perched on the edge of the sofa, flicking through a catalogue irritably. It was unusual for her not to still be at her sewing-machine. René was in the arm-chair drinking Scotch.

'Where's Debbie?' she asked.

'Upstairs, putting Caitlin to bed,' said Josie.

René was wearing a black shirt with cuffs unfastened, and his gold chain bracelet dangled from one wrist. It had a small gold padlock fastening which clinked occasionally against his glass. Christina glanced at it, recalling the inscription on it, which from that distance she couldn't read, but knew her sister had had it engraved. She had given it to him for their wedding anniversary; it read: '*Love conquers all*'.

Tempted to go straight upstairs, Christina decided to linger a while and test the air — something was most definitely up. To make conversation, she said:

'I've been thinking, Mum,' she began, 'I think we should change the menu a bit. Not use that Cash 'n' Carry stuff anymore, but offer some fresh local produce, and shellfish. It wouldn't take too much extra work.'

'The Cash 'n' Carry's cheaper, that's why we use it,' said Josie stiffly, peering up at her over her reading glasses. 'Most of our customers don't know the difference anyway, let's face it.'

'Oh, they're not that ignorant, Mum! It's what visitors are looking for these days — they've started asking for it — Cornish cream and locally caught shellfish. They've got more money to spend than locals so we ought to take advantage of it.' She eyed René as she spoke, deliberately inviting a comment. But he appeared not to be listening.

She took a deep breath. 'I was also wondering whether we should start selling crafts as well. What do you think? We could take in some pottery, jewellery and paintings and stuff from local artists and have them on sale or return. Tourists like having something to look at. It wouldn't cost us anything. We could even get one of the artists to work in there, doing portraits or something.'

'Hold on a minute!' interrupted René. 'Who's put all these bright ideas into your stupid head?' He slammed down his glass, spilling some of the contents. 'How bloody ridiculous!' he drawled, pulling a handkerchief out of his trouser pocket and mopping the table.

'Do you mind, René? I don't think it's any of your business,' said Christina.

'What are you trying to turn it into now, Sister-in-law? A pretty little arty crafty tea-room?' he smirked. 'You really haven't got a clue have you, mmm? That's the trouble with you women — you're so out of touch it's not true. You want to go and take a look around London's West End; that would soon buck your ideas up.'

'You're not in London now, René, or haven't you noticed?' snapped Christina. 'I think they're good ideas. It's not a big deal. It wouldn't take much investment, and investing in local growers might give the café a bit of publicity too. We might even get an article in the Gazette.'

Josie had developed a peculiar interest in the catalogue and kept her head down. But when she did raise it, her expression was one of steel. Christina realized it was too late to back down. She hadn't predicted such a hostile reaction, and anyway, it was only an idea. Her father wouldn't have minded, she reflected. He'd probably have enjoyed juggling with the possibilities, and had a laugh, and maybe called up one of his mates. Why were René and her mother always so confrontational?

'It's better to support our own fishermen and farmers though, don't you think,' she said, believing in what she was saying more every minute. 'Why should we keep wasting money on all that imported stuff that's in that catalogue? It's rubbish, most of it, full of preservatives and chemicals and it's all tinned or frozen.'

'Who cares?' snapped René. 'It pays the bills. That's all we're worried about at the moment.' Taking a gulp of Scotch, he swallowed hard.

'What is it with you, René? Do you think you run the place or something?'

His eyes seemed to bulge as he looked at her.

'Yes, Sister-in-law, that's exactly what I do think.'

'What on earth do you mean by that remark?'

'You'd better ask your mother there,' he replied, giving a sickly smile and inclining his head with a smirk. 'You'd better tell her, Josie dear,' he said. This unexpected form of address Christina felt in her stomach as sure as though he had punched her. Something in the relationship between her mother and René had shifted.

'What's going on?' She felt panicky now;

the blood rushed to her cheeks. 'What does he mean, Mum?'

The sharp, sudden flicking of the pages seemed to mark out the time like an hour between each second. 'What does René mean?' shouted Christina. 'Mum! Come on!' Josie closed the catalogue. Her thin lips were tightly shut as though they held a row of pins. When she finally raised her face and focussed, Christina felt a shiver of fear run down her body.

'Actually,' said Josie, 'René owns sixty per cent of the Sea Café now. We did a deal. I didn't like to tell you before, well, I didn't think it was necessary.'

René smiled smugly and held up his hands in a gesture of false humility. 'C'est la vie!'

Christina looked at him, looked back at her mother, and took a deep breath. 'You sold us out, Mum?' she asked. 'You sold us out and never even told me?'

Josie shrugged. 'I didn't think it would matter to you, he is family after all. It's not as though I sold a part-share to a stranger or anything. The café's losing so much money, Chris. You couldn't make it pay — I mean, we couldn't make it pay. You know I'm doing all the hours God sends on this out-work. If it wasn't for that sewing-machine we'd never get the bills paid.' A flush spread across her cheek as the expression on her daughter's face changed from initial shock to one of hurt. 'René knows about these things. He's a businessman. I had to do something.'

But Christina had inherited her father's protective spirit. When an injustice was seen to be done, Charlie would lay down his life to put it right. It was only his confidence which had failed him. When Christina realized that René had invaded their home and taken control of the café in such a slick, underhand way, she leapt to the defence, tore the catalogue from her mother's lap and hurled it across the room.

'You can't just hand it over to him. We haven't talked about it! I told you I've got some new ideas to try out. Well, you want to see it pay? I'm going to make it pay! I can do it alone! You just watch me!'

René broke into a humourless laugh. 'Watch you? I haven't got time to sit around watching you, Sister-in-law! I tell you what.' He heaved himself out of his chair and stood up. 'I'll be in that café first thing Monday morning and you'll be seeing some changes, my girl. Don't you worry about that!'

'Monday?' Christina felt she had been stabbed.

'Listen to me!' he said, patronizingly, lifting a stubby finger. 'Food is a currency, it's as simple as that.' He gave a twitch of a smile; he was in his element now. 'You can win or lose with it, live or die by it, invest in it, or throw it away — it's up to you.' He shrugged. 'Your mother here, she realizes an opportunity when she sees it. Of course, I forgot — you don't care about little things like turnover and profit!'

Christina stood staring at his performance in horror. But he wasn't finished yet.

'Take a grain of rice, for instance; you can eat it, and it's wasted, zap! Gone!' He snapped his fingers right in front of her face. 'Or you can plant it, cultivate it, sell the harvest and multiply it a hundred times over! It's Biblical! One thing you need to learn, Sister-in-law, is that food is money. Right? It's cash. Right? You don't mess with it. That's the lesson you've got to learn. So, from now on, I'll show you what it's like to run a profitable business.' Pleased with himself, he sat down again and picked up his Scotch. 'And the first thing that's going is that bloody dog!'

At that moment, the door flew open and Deborah entered, dressed-up as though for the stage in an off-the-shoulder dress studded with sequins. 'René!' she scolded. 'What the hell's all the noise about? I can hear you all over the house! Caitlin's trying to sleep upstairs! I thought we were going out tonight. Can't you lot sit in the same room for five minutes without bickering?'

'We are going out, dear,' replied René soothingly, 'just as soon as I talk some sense into your big sister here. Personally, Debs, I think some of your relations live in cloud-cuckoo land. The sooner they all wake up to the real world the better.'

'Oh for God's sake!' said Christina. She had had enough. She brushed past Deborah and started up the stairs, the sound of René's sniggering laughter followed her.

Entering Caitlin's room quietly, Christina whispered a few comforting words to the little girl who lay in bed wide-eyed. As she eased herself onto the edge of the bed, Caitlin sat up and snuggled against her. Christina held her close and gazed sadly out of the window over the yard to the distance beyond. She saw the lights from houses where other families, she imagined, were enjoying a meal together, perhaps watching television, and living normal lives. A part of her inner self wept for some affection too, for that peaceful family existence neither she nor Caitlin had experienced for a very long time. Caitlin needed someone she could depend on, like a loving understanding grand-dad. Immediately, her thoughts turned again to contacting her father. She wasn't the only one who needed him desperately.

3

Teagan arrived the following afternoon at her parents' homely cottage with its creative atmosphere. She could hear Beethoven's Fifth Symphony booming from down the street. Their old springer spaniel was asleep in the doorway. He raised his head and fixed her with solemn brown eyes before recognition caused him to stumble to his feet, wagging his cropped stern.

'Hello, old thing,' murmured Teagan, as he pressed his warm muzzle into her hand. Stepping in through the open door, she found no-one there. 'Anyone at home?' she shouted.

'Up here, love, just coming!' Olga came down the stairs breathing heavily. Her waist-length hair was plaited in a chunky rope which hung over her right shoulder like rats' tails.

'I was just putting some sheets away, dear,' she sighed. 'They've been hanging up in here for three days — it's so damp everywhere.'

'You need a tumble dryer, Mum!' Teagan said and smiled, knowing it was a useless suggestion; the couple didn't even possess a washing machine. Funds were limited, but their house was crammed with things which might be deemed useful at some stage, if for nothing else than for burning as fuel.

Their home was a tiny, terraced cottage set back from the harbour in St. Ives. As the attic had a sky-light and was flooded with light during the day, they had chosen this space for Quinn's studio. The rest of the cottage was dimly lit, though, being joined to its neighbours on each side and at the back. It had become his haven, and while he painted at the top of the house, Olga did her weaving on the full-size floor loom which dominated the sitting room.

Olga's hands were knobbly with arthritis. She worked on commission, making beautiful shaggy rugs to lie in front of old Cornish fireplaces. Weaving bold sweeps of colour, she worked with sheep fleeces that arrived in big bouncy parcels and were still tangled with thistle and grasses. Most dyes she made herself, gathered from the wild flowers she collected along the coastal path and spent the evenings carding her wool, teasing it out and removing the dirt and thorns while listening to the radio. The fleeces gave off a musty animal-like odour and clouds of dust when handled. Her work-in-progress was a rug in orange, brown and cream wool, shot through with strands of cobalt blue.

'Want a cuppa, dear?'

'Yes, please Mum, I'll make it. You sit down.' A kettle was already simmering on the Aga.

'Oh, if I sit down I'll never get up again,' said Olga. 'But if you're happy to make the tea I'll carry on. I'd like to get this finished before the weekend. It's for a young couple from up-country; they want to take it back with them.'

'What colour is their room?' asked Teagan, eyeing the multicoloured rug dubiously.

'I don't know. I never thought to ask that, dear. Folks as want things to match everythin' get on my nerves. I can't understand 'em myself.'

Teagan stifled a giggle and poured the boiling water into the teapot. Olga began weaving; a sleepy rhythmic manner seemed to take hold of her as she stood with her broad hips swaying, moving her foot and flicking the shuttle with her hand. As the warp lifted, the shuttle shot across the weft making a satisfactory clunk as it hit the other side.

'Mum?' began Teagan. A lot must have been expressed in that one word because it caused Olga to stop.

'What's up, love?' She peered at her daughter before picking up a pair of scissors and snipping some end threads.

Teagan drew the letter from her pocket. 'I've heard from Peter,' she said. 'He's a bit down. Things are difficult between him and Nicola at the moment.'

'Oh? Why's that, dear?' She re-started her work.

'He doesn't give a lot away, but something's happened between them.' Teagan paused, finding it difficult to explain.

Olga stopped again and gave Teagan her full attention. 'Come on then, out with it!'

'It's serious, Mum. Nicola's found someone else. She's told Peter to get out. He's asked if he can come down here to stay for a bit. He just needs to get away.'

'Found someone else? But they've got the boys!'

'That doesn't make any difference apparently. It's true, Mum. It doesn't seem possible, does it?'

Placing Olga's mug beside the loom, Teagan sat down, cupping her own tea in both hands. The room fell silent.

'The flighty so an' so,' said Olga finally. 'I always thought she fancied herself, that one. Wait till your father hears about it.' She resumed her weaving, but this time it wasn't in a relaxing rhythm. The shuttle went rattling across at an ill-tempered speed.

'If Peter comes down here it'll give him

time to gather his thoughts. Think I'd want a break too, if that happened to me.'

'Huh!' scoffed Olga. 'Not likely your Connor would give you reason to run away, dear, thank goodness. He's devoted to you and you to him — it shows.' She paused and stood resting a hand on her hip in indignation. 'So what about the kids?' she demanded. 'The selfish hussy! Suppose she hasn't stopped to consider the affect it'll have on them, the poor little blighters!'

'I don't know, Mum. We'll find out more when he gets here. I'm so lucky to have Connor, but I just wish . . . ' Teagan fell into a reverie and when she didn't continue, the clunk, clunk of the shuttle was drowned out by the opening strains of a Wagner opera from upstairs. Through the open doorway, snatches of banter from tourists passing by in the street lightened the mood.

'You're lucky to have Connor, but what dear . . . ?' prompted Olga eventually. 'You're wishin' you had a family again, is that it?'

'Yes, I suppose so.'

'There's still plenty of time, love. When you least expect it, there! Before you know where you are, there's a baby in your arms!' Clunk went the shuttle again. Olga cut the yarn and rejoined it adding emerald green. 'That's how you came along anyway, dear. You took me and your father completely by surprise!'

'Did I?' Teagan said and smiled. 'Mum, a family would make our lives complete!' she announced, as though having just made a new discovery.

'Well, it hasn't helped our Peter, has it?' replied the practical Olga. 'What's going to happen to those poor boys, I wonder?' She left her work and sank her abundant hips into the small settee next to her daughter. 'When's he coming down? We'll fit him in here somehow, but I don't know what your father's going to say. If he has to give up his studio he'll go mad — or he'll drive me mad at least.'

'Mum, you've no need to worry. Peter will stay with us in the spare room. It'll only need a bit of sorting.'

'Are you sure? He's a big lad, our Peter.'

'I know.' Teagan got up and went to fetch some more milk from a stone jug which was kept in a bucket of water outside the front step. A fridge was another convenience of the modern age which had escaped them.

'I think we've got a bit more room than you, Mum. I'm having a top up — do you want some more? We couldn't throw Dad out of his studio — just imagine!'

'Oh, he paces the floor like a flippin' tiger in a cage sometimes. It'll drive us mad one day, this cottage, it's so cramped.'

'But it's cosy and peaceful.'

'What? Music on full blast, sawin' an' hammerin' and goodness knows what all the time! He makes so much noise when he's here, but he still complains about kids makin' a racket outside. Mad? He's like a ravin' lunatic, your father!'

Teagan smiled. Her mother had been complaining for as long as she could remember, but she knew she would never leave in spite of all she said.

★　★　★

Christina, walking home from the café, wondered if John Madison was back from sea and even allowed herself to imagine him asking her out, until she pictured trying to keep up with his long strides — and with a sense of sadness reflected on her bad leg. Her romantic illusions never lasted long. Letting herself in the front door, Christina listened for the familiar sound of Josie's machine trundling its way through mountains of suffocating cloth.

'Hi, Mum,' she shouted, sticking her head round the door and addressing her back bent over the machine. Josie stopped the sewing-machine abruptly and tugging the fillet of cloth from its jaws, turned round to face her.

'I'm all behind, Chris. Caitlin's sulking in her room; your sister's not back yet and I haven't even started the dinner.'

'What are we having?' replied Christina.

'Whatever you like, have a look in the freezer.'

Unimpressed with this piece of information, she went through to the kitchen. Flies buzzed around dirty dishes from the night before and breakfast bowls were still piled up in the sink. She sighed, picked up a greasy saucepan, looked around and slammed it down again. Ginger hung his head and retreated into his basket in the corner by the Aga. Abandoning the kitchen, she went upstairs to find her niece.

Caitlin's room was at the top of the house, set under the eaves opposite Christina's bedroom. The stairwell and landing separated the two rooms; Caitlin's, overlooking the back of the house, was slightly larger. It was decorated in dusky pink Regency wallpaper, the furniture was white, and the long velvet curtains were faded. From her window, she could look out on a row of ramshackle back-gardens. A crumbling stone wall was over-run with clematis, but it was the only redeeming feature in this otherwise neglected concrete yard. Ivy wove its tangled way

66

through abandoned lobster pots, a dustbin, broken chairs and an old rusting boat. The wall of a nearby house still showed traces of the mural painted by an artist years before; it was of a mermaid with seaweed and shells. Beyond these gardens lay an alleyway, climbing in shallow steps up the hill.

If the little girl had looked out of the window at that moment, she would have seen an old man struggling to push a sack-barrow carrying a beer-keg up to the pub on the corner. He was easing it up over each step, backwards, like a mother pulling a pram. A tabby cat, sitting on a nearby wall, watched the man's progress in a bored fashion. Somewhere, across the rooftops could be heard a beginner's attempts at playing the trumpet. Its feeble voice drifted off towards the centre of the town, where a few lights twinkled in the growing dusk. Voices rose occasionally from the street and were joined by the seagulls' plaintive mewing.

Christina stuck her head round the door. 'Caitlin? Didn't you go to your dancing class this afternoon?' The little girl, wearing a pink leotard, tights and ballet shoes, was sitting on her bed playing. Some tiny clothes were set out before her and she was sorting them and whispering to a Barbie doll on her lap. Ignoring Christina, she carried on placing the items in rows, inspecting each one with exaggerated concentration. Her petite face was accentuated by her hair being drawn tightly back into a ballerina's bun. 'Caitlin?'

The child shrugged her shoulders as though tossing the question aside.

'Do you fancy coming to buy some fish an' chips with me?' She shook her head solemnly.

'Come on, Caitlin, just you and me! We can have a look at the harbour on the way and see what boats have come in. Come on!' she urged gently.

'Mummy didn't come an' get me,' Caitlin said and pouted. Her voice was distinct and crystal clear. Only the slightest twitch to the corner of her mouth revealed a suppressed cry. 'Granny met me from school. Mummy was supposed to fetch me for my ballet class — so I couldn't go.'

'Oh! Never mind! Perhaps she was too busy,' said Christina. 'We'll make sure you get there next week. Come on, Caitlin, let's go an' get ourselves some nice fish an' chips!'

Turning away from her toys for the first time and looking straight at Christina, she said: 'It's because Daddy's here, that's why she didn't come. She forgot.'

'Not necessarily, little one; your Mummy's busy, that's all.'

Rising from the bed, Caitlin's doll fell to

the floor but she ignored it. 'Granny said Daddy's got a new car, that's why she forgot about me,' she said matter-of-factly, sweeping past Christina and going towards the door. 'I hate fish. Can I have sausage with mine?'

'Hang on! Let's change your ballet shoes first!'

The evening was light and warm as Christina, holding Caitlin's hand, and with Ginger at her heel, walked down to the harbour through cobblestone streets. They passed noisy restaurant kitchen windows and cheerful gift-shops with their doors still open, and made their way towards the harbour. Caitlin clung tightly to her hand, her eyes darting from right to left as though she was walking on a tightrope. Christina glanced down fondly on to the top of her dainty head and wished for a moment that Caitlin was her little girl. She would look after her and not leave her neglected. She wondered how her sister could still fall for the fake charms of a man like René. And how could she give attention to her pupils, a bunch of tinsel-clad dancing girls, but forget her own daughter?

★　★　★

When they arrived home clutching their warm parcels, the aroma of fish and chips soon permeated the house.

'Mum!' shouted Christina. 'Come and get it!' She switched the television on and they sat in the sitting room eating straight from the newspaper, watching Coronation Street and enjoying their meal. Caitlin poked her fingers into the parcel, pulling out chips and licking her fingers.

'No, Ginger, it's hot!' shouted Caitlin. But the dog continued watching her keenly, with his ears cocked and stump of a tail wagging.

'My tooth's loose, look!' said Caitlin, turning towards Christina and showing her sharp little row of milk teeth. She pointed to one tiny pearl, wobbling it. 'I'm going to put it under my pillow tonight,' she said.

'OK, if it comes out tonight we'll have to tell Mummy to look out for the tooth fairy.'

Caitlin nodded happily. 'I can't eat my chips properly,' she lisped. 'No!' she shouted again. 'Stop it, Ginger, naughty boy!' and swung round, bringing her food away from the dog's nose. 'He keeps snatching it out of my hands, Chris!' she scolded. 'Tell him!'

Christina giggled. 'Perhaps he's afraid he won't get any supper! Here, Ginger!' she called, 'Sit!' and she tossed a piece of batter towards him which he gobbled greedily. At that moment Josie came into the room.

'Yours is over there,' Christina nodded to a

package on the table.

'Haven't you got plates out or anything? Honestly, do you think we're camping or what?'

Christina ignored her. Josie took her parcel and disappeared into the kitchen, but within minutes, she returned. 'Didn't you get your sister any then?'

'No,' Christina looked at her curiously. 'René will take her out for a meal, won't he?'

'Not necessarily, in fact they both might want something.'

'Well, tough!' said Christina, screwing up her fish paper and flinging it into the empty grate.

★　★　★

Maudie Peacock was an ageless lady. She cared little for her own appearance, was well nourished, and had a downy face that was puckered like an old balloon. She usually wore a tweed skirt with bare legs in all weathers. Somewhat eccentric, there was no disputing her good intentions and sound common sense. People respected her local knowledge, children adored her and parents sought her grandmotherly advice.

But Maudie had a weakness — cats. She simply loved them. If a stray was to cross her path, it would be swept up and carried home under her ample bosom like a trophy. No matter if it had fleas or ticks or was riddled with worms; if it was homeless and hungry it would be cared for, nurtured and smothered with love. Children she treated in much the same way and her face, on these occasions, was always radiant with joy. She believed one could cure anything with love.

Cats were her priority though, taking precedent over everything including her husband of thirty-five years. Arthur Peacock was a retired policeman and dutiful bread-winner to the Peacock menagerie. He kept a low profile, eating his dinner alone in front of the television while his wife pottered about in the kitchen and fed her protégés. More recently, he had vacated the marital bed and taken to sleeping on a put-u-up in the sitting room. Tall in stature, Arthur now worked as a night-watchman at an engineering company in Truro.

When he came home at seven in the morning, he would cook himself a fried breakfast on the blackened stove, soaking the fat up with a generous slice of bread. Eating this in front of the television in the sitting room, he would retire to his bed in the same room, blissfully undisturbed by the sleeping cats around him.

Maudie would rise at eight, feed the cats,

currently nineteen of them, before going to collect any little charges she had of primary school age to take them to school. Invariably, one of these was John Madison's daughter, Sylvie, who often slept over in the Peacock household while John was at sea. She occupied a spare bed in Maudie's bedroom. Maudie's concern for the widower John Madison caused her to clean his house and do some of his washing too. Meanwhile, uncomplaining Arthur would sleep like an old tom-cat, all day, waking only occasionally to eat or drink or scratch until nocturnal commitments roused him from his slumber.

★ ★ ★

When Maudie called into the Sea Café one morning she had an idea to put to Christina. 'I've been thinkin', dearie,' she said. 'I'll have a cuppa, girl, by the way, if you've got one handy.' Settling herself into a chair she continued: 'Your Caitlin might like to be proper friends with our Sylvie, now she's started school full-time. Be nice if they could come home together with me sometimes. I'd fetch them both and it'd save your sister a journey.'

'That sounds a great idea,' replied Christina, 'but I don't think we could afford anything extra at the moment. Thanks anyway.'

'Oh, I weren't going to charge you, my 'andsome, just thought she'd be a nice little playmate for Sylvie.'

'Wouldn't John Madison mind? He pays you to have Sylvie, after all,' said Christina.

'Mind?' chuckled Maudie. 'Why should he mind? He needs her bringin' up to be a young lady, an' she ain't got no female company at home. No, dearie, he won't mind. He said to me only the other day she ought to be havin' some friends to play with, seein' as she's got no mother at home. It might help pass the time for 'er, especially when he's away at sea. It can't be much fun, havin' the company of an old woman like me all the time!'

Christina regarded her soberly. 'I'll see what my sister says,' she replied. 'It's often left to me to collect Caitlin anyway. Debbie's so busy with her dance classes, and Mum's always working. Teagan steps in to watch the café for me.'

Maudie shook her head at the mention of Teagan's name. 'Ah, yes, that poor girl,' she mumbled, without giving an explanation.

Taking the tea to her table, Christina's mind spun with the opportunity of having closer contact with John. The memory of the evening he had cooked her herrings haunted her.

'Sylvie's been goin' to school near on a year now,' Maudie's voice came breaking into her thoughts. 'She's startin' to find her feet an' she's an independent little madam, that one. Growin' up a bit too quick if you ask me, but just as well I s'pose, seein' as how her mother passed away so sudden. Ah, 'tis a rum life.' Her good-natured face crumpled slightly and her massive frame wobbled on the small café chair. 'Life's too short, dearie. You should be goin' out a bit yerself, findin' yerself a young man. You're too serious, that's your trouble. Take a leaf out of your sister's book an' go out dancin' an' havin' a bit o' fun. Don't want you gettin' left on the shelf.'

'Dancing? What, with my leg?' Christina smiled. 'The shelf has a certain appeal, you know. I'm all right as I am, Maudie, honestly. I don't think I'm the sort to go out hitting the town really, do you?'

'Come now! You've still got a pretty face on yer! If you can't enjoy life when you're young, when can you? That John Madison, now he'd be a fine catch!' Her eyes sparkled with mischief. 'You mark my words, dearie, he's got a good sensible head on him an' he owns his own house. You could do a lot worse.'

'Maudie! Shame on you!' she exclaimed, with a giggle. 'It's just as well there's no-one in here to hear you!' A blush was spreading on her cheek and she turned away to conceal it.

'You think on it, girl. He's got a ready-made family with Sylvie. That poor little 'un, she don't know what it is to have a mother's love.'

What Maudie said had hit a nerve. The idea of putting her and John Madison together as a couple sent her heart racing.

'Oh well, I'd best be gettin' back to the family,' declared Maudie, finishing her tea. She slapped some change on the table and roused herself from the chair.

By 'the family' Christina knew she meant the cats and wrapping some scraps in tin-foil she gave them to her. 'Here,' she said. 'Take these; it'll fill a few tummies!' Maudie's face lit-up in delight. 'Oh thank you, dearie!' she exclaimed, and immediately despatched the package down the front of her jumper.

Later that morning, Josie arrived with provisions, having just been to the warehouse. Impatient and businesslike, she began unloading boxes of food from the boot of her car parked out on the road. Christina noticed there was an agitated sternness about her, as though she had better things to do.

'Take these. I'll fetch the oil,' she said, disappearing out of the door again. Thin to the point of looking undernourished, Josie always wore black clothes; her once auburn hair was greying and tied back, presenting a severe face to the world. She looked worn-out. 'I don't know how these companies expect us to make a profit!' she complained as she came bursting into the café again loaded with more boxes. 'Been busy?'

'Not really,' replied Christina, resenting her noisy invasion. The few customers she had, had been enjoying a quiet cup of coffee before her arrival.

'Shall I do that?' she asked.

Josie ignored her and started putting the food away, tearing the cardboard boxes open and stashing crisps in the cupboard. Leaving her to it, Christina went into the storeroom to check off the stock. Returning a few minutes later, she said: 'I don't think you needed to get more crisps. We don't want them going soft or we'll have to chuck half of them away again.'

'Remind me not to get any next week then, I'm not a mind-reader. How many biscuits have you got left?'

'Oh, enough,' said Christina, wishing she would go and leave her in peace.

Josie cast a look around the café, 'Not many in for elevenses then,' she said.

'No, where is everyone these days?' replied Christina. 'Are they all stopping in the town?

Don't people like walking anymore?'

'Flying off to Sunny Spain or Florida, more likely,' replied Josie.

'So, what exactly has René got planned for the café then, Mum? I dread to think!'

Josie was tight-lipped. It was as though Christina hadn't spoken. She continued counting boxes of tea-bags, staring intently at her list before rooting through a box as though searching for something.

'Mum? What's René planning to do here? I'd like to know.'

Josie straightened-up. 'Didn't they send four packets of mustard last week? There's only one here. We couldn't have used all those already.'

'I can't remember. I'll have to check with the order sheets at home. Mum! I asked you what René's up to. He must have told you something!'

Josie looked at her. 'Where's Debbie this morning?'

Christina sighed and turned away. 'Out shopping in Truro for tap shoes apparently,' she replied, 'and taking rehearsals for the show this afternoon.' Her voice had a despairing tone, reflecting her confusion. Why wouldn't her mother talk to her? She waited, busying herself with the order-sheet, but still no response came. Obviously Josie had no intention of answering her question. She decided to change the subject.

'You know Maudie looks after John Madison's little girl?' she began. 'Well, Maudie made a suggestion this morning: Would we like her to collect Caitlin for us and take her to play with Sylvie sometimes?'

'Why, what for?' asked Josie absent-mindedly, pen in hand, intent on her paperwork.

'She says Sylvie needs the company. I think it's a good idea, don't you? John Madison apparently told her it would do his daughter good to have someone her own age to play with. Probably do Caitlin good as well, don't you think?'

'I don't like that woman, she's a bit, well,' Josie lowered her voice, 'bit of a gypsy, I always think.'

'A gypsy?' Christina stopped herself, realizing the customers might have overheard. 'She's a bit of a yokel, yes,' she added in a whisper, 'but she's a kind-hearted soul. Sylvie adores her.'

Josie gave the paperwork a couple of ticks. 'Don't you think she, well, smells a bit catty?'

'Maybe, but I like her. I think it would do Caitlin good. It might bring her out of herself a bit; she does need to mix more, poor thing, she's still so shy.'

'It depends how much this woman wants

paying,' Josie added. 'I certainly can't afford it and I don't expect René — '

'She doesn't want paying. All she wants is a playmate for Sylvie because her dad's away at sea so much.'

'Best speak to Debbie about it then.'

'Mum, please tell me what René's planning.'

Josie gave her a quick look. 'Not now, Chris! We'll talk about it later.' Chucking down the paperwork, she closed the storecupboard and minutes later, she left.

★ ★ ★

That evening Christina went to call on Maudie Peacock. She left Ginger at home and took some more left-overs for the cats. Maudie's cottage had only one bedroom, which was in the roof, accessed via a wooden ladder; something which caused a degree of difficulty for a woman of her age and stature. It was furnished with an iron bedstead and a wardrobe wedged under the eaves of its sloping roof. Under the window, there was also a small put-u-up bed where, on the occasions that were deemed necessary, a small child could comfortably stay. Apart from Sylvie, who was a regular guest, numerous other waifs and orphans had occupied this little bed over the years. It was a secure corner with a window overlooking St. Ives Bay. Many a child's eyes had been fascinated by watching the boats out at sea, twinkling like fairy lights, and the comings and goings of the busy harbour.

The bathroom and toilet were downstairs adjoining the kitchen. The bath was almost always full of washing soaking in suds, indicating that it wasn't often used for its intended purpose. But what the cottage lacked in mod-cons it made up for in homeliness. There was a general aura of warmth. In the thirty years Maudie and her husband had lived there, it had managed to evade the progress of science. The cottage existed in its own time, with its own values and its own sense of survival. Nature crept in from the garden, winding its tentacles of ivy through the doorway. Every day, summer and winter, the back-door was propped open to accommodate the many comings and goings of cats of all shapes and sizes. Ants crawled on the kitchen floor, wasps hovered, and birds, chickens and even seagulls hopped into the cottage to help themselves to crumbs of bread from the bread board or pieces of pastry from the edge of a pie. If seen, Maudie would wave her apron at them and shush them off, beaming her hearty smile.

A cramped sitting room with a low-beamed ceiling, housed an enormous broken-backed chesterfield sofa, a sideboard dusted only by the fur of sleeping cats, and a black-and-white television, always switched on. The window-sills were covered in letters, bills, faded photographs, potted plants, candles, and coffee mugs. On top of this collection sat two cats grooming each other. Five were curled-up asleep on the sofa and three more perched along its back. On the floor in front of the fireplace was a large wicker dog-basket lined with blankets. This housed a queen cat with a litter of new-born kittens squeaking and kneading their mother's soft abdomen with pink pointed paws.

Maudie led Christina out into the garden. It was a warm balmy evening. 'You come an' have a look at this, dearie,' she said. Bees buzzed in the lavender. Long grass wafted in the breeze. The air was heady with the musky scent of chicken manure and sheep's parsley. 'Look 'ee here,' she whispered as they approached the wooden sheds. Christina stepped into the gloom behind Maudie's bulky form. When Maudie turned round she was holding a shoe box; a shaft of sunlight sliced across her shoulder straight into the box. What Christina saw took her breath away. Four tiny kittens, not more than a few days old, were just stirring from their sleep.

'Beauties aren't they!' Maudie whispered. 'They're our Tabitha's. A terrible mother she is. I says to my Arthur at the weekend: 'She looks as though she's dropped them kittens, don't she?' I spent all mornin' lookin' and then I finds 'em in the garden under the hedge — she won't go near 'em, naughty girl! So I've been feedin' them myself with a little baby-milk from a dropper. I've been up half the night with 'em. Their mother don't want nothin' to do with 'em. You can't tell cats nothin' these days — they please 'emselves.'

'Bit like teenagers then, Maudie?' said Christina stroking their velvety heads.

'Oh much worse, dearie.'

The evening started to lose the sun's warmth and Maudie and Christina made their way back to the house with Maudie bearing the box full of kittens and escorted by a troupe of cats. Some darted ahead and some brushed affectionately against their legs. Tabitha, the wayward mother, was among them.

'Let's have ourselves a cup o' coffee,' said Maudie, 'an' I'll show you our new babby.' In the lean-to, enthroned in a cardboard box, sat a big, brown tabby cat. Its eyes were half-closed like a broody chicken. 'This is our new addition,' said Maudie. 'He was brought here last night by the Cats' Rescue. Found on a boat in Penryn he was, hiding down by the engine to keep himself warm, poor thing. I won't disturb him to show you, but he had his foot caught in a gin-trap an' it's all swelled up, poor boy!' she crooned. 'Cruel gadgets those things, I hate 'em.'

'They're illegal, Maudie,' said Christina, stroking the cat's broad head and hearing a loud purr start up, like a rusty old generator.

'Some folks don't take no notice o' the law, dearie.'

'Maudie?' began Christina. This was the subject which had been on her mind. 'I've talked to my sister about Caitlin playing with Sylvie. The only thing is — she said we ought to give you something for your trouble, but business is so bad at the moment, all we can offer you are some left-over scraps for the cats as a sort of payment.'

'I don't want no payment, dearie, I told you that, but some scraps would be 'andy. I just thought it'd be nice for 'em,' she replied. 'Seems little ones need to be together in this big world, don't they, old boy,' she replied, stroking the old cat fondly.

4

Christina and Teagan, waiting at St. Ives railway station, had their eyes fixed on the curve of the bay, watching for the branch-line train which runs within splashing distance of the waves between St. Erth and St. Ives. The small train arrived, bringing passengers off the night train from London and day-trippers from other parts of the West Country. Crowds of people spilled onto the small platform and Teagan immediately saw her brother. 'There he is!' she cried.

Looking every inch the Cornishman he was, he wore jeans and a rough shirt unbuttoned to the waist. His bushy chestnut beard and hair gave him an unkempt masculinity. Heavy walking boots accentuated his six feet in stature so that when they reached him, Teagan had to stand on tip-toe to embrace him. 'You must be ten minutes early at least!' she exclaimed, laughing in delight.

'I'm a year or two late, girl,' he growled. His manner was brusque and he paused, scrutinizing his sister's companion. 'And who's this you've brought to inspect me, eh?' he asked, turning two searching eyes on Christina.

'You know Christina, Peter!'

Examining her face, he said, 'Not that I remember.'

'We've met before,' said Christina, 'a few years ago, at school.'

'Ah, my memory's hopeless these days. I'll try to make amends from now on; sorry! I'm pleased to meet you,' he said, offering a big hand and a warm smile. Throwing down his rucksack restlessly he stood facing the sea squarely, forgetting them both. Drawing breath into his broad chest noisily, he savoured the sea air. 'My, that smells good. I'd quite forgotten how fresh that air feels!' he roared. 'It's great to be back.'

'I was sorry to hear about what happened,' began Teagan. 'Hope you don't mind, but Chris sort of knows how things stand.'

'More than I do then! Damned if I can understand the woman. Aah!' he grunted savagely, and picking up his rucksack, he slung it over his shoulder. 'Don't go spoilin' my appetite talkin' about that now, sis! Hope you feel up to cookin' today, I'm starving!'

Soon, Christina left them so she could go and open the café. Looking over her shoulder briefly, she saw them climbing the hill together; Teagan running to keep up with Peter's long strides like a small child.

Leaving the town behind them, Teagan and her brother made their way towards Bent Cross; as soon as they were indoors, Peter seemed to dwarf it all. His broad shoulders almost touched the sloping ceiling. Throwing down his things, he went to look out of the window, his massive form filling the tiny sitting room and blocking out the light. Several times he had to duck to avoid hitting his head on a beam or a low door frame. Teagan began to explain that she had moved all the junk and sewing paraphernalia from their spare room, and furnished it as best she could.

'I hope you don't mind roughing it for a bit, Peter? We're a bit basic here. It's rather cramped, not what you're used to.'

He swung round to face her. 'Don't you go feelin' all inadequate on me, sis. I ain't askin' for nothin' grand, I told you that, didn't I? Hey! I'm pleased enough that you could find any room for me at all, big oaf that I am.' He gazed at her face in concern before his eyes softened and he cast around the room in genuine distress. 'I didn't know where else to go.'

'I'm so sorry!' she exclaimed, 'You're welcome to stay as long as you like. It's lovely to have you, honestly! Make yourself at home — promise?'

'Thanks, sis,' he said, and gave her a bear-hug. 'You might change your mind though, come night-time,' he chuckled, releasing her and kissing the top of her head. 'Folks tell me I snore like a pig!' Within minutes, his possessions were everywhere. His rucksack was spilling its contents across the floor, his jacket was thrown down and his big walking boots stood in the fireplace. But when she saw her brother stretch himself out on the sofa giving a big sigh of contentment it was evidence enough that he felt at ease.

Peter did indeed snore. That night, she heard his deep slumber coming from the spare bed-room and rumble around the cottage. Finding some comfort in her brother's presence, she lay thinking about Connor miles away on the open sea, imagining the roar and swell of the waves, and praying for his safe return.

★　★　★

Shortly after Christina had opened the café the following day, she was pleased to see Peter and Teagan stroll in together. Peter stood gazing about him with an animal-like passivity, but his face bore traces of strain. It was early, but already several customers were sitting at tables eating breakfast. He approached the counter where Christina was busy making sandwiches and ordered coffee and hot 'bacon butties' for himself and Teagan. While she prepared it, he confided in her:

'I'm glad my sister's found a shoulder to cry on,' he said. 'She's told me you've always been there for her. It's good of yer. She's at a loose end sometimes with her man at sea so long.'

Christina nodded. 'She helps me out here too quite often, and she'll never accept anything for it. I do appreciate it. Actually I'm at a bit of a loose end myself at times — and no husband away at sea either as an excuse!'

'You're not spoken for then?' he teased. 'There's still time!' He winked at her. 'It's not all it's cracked up to be though, marriage, I mean, believe me.'

She smiled at him. 'So they tell me.'

A rugged looking woman, apparently on her paper-round delivering the Western Morning News, sat having coffee with the bag of newspapers beside her. Carrying their breakfast back, Peter asked her if he could buy a copy and minutes later a restful peace ensued as he settled down to read and his sister began writing her diary.

Within minutes an over-bearing voice was heard outside, transforming the atmosphere in a split-second to one of tension. It signalled the arrival of René. Christina busied herself tidying the counter, bracing herself for when he made his entrance. But René was still outside — talking to himself, it appeared. While he seemed to be inspecting the framework of the door, she could see he had an expression of mild irritation on his face. Presently he stopped lingering and entered the café, humming to himself in a distracted way. He didn't acknowledge anyone.

'Good morning, René,' said Christina. He didn't respond. Instead he started kicking the bottom of the French-doors. Christina glanced across at Teagan nervously before going over to him and hissing under her breath:

'What exactly do you think you're doing?'

'We'll have to get that seen to, Sister-in-law, there's wet-rot on the bottom of that door. Wouldn't be surprised if the whole place isn't riddled with damp,' he added, wrinkling his nose as though he could smell it. On saying this, he swaggered about, glancing first at the ceiling, then the walls, the floor, as though entering a poor widow's house. He had a bemused smile on his face. When he inadvertently made eye-contact with a customer sitting at one of the tables, he responded good-humouredly. 'Good Morning!' he said breezily, with a broad sweep of his eyes. Peter had stopped reading and was eyeing him suspiciously. René's presence seemed to suck the oxygen from the room.

Hidden from view behind the counter, Ginger began to emit a long low growl. Hearing this, René barged past Christina and stood staring down at the dog that now sprang from his basket with full force, barking ferociously. René kicked out and struck him with his foot. Ginger yelped, ran past him and through the inner doorway towards the storeroom, where he turned to face René, threatening him with a tirade of barks.

'Shut that dog up!' yelled René. 'Bloody hound!' The customers looked on in amazement. Peter scraped back his chair and stood up. Christina, rushing to check Ginger, saw that his mouth was bleeding and she closed the inter-connecting door, shutting him in the storeroom.

'You shouldn't be keeping any dog in the café let alone a vicious little runt like that,' said René. 'Look! A bloody dog basket as well! Can you believe that? Wait until the Health Inspectors discover that — they'll close us down just like that, girl.' He snapped his fingers right under her nose.

'I'd like you to leave, René,' said Christina. 'My customers are trying to have a quiet cup of coffee.'

He gave a snort of laughter. 'Suppose your customers don't mind a rabid dog slinking around the place. Ever asked them, mmm?'

Christina shuddered. She began to wonder if he was drunk and caught Peter's sympathetic gaze with a degree of helplessness. René continued to totter around the café, poking at things and muttering to himself until he stopped, holding up a menu in a shaky hand.

'Hum!' he declared, scanning it quickly. 'Very nice! Rather them than me,' he said. 'Can't say I'd like to take my refreshment in a dog kennel, but it's up to them.' He cleared his throat and, turning his heavy body towards the door, seemed about to leave. But Peter stepped out towards him, towering above him and blocking his exit. René stared up at his opponent with a bored smile.

'I think you owe the young lady an apology,' said Peter. 'I'm new to this place, but I bet it's not often this café's disturbed by such a loud mouth. I don't know who you are, but I suggest you shut your mouth and take yourself back to where you came from.'

René looked up at Peter in utter astonishment. 'Who the hell are you, telling me what to do?' he demanded. 'Do you know who I am? I could have you thrown out of this place, do you realize that?'

Peter took a step closer, folding his muscular arms across his chest. 'Go ahead,' he said.

René abruptly turned his back on him. 'I suggest you buck your ideas up, Sister-in-law. I'll speak to your mother. Bloody useless way to run a business.' With that parting shot he brushed past Peter and walked out.

★ ★ ★

It was almost ten o'clock that night, and the summer evening buzz of people out on the town had died down. Christina, from her vantage point on her window-seat, saw René's open-topped sports-car draw up outside. Her sister's giggles, slightly hysterical after too much wine, rang above René's deceptive laugh. His was a laugh studded with fake diamonds, and the rustle of twenty pound notes. The whole artificial package spilled out of the car onto the street. Simultaneously, Ginger exploded into a frenzy of barking beside her. Every hair on his back bristled. She tried to restrain him, refusing to open her bedroom door to let him take his jaunt down the stairs. Reluctant to face René at that hour, especially if he had been drinking, she tried to quieten the dog. But before she could, there was a quiet tapping on her door and it began to open. Caitlin's sleepy head poked through.

'Is Mummy back?' she lisped. Ginger shot

straight through the gap and raced down the stairs on the attack.

'Yes, love, your Mummy's come home but it's late now. Go back to bed, there's a good girl.' She was about to go after Ginger when the little girl began to cry.

'I wanted . . . ' she sniffed. 'I wanted to ask Mummy something.'

'Mummy will be up presently,' she coaxed, taking the sleepy child's hand and leading her back into her room. Before long, she knew, Deborah would be creeping into Caitlin's bedroom, duvet under her arm, in retreat from René's embraces.

'She'll be too tired to talk tonight, Caitlin. Ask her in the morning.'

'But I want to ask her now!' grizzled the little girl, pale with exhaustion, but driven by her need.

Tucking her up in bed again, Christina kissed her forehead. 'Close your eyes and you'll be asleep again in two minutes.'

Just as she was leaving the room however, her voice piped up again through the darkness. 'I wanted to ask Mummy if I can go with Mithus Peacock after school tomorrow to play at Sylvie's house 'cos her daddy's come home.'

'We'll ask her in the morning,' she whispered, feeling her heart quicken at the possibility of seeing John again.

The following morning Deborah appeared in the kitchen, followed by Caitlin, still sleepy, dressed in her pyjamas and carrying a pink blanket

'Any coffee brewing?' asked Deborah, lifting the filter jug and wrinkling her nose. 'I've got such a headache!'

'There would be if anyone could be bothered to put some on,' replied Christina who was washing dishes left from the night before. It made little difference to Christina how unfair the work-load appeared to be. In some quiet part of her mind, there remained a sanctuary where eventually she could recapture her own peace of mind. After all the domestic chores were done, she would go for a walk along the beach to open the café. On the way she might compose a poem in her head. In the evenings she looked forward to taking herself off to her room to read. More than anything, she liked to sit on the window-seat in her bedroom at night with Ginger on her lap and watch the world go by down below. There, tourists dawdled through cobbled streets on their way to the pubs and restaurants in the town. She always closed the Sea Café early so at least her commitment there ended soon after six.

'Mummy!' Caitlin whined. 'She said I could have my tea there. Her daddy's making her a doll's house wiv' proper furniture an' things.' This was apparently the continuation of a conversation started upstairs, assumed Christina, and she listened intently for her sister's reply.

'You've got a nice doll's house of your own. I've never seen you play with it, not once!'

'I do! I do play with it,' complained Caitlin. 'Sylvie's got real lights in hers, and it's got — '

'All right, but ask Granny, I won't have time so she'll have to fetch you. Where is Mother anyway?' she asked, turning to Christina.

'I'll collect her from John Madison's if you like.'

'There you are, pest, Chris will fetch you, so off you go and get dressed.'

Caitlin skipped out of the room humming to herself. Deborah had raised her eyebrows. 'Well, well, why are we so keen all of a sudden?'

Christina blushed. 'I'm just trying to keep the peace, that's all.' She dried her hands on the tea-towel and tried to look busy. 'Poor thing, she's been going on about it for ages,' she added.

'Nothing to do with going to see John

Madison, I suppose!' teased Deborah, scrutinizing Christina's burning face.

'Why should it be?' she retaliated.

Deborah only smiled.

★ ★ ★

Half-an-hour later, before Christina left to open the café, she poked her head round the door.

'Where is everyone, Mum?' she asked.

Josie stopped the sewing-machine and turned round to face her. This was unusual. 'Debbie's taken Caitlin to school and she's got classes all day,' she said. 'But your brother-in-law, you'll be pleased to hear, has taken himself off back to London.'

'Oh? What brought that on so suddenly?' she asked, relief flooding though her.

'He said he's got a meeting in the City, but it sounds as if he wasn't too impressed by his reception in the café yesterday.' Josie was staring at her suspiciously.

'He's impossible, Mum!' exclaimed Christina. 'He was so rude in front of the customers. He's really got no idea! How can anyone have a civilized conversation with him?'

'René does have a lot of experience in business, dear,' Josie emphasized, looking over the top of her glasses, 'and he does have money.'

'But he's so heavy-handed. He'll barge in and spoil everything. He's so arrogant! The way he spoke to me yesterday in front of the customers, you should have heard him! He hasn't got a clue, Mum.'

Josie removed some pins from her work and looked at her daughter with resignation. 'Sooner or later, we may have to bow to his demands. The café's not paying its way. We've got to do something. It's not just a place to have a few friends to hang around, you know.'

'I know that! Credit me with a bit of common sense, Mum! Anyway, I've got plenty of new plans of my own. He'll see changes; he doesn't need to throw his weight about.'

'Changes need money, and money to invest is something we just haven't got.' Josie looked at her daughter steadily, watching her message hit home. 'It's time you realized, Chris. We're at the end of the line. It's over.'

★ ★ ★

Christina walked up the High Street that evening with a heavy heart. She was on her way to collect Caitlin from John Madison's, but even the prospect of seeing John again hadn't cheered her. Many of the shops were still open, with holiday-makers strolling around. Pleased at the slight reprieve she had by René's departure, she feared sooner or later her routine was bound to change.

Her thoughts kept going back to when John had come into the café and filleted the herrings. The closeness of his body had overwhelmed her that night, and caused her pulse to beat wildly; it was as though she was drawn to him like a magnet. His natural scent of fish and wood-smoke and tobacco, suddenly came back to her and her heart leapt at the recollection. The way he had touched her face!

Following Maudie's directions, she soon came upon the terraced cottage, the first in a row of three whose front-doors opened straight onto the street. Within moments, failing to find a doorbell, she lifted the letter-box and let it spring back noisily. There was a scramble of activity inside and she heard John call: 'Come round the back!'

Following the side alleyway, she found herself in a pretty cobbled courtyard. Climbing roses and honeysuckle created a secluded haven where a cast iron table and chairs stood. Some papers lay on the table and beside them half a tankard of frothy beer. The back-door opened and John appeared. He said quietly: 'I see you've discovered my sanctuary.'

'It's lovely,' Christina replied. 'Our back-yard's just a dumping ground. It must be wonderful to sit here and read. It's so peaceful.'

'I planted it in memory of my wife, Kate. It took my mind off things to be able to do something, you know, just for her. She collected those pebbles and shells off the beach before she . . . '

'I'm sorry,' said Christina gently, seeing the small fragments of sea-washed glass and tiny shells that decorated the concrete path. 'I didn't mean to intrude. It's beautiful.'

'No need to apologize. Want a beer or cider? The girls are still busy playing with the doll's house upstairs. I don't think they'll mind carrying on a bit longer.'

'Then I will. Cider, thanks.'

'Good! Take a seat; I'll be back in a minute.'

'Sylvie?' She heard his voice within the house: 'Come and take this lemonade, please!' There was the thunder of feet down the stairs, causing her to smile to herself. She relaxed, and leaning back, gazed upwards at the sky, letting the last of the sun's warmth play on her face. John came back into the garden with a tall glass of cider for her.

'Cheers,' he said, sitting down near her.

'Cheers! I didn't interrupt your work, did

I?' she asked, looking at all the paperwork laid out on the table.

'No, this is . . . well, it's the stuff I sent for, about decommissioning.'

'But it won't really come to that, will it John?'

'It's an option I can't afford to ignore.' He took a long draught of beer and sighed.

'But you've got to stick to your principles. Don't let them beat you too easily.'

'Principles?' He laughed bitterly. 'I can't afford to have principles, not any more. If they've chosen to destroy the market for us, who am I to talk about principles?'

If Christina hadn't seen his face, she would have thought his words were loaded with sarcasm.

'John!' she pleaded. 'Don't give up, not just yet.'

'No,' he replied, 'not just yet.' But when his eyes came to rest on hers she could see he was closer to it than she realized.

5

Josie sat in front of her dressing-table. It was her birthday and she was getting ready to go out. Her bottles of perfume and cosmetics were all covered in dust, as was the mirror. She raised a hand, making a window in the dirt. Her thoughts went back to the days when she had such high expectations for her daughters Christina and Deborah. She thought of her estranged husband Charlie. What a fool he was, and yet — since he had gone, her reason for living seemed to have deserted her.

How she had blamed him for Christina's accident! One moment of careless distraction while he stopped to talk to Theo and tragedy had struck. He was sorry and he'd begged for her forgiveness, but she hadn't been able to forgive and forget. She could still see little Chrissy falling in her mind's eye, even now.

Christina, only three years old, was with Charlie watching the fish being landed from the top of the harbour wall. She was a quiet thoughtful little girl with dark primeval eyes. The bark of a terrier caught her attention and peering down she was fascinated by the colourful plastic pallets the fishermen slammed down on the ground. Reaching out, she grabbed the rail to steady herself as her new shoes slipped on the slimy green algae that clung to the sea wall. The railings finished further along, where stone steps led down twenty feet or so to the landing jetty. There was such a din: the seagulls, the men yelling at each other, the dog yapping. Waves, swelling towards high-tide, beat against the harbour wall below and caused the trawler to bump against the rubber tyres that were slung there to cushion the boats. Wood against rubber creaked and groaned.

Charlie had taken Christina for a walk along the harbour wall while she went shopping. Returning a while later, she saw Christina toddle away from him and shouted a warning. But it was too late! The child fell over the edge and hit the deck of the trawler below with a thud and her screams joined the sea-gulls' cries in a desperate bid for survival.

'Don't move her, man!' Theo yelled, as he and Josie raced down the steps after Charlie, and found him kneeling beside her, 'Where do you think you were goin', my little one?' he cried.

Josie snapped back to reality with a shudder. 'All those years ago,' she said, 'and still I can't forgive his carelessness! And yet — it could just as easily have been me.' Sadly she spoke to her reflection: 'I know, Charlie, one minute she was there, the next she was gone. I can see that now.' She sighed a sympathetic sigh, and half-smiled to herself. 'Never mind! I know you didn't mean it, Charlie — none of us mean to do what we do.'

She began to apply her make-up. 'So, this is where we're at, old girl,' she said, taking a deep breath. 'You're fifty years of age and the colour's gone out of your hair.' Tearing a piece of cotton wool from a jar, she began to apply some toner to her face. 'Not married, not really single either, not even divorced!' She peered closer into the mirror at some spot or blemish and gave it a rub. Next, she applied a little eye-shadow, a touch of mascara and a dab of rouge on each cheek. 'No money,' she said, 'no security, no savings to speak of, for your old age.' Finally she put on her lipstick, smoothed her hair and stared at the over-all picture of her face. 'And do you know what, Josie love? No-one gives a bloody damn.'

She left the dressing table, and tucking her emotions back where no-one could reach them, she went downstairs. Her daughter Christina had suggested they go to the cinema together; a rare occurrence, but a kind thought neverthe-less.

While Christina waited for her mother, she considered how difficult it had been dragging her away from her sewing-machine. Getting Deborah to stay in for the evening with Caitlin for once was in itself a major achievement. The film she planned to take her to see was 'The Godfather Part II' starring Al Pacino and Robert Duvall. It was showing at the small cinema in St. Ives.

Once they had set off together, they climbed the hill through the town in virtual silence. Christina attempted to talk — it was so rare to have her mother's attention. 'Mum,' she began. 'Would you mind telling me a bit about my dad?'

'Your father? There's nothing to tell,' Josie replied with some annoyance, looking away from her, tight-lipped. 'You know he made his choice, left me alone with you to support, and the café to run. That's enough, isn't it?' Immediately Christina regretted raising the subject and tried to make amends. After all it was supposed to be her mother's birthday treat.

'I'm sorry, never mind. It's just I worry about him sometimes, that's all.'

'Well he doesn't worry about you, or me, Chris,' replied Josie. 'He could be dead for all we know.'

'But he's not dead though, is he, Mum. He's living in Plymouth. Theo told me.'

'Why did Theo go and tell you that? Stirring up old hurts and memories! What good does that do? I'll have a word with that man; give him a piece of my mind.'

'No, it wasn't Theo's fault. It was only because I asked him. I want to see Dad again one day, Mum, I ought to really.'

'Ought to? There's no 'ought' about it. He's best put out of your mind, Chris, and forgotten. That's what I've done.'

★ ★ ★

To Josie's relief they turned up a side street and entered the foyer of the cinema. The bright lights and glamour of the place were a contrast to their conversation and a welcome distraction. Josie remembered only too well her first date there with Charlie. She had been so excited and he, looking so shy and pink and well-scrubbed. It was 1962 and they were showing a fashionable new film called 'Dr No' starring Sean Connery. It had been a fast moving, slick film she thought, and she had hated it so much that when she stood up before the end and picked up her coat, Charlie had mistakenly thought she was leaving because he had tried to hold her

106

hand. He had been so apologetic she hadn't told him it was the film and not his touch which had upset her.

'I used to come here often with your father,' she admitted.

'Did you! Before you were married?' Christina looked at her in surprise.

'Yes, and after. We had our first date here. It seems like only yesterday.' Josie clicked her tongue and gave a flick of her head as though wanting to shake off the memory. As they were carried through with the crowd, she felt glad to sit in her seat where, under cover of darkness, she could hide her tear-stained face.

* * *

Teagan was awoken by a voice she had longed to hear.

'I'm home, Tig!' Instantly wide-awake, she slipped from the warm sheets, draped a dressing-gown around her shoulders and fled down the stairs into his arms.

'Ssh!' she giggled. 'Peter's here!' Connor kissed her and hugged her tenderly. 'Too bad,' he murmured. 'A man's got to kiss his wife when he gets home from sea!' Dragging the heavy oilskins from his perspiration soaked body he eased off his boots and ran a hand through his black hair.

'I got a fair price at auction this mornin',' he said, 'an' I've paid the men. Ah, 'tis good to be home! A sea mist's blowin' up from the west; we could hardly make out Godrevy Lighthouse on our way in. This weather's a hellish beast an' the winter's not upon us yet, girl!' he exclaimed. 'How have yer been, eh? Missed me?' he teased, kissing her again.

Sweeping her off of her feet, Connor carried her up the creaky narrow staircase to their bedroom. He kicked the door closed behind him, and lay her gently down on the bed. Stifling her giggles with more kisses, he stripped and flung himself down beside her. The ocean rolled over her warm sleep-scented body, waking her dark lonely nights. She felt the motion of the waves and gave herself up to the strong current, languishing in the rhythm of the tide. Strength that had moved continents shot through her, tingling right through to her fingertips and she clung to him; their mouths and tongues dissolved together until her whole being became intoxicated with the physical reality of his closeness. She loved everything about him: the rough salty taste of his lips, the crushing strength of his arms, and even the strong aroma of fish that enveloped her when he held her. She filled the aching gap in her soul with his masculine presence.

'Oh! I've missed you so much!' she sighed, kissing his bristly cheek and burying her face in his neck.

When their surging tide had raged, peaked, and turned, Connor lay back on the bed. It was after nine and the early morning mist had lifted, letting the warm sun stream through their bedroom window. Teagan lay quietly in his arms, passive and content. The cottage was quiet. Outside the window, sea-gulls were softly mewing and now and again a car drove past. There was the sound of milk-bottles chinking, and the occasional call as passers-by greeted each other. She stirred, reluctant to leave Connor's warm embrace and begin the day. Finally she rose, went to the bathroom, returned, and began to dress.

'Ready for some breakfast?' she asked. 'Peter will be downstairs soon, looking for something to eat I'm sure.'

'Teagan?' Connor's voice had a strange urgency. His eyes were wide-open. 'Next week I'll be going further out. I've a mind to play the Spanish at their own game! We'll show them what we're made of.'

'You won't put yourself in danger, will you Connor? I'd rather you stayed close to shore, really, even if it means you don't get the best catch.'

'Why shouldn't I get the best catch? Surely to God, me and the men work hard enough without it being stolen from right under our noses. Listen, Tig! If we don't fight for it we'll lose it! The ministers don't care. They seem happy to let those bastards take the fish from under our noses rather than give us a decent quota.' She studied his face. He looked exhausted, but he was so angry. Tidying away his clothes, she went downstairs to fry his breakfast. For the time being she was just relieved that he was home. When she went back to him ten minutes later, he was fast asleep.

★　★　★

In the café later that day, Peter was repairing a table which he had upended on the floor. His head was bowed, as he contemplated a loose joint. An array of tools lay before him. It was Teagan's idea that her brother could help out in the café with a few odd jobs.

'I'm afraid Maudie Peacock's frame was too much for that old table,' explained Christina. 'She tried to sit on the edge and it capsized!'

'It won't take long to fix. Anything else you want me to do?'

'Several things I think, if you don't mind.

Those shelves need putting up. Not much more we can do today though.'

'I'll be getting off home now to start dinner,' said Teagan. 'Are you stopping here, Pete?'

'Yep, I'll be along later!' His voice came from under the table where he was tightening the bolts. Smiling, Teagan left the two of them and went through the French doors onto the beach.

Christina watched the comfortable way Peter worked, whistling and humming to himself. No one would believe that he had so many sorrows, with a wife who had cheated on him and a home he could no longer call his own. His hairy, bear-like demeanour fascinated her.

'Have you always been good with your hands?' she asked.

He turned his head as though surprised to find her still there.

'Don't remember a time when I wasn't fiddlin' with summat or other,' he said. 'Depends what you mean by good. I haven't fixed this yet!'

'Oh, but you will, I can see that,' she replied.

He smiled. 'Don't suppose people should go sittin' on tables. Perhaps you should put a sign up!'

A giggle escaped her, and changing her mind about locking up, she turned the lights on so Peter could see better. It was August, but the days were shortening rapidly.

'It's all right, I've finished now; there she is!' With one swift movement he swept the table back on its feet. Good as new!' he declared. Replacing the chairs, he began collecting his tools together. 'Think that'll do, till next time,' he said. 'I'll see to them shelves tomorrow if you like. Are you ready to go?'

'Yes, thanks. Are you going back my way?'

'Is that your usual chat-up line?' he asked, glancing at her over his shoulder.

'No!' she protested, flushing.

'Only teasing,' he said. 'I could be goin' your way, if you want an old fool's company, that is.'

'You're not so old yet, I don't think,' she replied. Christina couldn't help feeling attracted to him. He had such an honest physicality about him with his clumsy yet caring demeanour. Taking his tool-box, he opened the door for her. She switched off the lights and whistled for Ginger who had been fast asleep in his basket. They set off together in the direction of the town. But hampered by her limp, she found trying to keep up with Peter's huge strides soon had her out of breath.

'Do you always walk this fast?' she panted. He immediately apologized and dropped back a pace. 'Sorry,' he said. 'I'd forgotten about your . . . '

'That's OK. So how are things going with you? I mean, will you be staying down here for a while?'

'Yep, there's plenty to do apparently.' He shot her a teasing look, before replying more seriously. 'I'll put an ad in the paper and do a few odd jobs, but I don't want to take on anything big in case I can't stop down here to finish it.'

'You could go home then? If Nicola would have you — '

'Have me back you mean?' Peter tossed his bear-like head. 'She won't have me back, Chris! The truth is, I don't want to go back to her now. I don't know who she is any more. The young girl I loved and married, the mother of my two boys, she's changed so much!' He nodded towards a group of young women on a street corner, dressed up for a night on the town. 'See those girls there? Any one of them could be my Nicola an' I wouldn't even recognize her! No,' he said. 'I won't be going back to Nicola. The girl I knew and loved has gone forever.'

The silence between them was electric. Christina was struggling to think how to change the subject.

'I'm sorry, I shouldn't have asked about her.'

'Shouldn't have asked?' His loud response shocked her. 'I wish to hell more people would ask! I wish folks would ask 'Where is she? Where the bloody hell's your wife, what's she playin' at?' But they don't. They say damn all about it!'

At this outburst, something inside Christina hurt so much her eyes stung. She knew what it was like to be abandoned by someone you loved.

'Have you talked about Nicola with Quinn and Olga? They must have asked.'

'My parents don't say much,' he replied. 'The truth is we got married too young, I suppose. I didn't give her time to find herself, ha! That's what I tell myself anyway, it makes losing her a bit easier to swallow.'

Instinctively, she slipped her arm through his and gave it a squeeze. 'You'll come through it, Peter, don't worry.'

He turned his tousled head to gaze down at her face. 'You're all right, you are, aren't you!' he beamed. 'Wonder some chap hasn't scooped you up and carried you off by now.'

She laughed, loving this affectionate way he had of talking to her. But suddenly the dog stole their attention.

'Ginger!' she shouted and broke away. He had met a vicious-looking bull-terrier and the dogs stood dead still, challenging each other. Ginger's hair stood up on his back. The bull-terrier gave a slow menacing growl, bared its teeth and a blood-curdling whine came from its throat. Looking around, Christina saw who she imagined to be the dog's owner. He was dark and wiry, wearing cowboy type clothes and had an aggressive air about him. With a shout the man raised a stick and threw it hard, straight at the two dogs, narrowly missing Christina's shoulder.

'Watch it, you!' shouted Peter. 'You could've hurt someone with that stick! What the hell do you think you're doing?'

'Call your stupid mutt off then!' replied the cowboy. 'Get back here, Max, or I'll break your neck!' he yelled. The dog crept slowly back towards its master, looking a miserable object of guilt. Pain was obviously a frequent reward.

'You want to keep that mutt under control,' the man shouted, as he grabbed his dog by the scruff of the neck and cuffed it hard round the ear causing it to yelp.

'Who are you to go round telling people what to do?' Peter demanded, stepping up and confronting the man. 'There's nothin' vicious about our dog; it's yours that's tryin' to pick a fight.' At this point Christina intervened. She slipped the lead on Ginger and taking Peter's arm, gave him a gentle tug.

'Hey, Peter,' she said. 'Come on, let's go and get something to eat.' Reluctantly Peter turned and with one more disdainful glance at the cowboy, tore himself away. The man moved off and as he did so, Christina saw his dog following meekly behind him, its tail between its legs.

'Thanks for sticking up for us,' she said. 'I'm not used to anyone jumping to my defence.' Realizing that her arm was still linked through his, she released her hold.

'Oh, shame,' he said. 'I was just getting used to that.' He smiled down at her. 'You thought I was worth saving from a fight, did you?' he asked, with a twinkle in his eye.

'Well, I might have some more odd-jobs I need doing in the café.'

'I'm depending on it,' he replied, looking at her. 'Good idea of yours to get something to eat. Fancy coming up the pub for supper? I expect Teagan would appreciate me giving them the house to themselves now Connor's home.'

Something about the expression in his big brown eyes made her consent. 'That sounds a great idea, but we ought to ring and tell her not to expect you.' Before she knew it, they were on their way to the *The Old Ship Inn* down on the harbour.

★ ★ ★

News travels fast in a small fishing community. The next time Christina met John Madison it was her afternoon off. Arriving at his cottage early, she had arranged to collect Caitlin and go to the beach.

'Not with that hefty friend of yours today then?' he asked while Caitlin was finding her shoes.

'Who?' she replied, feeling the colour rush to her cheeks.

He didn't answer. In the awkwardness that prevailed, she watched an ant crawling up the wall until the silence was broken by Sylvie: 'Daddy? I can't find my sandals!'

Soon the girls were ready, but just as Christina was about to say she would bring her back by five, John said, 'Mind if I come along? I need a walk to clear my head.'

He ambled along beside her in a quiet, brooding mood. His long legs could easily have struck up a good pace and Christina became self-conscious of her limp.

'Sorry I walk so slowly,' she said simply.

'Don't be,' he replied. 'I'm not in a hurry.' The girls ran ahead skipping and singing to themselves. She made several attempts to start a conversation, but without success.

'I've been thinking about this decommissioning,' said John finally. 'There's talk of limiting the number of grants available. Either I go for it now, decommission the *Coral Princess* and go for a smaller boat while the government have the funds available, or I forget it.' He paused. 'I could use the rest of the money to invest in crab and lobster pots and work close to shore; and then I'd get home at night instead of being gone all week.'

She looked at his sullen face absorbed in thought. He wasn't even watching the children. They were far ahead now, running towards the beach hand in hand and in seconds they were out of sight. 'We'd better catch up with the girls, John,' she said, afraid that another lengthy discussion about his boat might delay them too long. She quickened her pace and soon they caught sight of them again, safely playing near the water's edge. She relaxed as Porthminster Beach came into full view, revealing a huge expanse of blonde sand with a strong head-wind blowing.

'Try not to worry,' she said, feeling that perhaps she had been too dismissive. 'Earning any sort of living's hard at the moment. Look at the café, it's running at a loss most of the time. Business changes from one day to the next. It's so unpredictable. As soon as the weather breaks, the customers disappear.' She wished his mood would lift. Moving away from him slightly, she sheltered her eyes to watch the girls. They were chasing each other, holding long ribbons of seaweed and swinging them round in the wind.

'It doesn't make economic sense,' came his voice again. 'You know the big factory trawlers? They land over eighty per cent of the fish in this country. Never mind they dump three times that amount back in the sea.'

Christina sighed. She had definitely had enough of his politics. 'Why do they keep doing that then?' she asked, trying to conceal her impatience. 'Why not keep it and sell it anyway?'

'Because the Ministry says so!'

'Why don't they refuse?' She shrugged her shoulders defiantly.

'Like Jim Telford, you mean? He got convicted and fined fifty thousand pounds for concealing it and landing fish illegally. He'll have his licence confiscated probably — he could even go to prison.'

'Go to prison? What — just for catching fish?' She almost laughed. His intensity exhausted her, but failing to notice, he embarked on a longer in-depth explanation of his problems.

'For catching certain fish and selling them, yes. None of us want to endanger the fish stocks, but what can we do? When the nets are full of cod, it could mean the difference between being able to pay the crew and going bankrupt. Like I said, the fish are dead anyway, makes no sense. You can't fix a sign on the back of the trawler saying: 'No cod allowed in the nets today'.' She glanced at him, hoping this was a joke, but his jaw was set.

'Perhaps you'll just have to make the best of it then?' she said.

He looked at her. In his eyes she saw a restless fire and it cut her to the quick. Never before had she seen such intense feeling in another human being. His forlorn expression reminded her of her father the morning he had gone away. The more he stared, the more uncomfortable she felt, almost claustrophobic. He was standing too close.

'Will you come to see me tonight?' he asked. 'Will you come up to the cottage to look through the application papers with me, help me decide what to do?'

'I don't know if I'd be any help, John. I don't know anything about it.'

'I'd appreciate your company, Christina,

please? We'll open a bottle of wine and try and make some sense out of all this.'

She hesitated, thinking hard. 'OK,' she replied. 'When Caitlin's settled in bed I'll walk up with Ginger. I can't stay too late, mind.' As soon as she had agreed, a sense of destiny filled her and she wondered where it would lead. His need for her, his air of loneliness possessed her.

6

'What if they wear white organza over the red satin? That would create more of a shimmer effect, wouldn't it?' Deborah was talking to Josie in the kitchen about her favourite topic: her dancing class production at the Town Hall.

'Yes,' Christina heard her mother's reply, 'but think of the cost! That's twice as much material, not to mention twice as much work for me having to make them!'

They were washing up while Christina and Caitlin played a board-game on the sitting room floor. She knew she ought to walk up to John's but Caitlin kept pleading, 'Just one more go!' So again, they threw the dice and moved the counter. 'Oh no, it's straight down the snake again!' Caitlin shrieked.

The door-bell sounded. 'I'll get it!' called Deborah from the hall.

'René!' they heard her shout. 'You didn't say you were coming down! Why did you ring the front-door bell? You've got a key!' His voice could be heard mumbling some response.

Caitlin looked up at Christina anxiously.

'It's Daddy!' she whispered.

'Don't bring me wine, René!' shouted Deborah. 'Don't bring me wine and flowers as though you're a visitor to this house! You're supposed to live here, remember?'

Caitlin's delight in the game was gone. Her face showed no trace of excitement at her father's return. Christina gave her a hug of encouragement. 'Come on, it's your go!' she coaxed. Caitlin shook her head and refused. 'Shall we go and say 'Hello' to your daddy then? You can tell him you've found a new friend to play with after school.' Her thoughts had turned to John who would be waiting for her. It was getting late; he would think she wasn't coming.

'Don't want to,' said Caitlin, but Christina took her hand and together they went into the hall.

'Evening René,' said Christina coolly.

'Good evening, Sister-in law!' René responded loudly, taking full advantage of the diversion. 'I'm pleased to see someone's got some manners in this house.'

'I thought you were going out, Chris,' said Deborah, folding her arms and pouting.

'Yes, I'm just about to.'

'Oh!' whined Caitlin. 'But I want to play snakes again now!' René's expression softened. His eyes lost their focus, and he dropped his attention to the child.

'Come here, Caitlin,' he said, snapping his fingers as though to a puppy. 'Let Daddy look at you.' He bent down to her but she hid her face in her mother's skirt.

'Say hello to your father, Caitlin,' commanded Deborah, pushing the child away from her.

'You're growing into quite a young lady, aren't you, mmm?' he mused gently. 'Going to school now too, I hear.' The child nodded with her chin tucked down, not looking at him. 'And what's your favourite thing at school eh? Drawing and painting, mmm? Stories?' he persisted, smiling at her in a curious manner.

'My friend,' she replied with sudden boldness. 'I like my new friend Sylvie the best.'

'Your *friend*?' crooned René, emphasizing the word and glancing up at Deborah.

'A friend's a person you get to know, René,' said Deborah. 'If you like each other you enjoy spending time together, believe it or not.'

'Oh, very funny,' he replied.

'I'll be off then,' Christina interjected before things became even more difficult. 'I won't be late. Come on boy!' Whistling the dog, and grabbing her jacket, she let herself out of the front door and closed it behind her with a sigh of relief.

★　★　★

It was beautiful in the twilight of the evening, walking away from the harbour and up the High Street. Christina was heading for the top of the town where John Madison lived. Looking down, she saw a thousand lights twinkling like glow-worms in slow procession along the harbour. She walked as fast as she could, her limp hardly hindering her progress at all. René's return had spoilt any excitement she felt in seeing John again, whose quiet nature was no match for René. Hard as she tried, she couldn't even imagine the two men in the same room. They were so different.

She found herself recalling her stroll into town with Peter, when they had encountered the cowboy with his bull-terrier and how the two of them had enjoyed a meal together. It had been a warm, funny sort of evening. Peter's conversation was punctuated by jokes and stories that made her laugh out loud. By contrast, the solemn broodiness of John crept into her thoughts like a ghost. Her walk ended abruptly when she found herself at his door. She slipped round the back. It was dark now and the lights were on in the cottage.

Tapping softly on the back door, she heard movement inside and the door opened. John stood there, wearing an open-necked shirt and jeans, looking freshly bathed. His long hair was neatly combed. It was very tidy inside and felt almost formal. In daylight, the girls were usually playing and shrieking on the stairs, with toys strewn about. Immediately she felt under pressure and regretted not having changed her clothes.

'John, sorry I'm late,' she said. 'I meant to come before but . . . Oh, family problems!' She abandoned the excuse.

'It's OK. Come in and sit down. I'll pour you some wine. Is red all right?'

'Yes, fine.' She noticed the bottle was already half empty. Beginning to wish she hadn't come at all, she felt the urgency of his invitation had evaporated and she wondered if she had imagined his need to talk.

'So, have you looked at those papers again?' she asked.

'Yes,' he replied, handing her the glass and immediately replenishing his own — strangely, a gesture characteristic of René.

'Cheers,' he said and resumed his seat at the table. Ginger was at her feet. She perched on the edge of the sofa and realized she still had her jacket on. He hadn't asked her for it, and now it seemed awkward to take it off.

'Have you had any more thoughts about it then?' She cast about, wondering why the papers weren't anywhere to be seen. Wasn't that the point of her visit?

'I've decided to apply. I might not be accepted anyway.'

So he didn't need her after all, she realized. 'What will happen to the *Coral Princess* if you are though?' she asked.

'If I get the grant? She'll go to scrap. I'll sell off my fishing quota too.'

'But she's a lovely boat!' protested Christina. 'I don't understand!' Suddenly she hated his attitude. Could he be seduced so easily by the promise of a cash pay-out? 'The *Coral Princess* isn't that old; she's not just a rusty old thing that's heading for the scrap yard, is she? You've only had her, what, since . . . ' She remembered then, when he had first bought the boat. His late wife, Kate, was pregnant with Sylvie and he'd said he needed a bigger boat now that he had a family to support.

'Since before Kate died, yes,' he said. 'I don't mind you saying it. Now I don't need income so much as time.' He sighed, ran a hand through his hair and for a moment she caught a glimpse of the gentle John she knew. He turned and looked into her eyes. 'The truth is, Christina, I'm afraid of losing what little family I've got left.'

'Sylvie?' she asked. 'You're afraid of losing Sylvie? Why? Who to?'

'To the world; I'm afraid of her growing up. She's changing so quickly, sometimes she leaves me behind. I could be away at sea for ten days and by the time I get back she could have grown up and forgotten me.'

'Don't be daft! A girl won't forget her own father,' she replied. Instantly she thought of Charlie, and a shaft of pain shot through her. 'Not after ten days anyway!' she added lamely.

'If anything happened to me, what then? She's got no other family to turn to. All she's got is Maudie Peacock! What a joke!' He stood up and kicked the table leg savagely, turning his face away from her, his cheek muscles working in tension. 'I should've sorted out a legal guardian for her years ago. What the hell would happen to her if — '

'If you were lost at sea? Folks would rally round and help if something happened to you. But nothing's going to happen to you, is it? Even if it did, we'd all help. You know we would! And Maudie might be a bit eccentric but she's kindness itself.' Why was he telling her all this? Ginger grew restless, whimpered and put his nose in his paws.

'I need to have something sorted, Christina; I can feel it in my bones.'

'Feel what in your bones?' she persisted. His conversation was so heavy it was difficult not to mock him slightly. She took a sip of wine and tried to concentrate. It tasted sour.

'Danger! Insecurity, if you like. I fear for my Sylvie, I'm afraid for her!' He flung himself down on the sofa beside her. 'I ought to make some provision for her, just in case.'

'If it would make you feel better,' suggested Christina carefully, 'why don't you ask Maudie Peacock to be officially on stand-by? Sylvie's always happy with her.'

'Would *you* though?' he asked. 'Would you want Maudie to be legally responsible for Caitlin?'

She thought for a moment. 'I might,' she reflected, 'but she's not my daughter. Maudie's a kind-hearted woman, I do trust her. She's a funny old stick I know, but she's caring and sensible.'

'Yes, but she's as old as the hills, and a bit odd, to say the least! No, it's just not practical.'

'But who else is there?' asked Christina, before meeting his direct stare and understanding exactly why he had invited her to his house that evening.

'Would you agree to be Sylvie's legal guardian? Put my mind at rest?'

'John! I couldn't!'

'Please?' he said. 'Of course it'll probably never happen, as you said, but you're young and level-headed. I'd love to know you'd be there for her if . . . if anything happened to me. Do you understand that, Christina?' Again, that slow pronunciation of her name, he seemed to savour the feel of it on his tongue. He put down his glass and laid his hand on hers. Something like an electric current shot up her arm. Her heart quickened; the pressure of his hand felt heavy, damp, and clinging. Suddenly she had an irrepressible urge to shake it off.

'There must be someone else more qualified than me, more financially secure for a start and more — '

'Please say yes,' he interrupted, staring at her intensely. 'I could get some papers drawn up so that it's all legal. I'd make sure there was financial security for her future.' He gave her hand a gentle squeeze. 'And for yours, too.'

Christina swallowed. Her throat felt dry. 'Have you discussed this with Sylvie?'

'No, not yet. Of course not. There's no need to frighten her with such things. All I want is your approval. If you agree, I'll see my solicitor in the morning. No-one else need know. Once the agreement has been signed and sealed, we need say no more about it.'

'Is that what you want, John? A secret pact?'

He paused, exhaling audibly: 'I was rather hoping for more than that, once we've got to know each other a bit more. But your agreement to the arrangement is all I'm really asking for.'

Why did she feel so uncomfortable? She felt torn between feeling genuine compassion for him, alternating with revulsion. 'You'll give me some time to think about it?' she said. 'It's a serious commitment. I can't take it on lightly.'

'Of course, here, let me fill your glass!' He rose from the sofa. Ginger raised his head and whined, perhaps sensing it was time to leave. What was she getting herself into, she wondered? She wished she could talk to Teagan or Peter about it. But John was already opening a new bottle of wine. 'I'll just nip up and see if Sylvie's gone off to sleep; I won't be long. Are you hungry or anything?'

'No, no I'm fine, thanks,' she replied. As he went up the stairs, she looked about the room. It was a lonely little room. There was a photo of Kate in a silver frame on the sideboard, smiling, carefree, and several of Sylvie as a baby. On the wall above the fireplace was a framed wedding photo of them both — a world lost to them now. She found herself wondering what it would be like to step into Kate's shoes, to be the woman of the house, as John's wife and mother to Sylvie. Slowly the hairs began to prickle on the back of her neck, and she shivered. But in spite of her misgivings, she found herself feeling surprisingly calm, and when John returned a few minutes later his relaxed smile drove away her fears. Within minutes they were both pouring over the decommissioning form and laughing at its complicated legal language.

★　★　★

When Christina got home it was very late and she had a headache. She couldn't wait to get to her room, fling herself down on her bed and have time to think. But as she let herself in at the front door, she noticed the lights were still on and heard loud voices. Sticking her head round the sitting room door, she called:

'I'm back! Goodnight everyone.' She was about to mount the stairs when someone shouted.

'Wait!' René's voice boomed out like a headmaster shouting after a child.

She sighed and went back. 'Yes, Sir?' she said.

'Come in and close the door,' he commanded.

Deborah was standing behind him. He was

sitting at the table with several files and papers spread before him. Josie was perched on the edge of the sofa. Christina stood in the doorway, longing to escape to her bed.

'Close the door, please.'

He was tapping a pen on the table irritably, his gold bracelet rattling. Josie refused to meet her gaze but when Christina caught her sister's eye, Deborah looked up to the heavens, as if to say, 'Here we go again'. Closing the door she faced René with a guarded expression.

'Your mother and I have been looking over the café's accounts. Why aren't they kept up to date, mmm?'

'They are up to date, René,' she replied coldly.

'Then where are the invoices for the Cash 'n' Carry these last few weeks?' he asked, looking up at her.

'I don't use the Cash 'n' Carry so much now. I like to buy locally, from the fisherman and nurseries nearby.'

'So where are the invoices for all those goods?'

'I pay cash. We get a better deal that way. If you look under petty-cash you'll see the difference. That's why those particular figures have gone up. You'll notice the others have come down.'

'So where are the receipts, Sister-in-law?'

he asked with a smirk.

'I don't get receipts for all of them. Well, you know what local people are like,' she replied.

'No,' said René stiffly. 'On the contrary, I don't know, or wish to know, what local people are like and I doubt Her Majesty's Tax Inspectors would wish to know either.'

'Well,' continued Christina, pulling at a thread on her jeans nervously. 'I've kept a record of everything I've spent. I've saved loads of money; they don't mind selling off their surplus cheaply, especially the fishermen. It's because they know me.'

'Huh! I bet they don't mind!' he snorted with satisfaction. 'Don't make me laugh! It's likely they're selling you the stuff they're supposed to be throwing back — the *discards* as they call them — that's why! They're breaking their legal quotas! They've seen you coming, girl, cash-in-hand; a nice little earner for them I bet, no questions asked!'

'No, it's not like that!' she cried, horrified. 'You think I'm stupid enough to be buying 'black fish'? You don't know what you're talking about, René! Why don't you get off back to London where you belong and leave us alone?'

'Because, Miss High and Mighty Sister-in-law, I'm going to be running the joint from now on. You're going to see some changes take place and you can take it or leave it. Someone's got to knock this business into shape or it'll be down the toilet before you know it.'

'Oh right!' she said and sighed, trying desperately to steel herself. 'And how d'you propose to do that?' she cried, tossing her head in disgust. 'You don't know the first thing about running a café!'

'I know how to run a successful business, girl, that's the difference between you and me. Now, give me the café keys and you can toddle off to bed and dream your dreams to your heart's content.'

'I won't give you the keys, René,' she replied. 'Mum? Tell him to stop being so heavy handed. He's not having my keys, I won't be able to go and open up in the morning.'

'Give René the keys, Chris, there's a good girl; we'll talk about it tomorrow.'

'No way! I'm not handing the café over to someone who can't even — '

'Christina!' roared Josie, rising to her feet with her arm outstretched. 'Hand over the keys, now! I'm not asking you, I'm telling you!' She lowered her voice as though attempting to remain calm. 'Not for my sake,' she almost whispered, 'but for the future of this whole family.' There was a tremor in her voice. Christina detected fear in her eyes, and suddenly realized her mother was afraid of René. She removed the keys from her belt, separated out the café keys from her own and placed them on her mother's palm without saying another word. As soon as Josie had them in her hand she passed them across to René.

'Right!' he said, snatching them into his plump fist. 'Progress at last!' Giving Christina a sly look he tapped the side of his nose with his index finger. 'Now! Sister-in-law: watch and learn, my girl, watch and learn!'

The loss of her keys came like a punch in the stomach. She fled from the room, slamming the door behind her and bursting with anger and frustration as she climbed the stairs to her room.

★　★　★

When Maudie went to fetch Sylvie to take her to school, John was sitting in the sun by the back door.

'Well, dearie, that hill ain't gettin' any easier on my old knees,' she gasped. 'Are y'all right then, my 'ansome? Where is she?'

'Ah, sorry not to have phoned you; I don't think she'll be going to school today. She's

136

complaining of a stomach ache.'

'Tummy ache, is it?' Maudie replied. 'Well, we'll soon see what kind o' tummy ache that is. Where is she, upstairs?' and with that she disappeared indoors. Presently, bustling could be heard, and she reappeared, breathing heavily. 'Got any Kaolin in the house, or gripe water or somethin' to give her?'

'No, I think she's best just giving her tummy a rest for a bit,' said John. 'Here, have a seat and I'll make you some tea.'

'Cup o' tea! My, am I the lucky one! It's usually me has to do all the fetchin' an' carryin'! Thank you, my dear!' She eased herself down with difficulty onto the garden chair, rubbing her knee joints through her old tweed skirt.

A few minutes later, Maudie was pouring milk clumsily, the flesh on her upper arms wobbling. 'Not often our Sylvie's poorly now, is it?' she commented.

'I don't think it's anything serious. She'll be up and about again this afternoon, I bet. She was perfectly all right last night. I sent her to bed a bit early, because I had a visitor.'

'Oh yes? A young lady friend was it?' asked Maudie, her eyes twinkling.

'It was Christina, actually.'

'Ah! A lovely girl! You won't go far wrong with her, my dear!'

'We're just friends, Maudie. Actually, I'm glad you suggested Sylvie and Caitlin got together, it's been very helpful.'

'For Caitlin too, I don't doubt, my dear. That child doesn't get much attention; it's not Chris's fault, it's those parents of hers. The mother's more interested in glitzy glamour and the father, well! If it weren't for Chris the poor kid might have got put out on the doorstep with the empties an' forgot about years ago.'

John smiled. A curious expression crept across his face and suddenly he said: 'I haven't liked to ask Christina, but how exactly did she damage her leg? She never talks about it and I don't like to ask.'

'Oh, it were her father's fault, so folks say. They say her father was stood talking and little Chris went down over the harbour wall; she were only three. She fell right down onto the boat below and broke half the bones in her little body. Her mother blamed Charlie, real hard on him she was. Well, maybe 'cos of that, maybe summat else, he walked out eventually. Haven't seen him since. Can't say I blame him for leavin' that woman, he never got a look in. Her an' her out-work — she's obsessed — not healthy I don't think.' Maudie shrugged, took a gulp of tea and sat back in her chair. 'My, you've made it right pretty round here, my lover,' she commented, peering around the garden.

'Christina's never spoken about that. I had no idea,' said John, staring into his tea.

'No dearie, she wouldn't have. She was too young, you see; she won't remember none of it. Where her sister gets her flighty ways from, I'll never know, with all her dancin' and troupin' about — not from Charlie, nor their mother.'

After a pause, John said: 'I'm not going to sea next week, Maudie. I've got some legal business to sort out in London. Would you mind — '

'Lookin' after your Sylvie? Course I don't mind. I can have her to stay at my place an' you can take as long as you like. No need to worry about that, my dear,' said Maudie, shifting her large hips more comfortably into the seat and helping herself to another biscuit.

'Thank you,' he replied. 'I might not always seem grateful, but I am, honestly.'

'You're all right, me 'ansome. Now I'd best be gettin' back along to the family. Hope the girl's feelin' better soon, dearie.'

John smiled, watching her bulky form make its way back through the gate before he sat down again, in a contemplative mood.

★　★　★

139

Before she arrived at her parents' house, Teagan could hear the gramophone playing. It was one of her father's favourites: Puccini's opera, Tosca. It was a sure sign that he was busy working. Walking up the lane, a certain melancholy filled the air as pigeons cooed from the rooftops; moisture dripped from gateposts and hedges as spider-webs lay white cotton shawls across every angle of thicket. Autumn first shows itself in the morning.

Teagan's mother, Olga, was in the kitchen.

'Hello, dear,' her mother said. 'Pass me that saucepan, will you?' She was peeling beetroot and the red blood-like juice dripped from her fingers and ran in ugly gashes down her wrists and arms. 'I'm saving this, it makes a wonderful dye. I tell you, your father's lucky to have any beetroot at all for his tea, I could use the whole lot in this new batch I'm doing.'

'Has Peter been up to see you lately?'

'He'll be here later,' she replied. 'He's gone into Truro to see his solicitor.'

'Is that the way things are going then? Will it be a divorce?'

'It seems so. He doesn't talk much about it, dear, but he did tell me he'd got a letter. They only discuss the future of the children, nothin' else. She thinks it's as good as over apparently. If Peter doesn't contest the divorce, it'll go through in the blink of an eye. I wouldn't have expected it of Nicola, that's the truth.' Olga moved the copper saucepan full of deep reddish-brown liquid onto the cooler part of the Aga.

'What grounds could she possibly have, Mum?'

'Peter hasn't discussed it with me, dear. Sometimes it's just a breakdown in communication; these things happen. Pass me that jar of salt, would you?'

Teagan watched her take two handfuls of salt, stirring it in methodically with a long wooden spoon. Having satisfied herself that the dye was ready, Olga began sorting through her baskets of wool and sighing to herself.

'Now,' said her mother, 'those skeins of wool are to go into the pot. Could you just test it for me, dear? The thermometer's on the table. If it's too hot it'll turn this lot into felt.'

Deciding the temperature was about right, Olga began threading each one onto the handle of her spoon. She lowered the first skein into the liquid, and hung it to drip over the sink. As each skein became immersed, it turned the wool a pinkish brown. 'I'll just leave them there to drip for a bit,' she declared with satisfaction. 'Right! Cup of coffee then, love?'

Teagan nodded. 'Yes please, I won't be getting one up the Sea Café, that's for sure.'

'Oh?' Olga took down the mugs. 'Got fed up with it? You haven't fallen out with Christina have you?'

'No! Something's going on up there, Mum. Debbie's husband just announced he's taking over the place. He's even taken Chris's keys away. He's closed it down, just like that!'

'Poor girl! How extraordinary!'

'Apparently he's got legal rights over the place now. Chris is devastated. I just saw her out with Ginger. She hadn't slept a wink.'

'What about that mother of hers? Where's she while all this is going on?'

'I don't know. When I was up the café a while ago, René came in and started laying the law down. He was picking the place to bits — all in front of the customers as well. He said she ought to get rid of Ginger too, you wouldn't believe it!'

Olga shook her head sadly. 'He's probably right about the dog. She shouldn't really have him in the kitchen when she's preparing food, dear.'

'Everyone loves Ginger though!' protested Teagan. Olga looked at her daughter with some amusement in her eyes.

'Yes, but he's still a dog,' she replied, 'and there are hygiene regulations after all. Want to

142

take this up to your father?'

Teagan climbed the stairs with the coffee and the sound of sawing and hammering competed with one of Puccini's arias.

'Thank you, darling,' said Quinn, sanding down a piece of picture frame.

'You all right?' she shouted above the volume of the music. He raised his eyebrows, looking at her quizzically until she reached over and turned down the volume.

'Is your brother with you?' he asked, sipping from his mug. Teagan shook her head.

'Don't go worrying yourself about your brother, girl. He's big enough to look after himself.'

She smiled. 'I know,' she whispered, gazing fondly about at her father's work. The sawdust and tools were all in disarray and she loved him for it. It was easy to see where her brother got his untidiness and his honest love of hard work.

'Not up the café with your friend today then?' he asked.

'No, Christina's not too good at the moment actually; things have happened.'

Quinn stopped what he was doing and looked troubled. 'Oh? Why, what's wrong?'

'Her rotten brother-in-law's come down from London and taken it over. He's going to give it a make-over apparently. He's taken her keys and closed the place down. She doesn't know what's happening to it yet.'

'Dear oh dear! It's not like Chris to let someone muscle in on the café without a fight.'

'No,' said Teagan, 'I found a notice on the door saying 'Closed for refurbishment.' There's a skip outside. It looked awful, like they're ripping it all out and gutting the place.'

'Oh, well that's not necessarily a bad thing. We all need to do a bit of sorting out sometimes,' he added with a smile.

'It's not as simple as that, Dad. Chris was really upset. She's got no say in the running of it any more or what's happening to it. It's not fair.'

'And this is her brother-in-law's doing, you say?' he asked, frowning. He held up a piece of framing to check the angle of the cut. 'Sounds a bit odd. That girl makes a right good sandwich, best I've ever had — don't tell your mother, mind.' Quinn's conspiratorial manner never failed to put Teagan at her ease; her father's individuality was like a rock.

Hearing her brother arrive downstairs, Teagan left her father and descended the spiral staircase. As she reached the bottom she smiled to herself as the opera shot up to full volume above her. Olga was hanging out skeins of wool to dry on a line slung along the

Aga and dripping blood-red liquid onto sheets of newspaper on the floor.

'Easy does it, Mother!' teased Peter. 'That's not some poor soul's hair you've got hangin' there, is it?'

'No, it's your father's beard,' she replied causing Peter's booming laugh to travel up the stairs.

'You sound happy! How did it go in Truro?' Teagan asked, as she sat down at the farmhouse table. He shrugged his shoulders. 'Who knows? Lawyers take their time — What's this I hear about the Sea Café?'

She began to describe the scene she had come across that morning and instantly Peter became agitated. 'The rotten bastard! Why's he bothering about a harmless little business like that. I was tempted to show him what I thought of him the other day!'

Teagan noticed her brother's clenched fists. Was his sudden anger really triggered by René's behaviour, or was it his visit to the solicitor?

'Christina doesn't deserve that!' he blurted out. 'The fat bastard's got no right to butt in and destroy it all.'

'No, but he has done. I don't know what she can do about it, if anything.' Teagan glanced back at him uncertainly and saw he was staring at his knuckles with a menacing light in his eye.

'Don't you worry about it though; God knows, you've got enough on your plate already, Pete.'

'Huh,' he growled, and rising from the chair impatiently he strode across the kitchen.

'Mother, I won't stop for dinner after all, there's something I need to do.' Turning to Teagan he added, 'Just see if I can't sort that man out.' Without waiting for her response, he was gone. The two women looked at each other in amazement.

'Oh no!' sighed Teagan. 'Now what's he getting himself into?'

★ ★ ★

Christina's morning hadn't gone well. Cast adrift on the empty day she felt useless, like a fishing boat that has lost its nets, she drifted aimlessly about. On her walk up the coastal path with Ginger, she would normally have picked a few flowers to fill the vases. Today she passed them by.

Leaving the well-trodden coastal path, she walked towards the cliff edge, seeing the deep wild sea beneath and the waves roaring, crashing their violent intent against the rocks below. Ginger gave a whine from deep in his throat and pricked his ears at the distant enemy who had unsettled them. His routine disrupted, instead of running around inquisitively in search of rabbits, he stayed close by her side as if sensing something was wrong.

Soon Christina could resist the tears no longer. The Sea Café had been stolen from her! She would do anything to get it back, but she felt helpless! Her one consolation, her one hope in all this turmoil was to seek out her father's help. With this in mind, she began to make her way down the coastal path. As she came down to the beach, her attention was drawn to a tall man walking along the water's edge with his back to her. When she stopped and threw a stone for Ginger into the sea, his sharp barks made the man turn round. He stood still, seeming to watch the dog, but as she came up closer, she was surprised to see it was Peter. He appeared to be waiting for her.

'Sad turn of events, I hear,' he said, as soon as she was within earshot. 'Teagan told me the news.'

Christina nodded, but all she wanted was to be alone.

'You can't allow him to bulldoze his way in and destroy the place,' he said. 'He hasn't got the right, you can't let it happen.'

She shrugged. 'What can I do? I'm rather outnumbered, don't you think?'

He walked along beside her in silence,

almost like a big dog listening and watching, his eyes were constantly returning to her face. She threw another stone for Ginger and they watched him running here and there. When she tired of it, Peter stooped and picking up a larger rock, flung it far out to sea. Ginger ploughed into the waves and stopped abruptly, panting and looking confused. It made her smile and Peter, seeing her, smiled too.

'That's my girl!' he said. 'Well, what d'you say to me going to speak to him, while the mood takes me? Seems to me he needs a talking to, or even a bit of persuasion.' Peter emphasized his meaning by drawing his hand up into a fist.

'No!' she cried, putting her hand on his arm. 'Please don't interfere!'

'He's taking advantage, Chris! That's no way to treat anybody, least of all your own family.' He stood so close to her now she could feel his body drawing her like a magnet. She swayed slightly, but didn't want to step away and when he looked her straight in the eye, there was no mistaking he sensed it too. She coloured; his directness had caught her off guard. 'I care about what happens to you, Chris. I think you can tell that already. I care about you and I want to help.'

'You can't, I'm sorry. Anyway, you've got

enough troubles of your own,' she said, flustered. 'Things are too complicated, there's money involved. The truth is the café's in debt, huge debt. I haven't been able to make it pay and my mum . . . ' She trailed off, hating to admit the truth. 'My mum's sold the café to René behind my back; sixty per cent of it anyway. It's enough to give him control. I don't own any of it. That's why he's acting like he is — because he's legally the joint owner now — apart from that, he's the only one with any money.' She gazed at Peter, touched by the concern in his big kind face and smiled, a sad whimsical smile. 'It's just a shame he's such a . . . '

'Bastard?' suggested Peter.

'Yes!' she laughed. 'Such a bastard!' Slipping her hand through his arm, a gesture that came so naturally to her, they walked further along the beach together. The tide was out and the wide expanse of sand spread out before them like a glistening path of diamonds.

'Isn't it beautiful here,' she whispered.

'Yes,' he said, 'it takes all your troubles away, doesn't it.'

'Does it take all your troubles away though, Peter?' she asked. He didn't answer and at first she thought he hadn't heard.

Then he started talking in earnest, using a

lower, more personal tone. 'My problems are
. . . Oh, it's all out of my hands! My life was
messed up by some geezer I've never met and
the stupid woman who used to call herself my
wife.'

'Teagan hasn't told me much, you know.
She didn't want to talk about it behind your
back. Your sister's been a good friend to me, I
trust her.'

'She doesn't know much more about the
divorce than I do. When Nicola decided to
leave the Design Studio and set up on her
own I thought she'd be happier, being
self-employed. The boys were starting school
and she had more time to devote to it. She
got quite a few commissions, going round
London with her portfolio, proper little
student she was!' He smiled sadly to himself.
'Then she took on a bigger project, kept
going out in the evenings for *business
meetings* as she called them.' His voice was
beginning to break now. Christina tightened
her grip on his arm. 'I lost count of the times
she got dressed up and went out, left me to
put the boys to bed. I couldn't handle it. So
one day, I told her enough was enough and
suddenly she just came out with it.'

'Oh, Peter! What did she say?'

'It doesn't matter now. We carried on for a
while, but there was a terrible atmosphere. I

thought if I hung on she'd see sense, but she'd changed. She said she couldn't afford to give him up. This geezer she'd met had loads of money and influence in the right places, a right clever arse apparently. What could I do? We needed the money and she said she couldn't afford to lose the contract. She was like another person — it wasn't my Nicola anymore. One night I said to her, she had to choose between lover-boy and this *once in a lifetime opportunity* or just plain old me.'

'And she chose the job?'

'She chose a man — and the man she chose wasn't me, put it that way,' he replied.

'I'm sorry.' Christina could see that he was struggling and longed to comfort him. 'Nicola's missing out on a good one,' she added, glancing at him, at once playful and sincere.

'Thanks,' he replied, catching her eye. 'Now, what's happenin' up there?' He jerked his head in the direction of the café. 'I came down with half a mind to sort him out, this brother-in-law of yours.'

Christina smiled; his warm-hearted passion amused her. 'Haven't you got enough of your own problems without taking on mine?' she asked with a giggle.

'Could just take my mind off them!

Nothing like a good punch-up to clear the head!'

'Peter!' she protested, laughing.

'No, seriously, let's go and talk to the bloke. They're all the same these city-types, think they own the world. Let's see if he won't listen to what you've got to say. He can still make changes if he wants to, but you're more than just an employee, you must have some rights.'

'It's between René and my mum. They won't listen to me.'

'No harm in trying, girl. Come on, let's go.' Suddenly he changed direction and letting her arm slip out of his, he was away off up the beach.

'Peter!' she called, trying to hurry after him. 'Peter! It's no use!' she shouted as she got left way behind.

'Better put Ginger on his lead!' he roared back to her as he headed towards the café.

As Christina made her way up the beach, she saw Peter disappear inside the French-doors. When she stepped inside, she found him talking to a workman who was demolishing the counter, ripping into the wood with hammer and chisel. Rubble obscured what remained of the floor. Dust filled the air. Christina looked around in disbelief. Every trace of her café had disappeared except for her table vases, broken and crammed into a box of rubbish.

Sensing trouble, she tugged on his arm. 'Peter, let's get out of here!'

He ignored her. 'So — is the boss about then?' he asked. The workman, a cigarette in his mouth, nodded towards the internal door and they found René in the storeroom, seated on a low stool. He had a laptop and papers in front of him. Sweat stood on his brow. It was a narrow and poorly lit room, and what remained of the stock was covered in plaster and dust.

'Yes?' He looked up as they approached.

'I'd like a word, if you don't mind,' said Peter.

'And you are?' asked René in a bored fashion. 'I seem to think we've met before.' He stared at Peter through narrowed eyes and then catching sight of Christina added: 'Oh, I see you've got yourself an entourage, Sister-in-law.'

Embarrassed, she stooped to stroke Ginger's head.

'My name's Peter Thomson — plumber by trade. I'm Teagan's brother.'

'Whose brother? I don't recognize the name.'

'My friend who helps out in the café,' prompted Christina. 'You do know her, René.'

153

'Oh, the voluntary worker,' he said. 'Yes, well, we're not a charity shop here, as I've told my sister-in-law more than once.'

'Oh, honestly!' Christina interrupted. 'Can't you hold a decent conversation for once without — '

René's eyes travelled about the small room as though he was hearing voices. 'You'll have to excuse my sister-in-law; she keeps forgetting who the boss is around here. Well, so you're a plumber? I might have use for a plumber as it happens. Give your number to one of the men on your way out. Thank you.' Dismissing them, his eyes reverted instantly back to the laptop.

But Peter stood his ground. 'I haven't come looking for work,' he said. 'What I wanted to say was: I think Chris here deserves to have some say in the alterations you're making. After all, she's been running the café here almost single-handedly for six years.'

'Almost?' René pounced on the word with glee. 'I'm so glad you said that! You can *almost* do a lot of things, sir; as you may well know. Unfortunately you can't *almost* run a business. If you're *almost* making a profit, then it's as good as making a loss and then, Mr What's-your-name Plumber, you find yourself in deep shit.' He gazed blankly at them both, in a manner both short-sighted, and vague. 'And what business is it of yours, may I ask,' he added, 'whether my unenlightened sister-in-law gets a say in what I plan to do or not?'

'I like to see fair play. I don't want to see people being trampled on,' said Peter, his voice quickly rising to the challenge. 'The café had a good following, regular customers, and nice atmosphere. I hate to see it all spoilt by some big arse like you who thinks they know better. You come down here interfering and full of big ideas. It seems to me you haven't got a clue about the locals and the way things are done around here.'

René stood up slowly, his face taking on a pasty pallor. When standing, he only reached Peter's chest. 'Suppose this is your idea, Sister-in-law? Think you can get your heavies to bully me into giving you a say in the business, is that it?'

A low growl began to emit from Ginger's throat. 'Sshh, ssh,' said Christina as she stroked Ginger's head nervously. 'I didn't ask him to stand up for me, René, but he's right. Me and Mum ought to have a say in what's done. You've ripped the place half to bits without telling us. You just came bulldozing your way in.'

'My, we are having a little tantrum aren't we?' chuckled René sarcastically. 'What makes you think I haven't talked to your mother, mmm?'

'You haven't talked to Christina, that's the point,' interrupted Peter. 'You could show her a bit more respect. Most of the customers are her friends. They are rather an important element in all this.'

'You think so, do you?' He was looking smug.

'You could at least have given them some warning that it was closing for refurbishment,' complained Christina. 'Maudie and Beefy and the others, they'll be wondering what's happened! What's the point of barging in creating all this bad feeling and letting all the customers down?'

'Because, my dear naive Sister-in-law, your poor little customers haven't got any money. Excuse me.' Giving an ice-cold smile, he shoved Peter aside and paused in the door-way. 'You can't run a business handing out cheap sandwiches to any odd-ball who wants to sit down and chat.' His bulbous eyes stood out like a bulldog's, steady and unblinking and cruel. 'Do you think we're running a bloody soup kitchen here for waifs and strays?' He stared at her, waiting for an answer. 'Well, do you?' he roared.

Peter grabbed him round the throat. 'You'll be sorry you ever came down to Cornwall, mate, you interfering money-grubber!' he hissed in his ear. 'We don't want your sort round here, thinkin' you can buy your way in here with your filthy money!' And throwing René back against the wall, he stormed out.

Pulling himself together and straightening his shirt, René cleared his throat and announced: 'Congratulations, Sister-in-law, I think you've found yourself an even bigger fool to fall in love with you, than I ever expected you would. Well done!'

Without another word, Christina turned and fled.

★ ★ ★

She found Peter standing near the water's edge, hands thrust deep in his pockets, staring out to sea.

'Are you always so impulsive?' she asked.

'I'm sorry,' he said, turning to her. 'I made a right pig's ear of that, didn't I! Trust me to put my foot in it!'

'Oh, it wasn't your fault. That man's impossible!' She looked up into his troubled face. 'Cheer up,' she said. 'At least you tried. No-one's dared to cross him before! It's nice to have someone sticking up for me for once! Thanks!'

A sad smile flickered across his face.

'People like you and me, Chris,' he said, 'we can have a go, but people like him — people like René — we can never change them, whatever we do or say.'

Suddenly he took her in his arms and, almost lifting her off the ground, kissed her passionately on the mouth. Her soul awoke under the unexpected pressure of his lips. Never had she been kissed like this! The sensation, the closeness, of his body pressing against hers stirred something so new in her that suddenly nothing else mattered. He kissed her with such urgency, the salty tang of the sea mingling with the roughness of his mouth. It was wild! It was like a storm inside her! When he finally released her, she felt something deep inside her had altered, like the world had shifted on its axis.

'You're quite something, aren't you!' she giggled.

7

In the town Hall, Deborah's dancing pupils were clearing up after the class. Christina was still reeling from Peter's kiss when she walked in and heard her sister giving orders: 'Stacy, stop swinging on that curtain! Has everyone collected their shoes? Who's left this jacket on the stage?' Suddenly a babble of children exploded out of the side doors, rushing past her into the arms of their parents.

Christina began reading some posters on the wall while she waited for her sister to finish. Finally, carrying a large hold-all in one hand and several files in the other, Deborah came across. 'Take these would you?' she said, by way of a greeting. 'Where is she then?'

'Who?' asked Christina.

'Caitlin? I do have a daughter, remember?' She was obviously in one of her superior moods.

'She's with Mum. I wanted to speak to you about something in private, before we get home that is,' said Christina, looking at her meaningfully.

Deborah frowned. 'It's not about money, is it? I really can't beg any more cash out of my dear husband at the moment; he's in such a foul mood these days.'

'Tell me about it!' replied Christina. 'He'll probably blow a gasket after what happened today. Peter went and had a go at him — roughed him up a bit.' This gained her sister's attention immediately.

'Wow! I'm intrigued!' exclaimed Deborah in delight. 'Tell me more!'

When Christina described what had happened, her sister was incredulous. 'Oh, brilliant!' she cried. 'Wish I'd seen it! Your chap must have had a job chucking René about — the size of him lately!'

'He's a foot taller than René at least, and he's very strong.' Christina couldn't disguise the admiration in her voice.

'Ooh! Sounds as though you're smitten! Is my big sister in love at last?' Deborah's finely manicured finger-nails were poised over the light switch — but she didn't receive a reply. 'So, is that what you came down to tell me?'

'Sort of.' Christina was keen to move the focus away from her love life. 'What I thought was — could you talk to René? Could you persuade him to leave the café alone? As it is I'll have to redecorate it now he's done so much damage. All I need is a bit longer to make it turn in some profit. I know I haven't done a very good job so far, but I've got loads of new ideas. Will you talk to him, Debs? Ask him not to rip any more out — and give me one last chance. Please Debs!'

'No-one can make René change his mind about anything, once he's decided. He's as stubborn as a mule, and bloody minded with it! He won't listen to me; you know what he's like. Once he gets an idea into his stupid head . . . '

Sadly, Christina looked at her sister and saw her slim Lycra clad figure, the glittery eye-shadow dusted over her eyelids, the shiny lip gloss, and thought it was like asking a fairy for a wish. 'Couldn't you just try?' she persisted.

'OK, I'll have to wait till he's had a few and mellowed a bit though, later on tonight, perhaps.' With that, she switched off the lights and the two sisters made their way outside. Deborah locked the door and tested it with a sharp twist of the handle. 'Want a lift home then?'

'No, I think I'd like the walk. I'll see you back home later. Hey Debs!' she added, 'Thanks!'

★ ★ ★

It was a cold autumnal morning a few weeks later. A thick mist hung over the sea when

161

Christina next visited the café. She went in response to what her sister had told her — that René was prepared to share with her what he was planning to do.

When she got there the skip outside was full to overflowing. She recognized bits of her tables and chairs crushed beneath a pile of rubble, and what remained of the dog basket; just as well she had left Ginger safely at home. Seeing all this, she realized there wasn't any hope left of getting the café back to how it was. Noise of drilling came from inside, and when she opened the door, the smell of wet paint filled her nostrils. There was a new counter, curved and topped with black marble and trimmed with chrome. A workman was applying mirror tiles which filled the whole of the back wall.

'Ah, you're here at last! Pass those drawings over would you, Sister-in-law?' It was René's voice but she couldn't see him at first — it was so smoky and dusty in there. Turning she found him seated near the window in a folding director's chair facing her. He was smoking a cheroot. She steeled herself.

'What drawings?'

He sighed, stood up, brushed past her and snatched something off the counter.

'These drawings,' he said. 'Sit yourself

down and I'll attempt to show you exactly what we're planning to do here.' He resumed sitting on the only seat available and seeing none other, Christina remained standing. René nodded to a nearby box. 'Bring that over, near me.'

Dragging the small heavy box across the floor and brushing off the dust, she sat down. He began with a quick smile. 'Your sister seems to have the misguided impression that I'm neglecting you. I shall therefore attempt to rectify the matter by explaining what we intend to do. I want you to be aware — ' he emphasized the words by puffing out his chest, 'I have no grievance whatsoever with you playing a part in all this. My wife's good at jumping to conclusions without knowing all the facts, but be that as it may, I *am* a reasonable man. If someone approaches me with an honest request, I will do all in my power to grant their wish, providing it is acceptable.' His two fat hands were clasped together as he made this speech, but his eyes roamed about the room without focussing on anything.

Spread before them on the floor were some pen and ink artist's impressions of the finished interior. These were not simply cosmetic changes; the overall effect was total transformation. Seeing them, she realized the

Sea Café she knew and loved was gone forever. In its place she saw a cheap wine-bar, like a night-club in the cheesier parts of London. There was a high bar area, with chrome bar stools on which the artist had sketched-in stylized figures wearing suits and cocktail dresses. An illuminated display stand was drawn next to the bar with glasses, wine, and spirit bottles lining the shelves.

'What do you think? Impressive isn't it?!' asked René proudly. 'Classy even!'

She paused to consider her reply. 'So this is the direction you're taking the café?' she said carefully.

'Mmm, I knew you'd be impressed, once you saw the effect I was after.'

'And you're changing the name as well I presume?' she asked, swallowing hard.

'Now yes, that would be an excellent idea!' he crowed, as though he genuinely hadn't thought of it. 'Well done, Sister-in-law! I'll tell Debs you're not as stupid as you lead us to believe. What do you suggest, mmm?' Pleased with this proposal, he stubbed out his cheroot and rested his chubby elbows on the arms of his chair to consider the options. 'What we need is something to catch the eye,' he mused. 'The Smugglers? No, there's one down the road. What did they call those rogues who used to lure the ships off the

Cornish coast and plunder their cargo? Umm . . . That's it!' He answered his own question with glee. 'The Wreckers!'

Christina groaned inwardly. The white-washed walls, the stripped pine shelves, and the sun-bleached tables were dissolving before her eyes. In their place was a sleazy establishment serving cocktails, with black leather seats, dim lighting, and an atmosphere thick with cigarette smoke.

'The Wreckers' Bar!' René's voice broke into her thoughts. 'Yes, I like that, it has a certain kick to it, don't you think? The name needs to suggest a bit of excitement to capture people's imagination! A bit of danger! Just the job! What do you think, Sister-in-law?'

Nausea swept through her. It was as though her body was being violated. She was afraid she was going to vomit. Jumping up, she rushed for the door. 'No, sorry, I can't stand it!' she cried as she fled outside.

Like a lover, the sea breeze caught her and she fell forward into its soothing embrace. Caressing her hair, the wind lifted her, relaxing her shoulders and taking her by the hand, it led her down to the water's edge. Waves rose up before her like a cooling balm to her burning pain and lashed against her jeans, soaking them. But she didn't care.

Wading into the sea deeper and deeper, she savoured the gentle tug and pull of the tide against her legs as her anger gave way to tears that welled up, hurting her throat like smooth pebbles. She wept in utter despair as the weight of the water dragged her in. Her strength was ebbing away. Gradually losing consciousness, she went down. The sea engulfed her. Again she was three years old, falling from the edge of the harbour wall. Within minutes she was fighting for her life. Choking and blinded by salt water, she was floundering and disorientated. Her lungs were scalded time and again by bitter salt water. In one final desperate attempt to live, she forced herself upwards, took a searing lungful of precious air, and screamed!

Suddenly something was lifting her, driving back the waves and letting the light back into her eyes. She felt herself being carried, floating above coral reefs; shoals of fish in a myriad of colours led the way to a turquoise cavern. She rose on a warm air current, like a seagull skimming across the surface. Now she was flying, like a dolphin, triumphantly riding above the sea as though on horseback. The thunder of hoofs took her to safety, cantering away with her across the sand.

'It's all right, Christina! I've got you!' Through a wall of water she saw a man's face.

It was contorted with exertion and anguish. Pulling her free of the waves, he held on to her, staggered back on the gravel and bringing her up the beach, laid her down on the dry sand.

'You're all right now, Christina! You're safe!' She felt the warmth of his coat wrapped around her. It smelt of fish and sweat and the heavy fabric was comforting. He came close, she could feel him breathing. It was a warm breath, closer than a kiss. His eyes, so clear and blue, were staring at her now as though they adored her. A tremble started deep down in her bones. Gradually it crept up through her body until she felt the shivering vibrations would tear her to pieces.

'Christina! Wake up! It's me!'

Coming to, she recognized who had saved her. 'John? Where am I?'

'Just as well I happened to be here. See if you can stand up,' he said.

She peered around, shivering, and found her clothes and hair were soaked. Trembling, she let John help her and tried to stand up. Looking about, she was surprised to see it was a familiar place — they were on the beach not far from the café. She felt as though she had been away for a very long time.

'Oh, John, I don't know what happened.' As she said this, she started to cry. Inexplicably a terrible fear came over her again and she clung to him as though she was falling.

'Thank God I came along when I did, Christina, you nearly drowned! What were you doing in the sea?' Taking her in his arms, he hugged her to him as though she was the most precious thing in the world.

'I don't know,' she sobbed, and then in a rush she remembered everything. 'I was in the café,' she began. 'I was with René and . . . '

'Right! We'll talk about it later. Come on; let's get you home, you're wet through. You need a hot bath and some sweet tea. Lean on me. I'll take you back to my place.'

With John supporting her, they made their way together across the beach towards the road, where he had parked his van. As they drew near the café, she caught sight of a figure watching them through the window. It was René. It occurred to her then, that he had seen the whole thing. He had seen the danger she was in, and he hadn't lifted a finger to help her.

★ ★ ★

Twenty minutes later, Christina was sitting in John's kitchen. She had stripped off her wet clothes and wrapped herself in the warm blanket he had given her. He was upstairs;

she could hear him whistling a tune, and running her a hot bath. It surprised her how easily he had taken control of the situation, how naturally he cared for her. His relaxed whistling made her think of better days, when she had been a little girl, sitting in the Sea Café with her book and colouring pencils while her father worked.

When John reappeared and put a mug of sweet tea in her hands, she found herself wondering whether their relationship would change since he had saved her life. Would he have some claim on her now?

'It was nice to hear you whistling,' she said. 'It reminded me of my dad.'

He looked surprised. 'Didn't realize I was!' he said. 'I mustn't do that on the boat. The men say it's bad luck, like calling up the wind.'

'You're not superstitious, are you, John?'

'Nah! I don't whistle though, just in case. They say you shouldn't take a Cornish pasty out to sea, and if you see a priest when you're about to cast off, you're safer staying at home. Anyway, into the bath with you — you're shivering! I'll be finding you some dry clothes.'

★   ★   ★

The weeks passed. Connor was preparing once again to put to sea. Down by the harbour, he was loading up supplies with his crew, food and bait and ice packs for the hold: they were all carried on board amidst a lot of shouting and hollering.

'How long will you be gone this time?' called Teagan. She was standing on the harbour wall with her coat wrapped tightly around her. There was a strong wind and droplets of early-morning mist clung to her hair. 'Long as it takes; need to get a good catch in before the weather breaks,' he yelled from a distance. 'We could be gone eight, ten days at the most.' He came closer. 'Don't worry. You'll be all right eh?'

She nodded, attempting a smile. 'Of course I will.'

'That's my girl!' Securing the ropes, he yelled up to one of his lads, 'Fetch those boxes off the side, will yer? Hurry up, before they get too wet to be any good.'

'But you will phone?' she persisted. 'I've no way of knowing when you're coming back, have I?'

He came up to her. 'Whenever I come home, you'll be here waitin' for me, won't you Tig?' he asked. 'Or do I have to come home to a cold empty house when I'm tired an' hungry eh?'

'No, no Connor! Of course I'll be here, it's just — '

'Well, then, take care of yourself and see to that brother of yours. See if you can't get his life sorted out for him. One o' these days it would be nice to have the place to ourselves again.' He opened his arms wide and gave her a big warm hug. 'Y'know, we might need to think about havin' a babby, if the time's right, eh, Tig?'

'Oh, Connor, there's nothing I want more in this whole world!' she cried, clinging to him and burying her face in his neck.

'Me too! I'll see if I can't bring back a bit of Irish blarney to make a bonny babby for us, eh?' He kissed her again, a long passionate kiss that stirred her body into a longing. She didn't ever want to let him go. These last moments were precious, every word, every sensation she would carry with her to remember him by, in the lonely nights to follow.

The days were growing colder and Christmas was approaching when Teagan told herself she must see the doctor. Connor was away at sea once more. With a thrill she counted the days again; there was no denying it now, she was at least a month and a half overdue. Other signs had begun to stir in her body too. Hastily she screwed the lid on the jar of Marmite her brother had left open and pushed it into the back of the cupboard, suppressing a feeling of nausea.

Later that day, walking home from the surgery, she could hardly contain her feelings as they fluctuated between excitement and fear. What if she miscarried? What if Connor said it was too soon? What if? What if? It was a heady feeling, like bubbly champagne rushing to her head, but she couldn't tell anyone until Connor was home. How could she share the news when even he didn't know? Oh, if only he would come home! Walking in a kind of dream, she found herself on the beach at Crystal Barr. The Sea Café — or what used to be the café — stood before her. If Christina was there, she wouldn't stop long for fear of revealing her secret which she felt sure was written all over her face! Her news was hers and hers alone.

'Can I help you?' A voice came from behind her. She spun round to see René coming towards her. 'We're opening on Saturday,' he added, as though she had enquired.

'Oh, no,' stumbled Teagan. 'It's all right. I was just looking for my friend, Christina; I thought she might be here, that's all.'

'You and me both,' he replied. 'She pleases herself, that girl, but you never know — she might be inside, waging war against the enemy.'

'The enemy?' she asked, confused.

'Some people won't accept change, even

for the better, if you know what I mean?' he mumbled as he opened the door. Inclining his head by way of invitation, he said: 'Step inside. Oh, surprise, surprise. No-one's here! They've demanded this damned meeting so you'd think they'd be here on time. Democracy! I'm all for democracy, I wouldn't mind it if it didn't waste so much bloody time.'

Teagan waited there reluctantly, watching the workmen whom René had ignored. She watched him waddle through to the back room, peering short-sightedly about as though Christina might be hiding behind a door. The two men continued working; they appeared to be stocking the shelves with alcohol, making quite a noise and apparently oblivious of her presence. 'I'd better go,' she said, as soon as he came into view again. The smell of paint was making her feel sick. 'I'll call back another day. Thanks anyway.' She couldn't wait to get out of the door.

'Please yourself. I bet they'll roll in any minute.' As he spoke there was a scuffle and voices. Christina appeared, followed by her mother. Josie's shrill voice rang out: 'Haven't they got any lights in here?'

'Oh, we have a committee at last!' said René. 'We are honoured. Bring that chair, Sister-in-law. Josie, you sit here.'

'How are you, Tig?' Christina asked. 'I haven't seen you for ages.'

'I'm fine,' whispered Teagan, eyeing the company nervously. 'Actually I'm not staying. I'll let you get on.'

'Stay a few minutes, please?' asked Christina. 'You don't mind Teagan listening in, do you, René?'

'Whatever,' he replied. Catching the eye of one of the men, he jerked his head towards the door. They both stopped what they were doing and left immediately. René sat toad-like on his director's chair, holding a handful of papers and looking at them with a benevolent stare.

'First of all, has anyone got any objections to these proposed new opening hours, mmm?' he gazed around, seemingly bored by the possibility of disagreement.

'I'm not in favour of opening until midnight if that's what you mean,' said Josie. 'We've never been that sort of establishment.'

'So I gather,' he replied.

'It might attract the wrong sort,' added Christina. 'I don't want to stay that late anyway. Seven-thirty is late enough for me. I don't like the idea of installing fruit machines either, they're expensive to insure, and cheap looking. They attract the wrong type of customer.'

'Yes, and if you're holding a drinks and

gambling licence, the overheads will be enormous. Our insurance costs will rocket. I don't see how we can do it, René,' said Josie, 'not on our budget. Well, we can't do it, frankly.'

'That's funny, Josie, I could have sworn I heard you say 'We can't do it'.' René's sarcastic comment was thrown over his shoulder as he reached for his cigarette lighter. Taking a cheroot, he lit up, and drew on it deeply. Letting his arm relax over the arm of the chair, his gold bracelet dangled over his plump forearm. There was an awkward silence.

Teagan stood up. 'I'm sorry, I really must be getting back,' she whispered and made to leave. Christina rose to apologize, and opening the door for her, caught a gust of sea air billowing though. She felt like a lobster trapped in a pot. It had been so easy to crawl in, to get ensnared in René's plans but now she couldn't find a way out.

'Good. So let's get down to business,' René prompted. 'It's all here: the insurance, VAT, rates etc. Everything's been drawn up by my solicitor; it's all been finalized. All you have to do is sign here, Josie dear. It's not a lot to ask. I am bearing full responsibility, so you needn't worry your head about it. All I ask, and I ask *most humbly*, is that you offer your services from time to time — to serve in the bar, welcome the clients, that sort of thing. I don't ask for a lot. I am aware you have your own work to do, fiddling about with that sewing-machine or whatever you do. But it's your prerogative, as you are both familiar with our clientele, I would appreciate a bit of input from yourselves. I am, admittedly, a novice in the field of tourist attractions. I much prefer the city life myself. But when it comes to running this kind of establishment, I have connections, and thankfully a little more business acumen than you two.'

He stopped talking and looked at each of the women expectantly, the cheroot temporarily abandoned on the edge of a nearby packing case. Christina felt awkward and suspicious of this new humility.

'When do you want me to work exactly?' she asked. 'I assumed I would be full-time, as before.'

'I have my own trained chefs and bar-staff, experienced in serving cocktails and the like — they're coming down from London and will be arriving on Friday. If I could ask you simply to help prepare and serve bar snacks, which are on the menu from six till nine, it would be a help, thank you.' He gave a flicker of a smile.

'What sort of bar snacks?' asked Christina.

'Oh, use your imagination girl! Not beans on toast for a start. I was assuming you would have some ideas on that score. Do I have to do everything myself?'

Christina sighed. 'What about breakfasts?'

'I don't do breakfast. We're opening a Wine Bar not a bloody bus-park caff. You'll be working between six and nine, six days a week, that's all I ask.'

'But that won't amount to many hours! I need to work enough to earn a living you know.'

'I'm looking for quality workmanship, not quantity,' he replied, picking up his cheroot and inhaling impatiently.

'While she was here, we could have asked Teagan if she wants to work occasionally,' suggested Christina. 'She likes to have something to do and she's very obliging. You wouldn't mind, would you?'

'What, the charity worker, you mean? I dare say there'll be some cleaning to do if she wants. Her approach isn't exactly — what shall we say — *professional* though, is it? Let's play it by ear, shall we?'

Christina longed to be a million miles away from René and his wine bar. When would he tire of this charade? Josie, who had been silent until now, stood up looking unusually flushed.

'René, Chris has struggled to keep this business in the family. I've not given it the time it deserved, but she's managed to keep going, mainly out of loyalty to our customers. The café has a good loyal following, doesn't it Chris? Local people, most of them. They aren't rich, I warrant you, but they've been regular customers for a long time.' She tossed her head nervously. 'My husband Charlie, he used to say some of these people are like family to us. The fishermen used to look for our lights before dawn, shining from the Sea Café when they were on their way back into harbour. And when they got here, there would be a good hot cuppa and a bacon buttie ready for their breakfast. It was something they looked forward to when they brought home their catch.'

Christina looked at her mother in amazement. It surprised her that she was suddenly speaking up so honestly, not only in her defence, but in Charlie's defence too! She never mentioned her father usually, never! But she was still speaking, her voice quivering with emotion and becoming shrill, almost hysterical.

'Are you telling me,' she demanded, putting her hands on her hips. 'Are you telling me and Chris here, that we're not doing breakfasts anymore? Because, you know what, René — they won't be looking for cocktails and nibbles when they come ashore in the morning, I can assure you of that!' There was a hush. René shifted in his chair, stubbed out his cheroot and stood up.

'They can have their tea and their bacon butties when they get home,' he replied. 'I don't want them coming in here stinking of fish anyway — not when I've put my life's savings into refurbishing the place. They'll be welcome to come when they've been home to shower and change. It's that little thing called respect, Mother-in-law, which I expect all our clientele to have.' He looked about him, restless and irritated. 'I think we've talked enough. There are a few minor details to cover, but I think I'll postpone that for now. We've got a business to run here, not a bloody welfare centre, and time's getting on. Sign here please — or this will be a wasted exercise and I for one don't intend to waste any more of my time — or money.'

He picked up the papers savagely and shoved them under Josie's nose. 'Sign here please, and here . . . and here,' he said, holding the pen out towards her like a dagger. Josie took it in silence, signed her name several times and threw the pen down. Satisfied, René whipped the papers away and tucked them into his briefcase.

'Right!' he said. Picking up his jacket and bunch of keys, he prepared to leave. 'Don't forget,' he said as he made his way to the door. 'We're opening on Saturday, so smarten up please, especially you, Sister-in-law, you look like something the cat's dragged in.'

'Oh, for God's sake!' Christina turned away in revulsion and caught her mother's eye. Josie, surprisingly, was shaking her head in disbelief. Something passed between the two women which went beyond words. Christina knew, at that moment, that her mother regretted what she had done. Now René was in charge, their lives would never be the same again.

★   ★   ★

'But he's so damn superior, Debs!' complained Christina that evening. 'Honestly, he made me feel like a lobster trapped in a lobster pot!'

Her sister laughed out loud. 'He's the lobster, darling, don't you think? Have you taken a look at him lately? He's so red and bloated with booze, I'm beginning to wonder if he shouldn't see a doctor.' She was sitting on the edge of Caitlin's bed manicuring her nails. 'I'm getting really fed-up with sleeping on the floor. I thought this café obsession he'd got would be an overnight wonder. I can't believe he's intending to stay on here

180

managing the place. Thought he'd soon get tired of it! He always said he couldn't stand this house, said it was claustrophobic. I wish he'd go back to London and get off my back!'

'You wouldn't recognize the place now, Debs. I don't think I can bear to work under him, he's impossible! I need to find another job.'

'Darling, I know he's a pig, but do you think you can just hang in there for a bit, just for my sake, please? The thing is, he's offered to buy me my own dancing-school!' Deborah purred, blowing on her wet nail varnish with pouting lips. 'You know it's what I've always dreamed of — I'd simply love it! I'll really feel I'm getting somewhere. All this hiring of town halls and making do with scout huts, it's really so disgustingly amateurish! Just think what I could do with my own premises! Imagine! Lovely oak floor, full-length mirrors, lighting! I can just see it!' She sighed dreamily as the vision lit up before her eyes.

Christina looked at her sister in utter astonishment. 'Do you really believe his offer's genuine?'

'Why shouldn't it be?' she asked indignantly. 'He told me when his precious wine bar's up and running he'll start looking out for a premises for me. Oh, I can't wait!'

'But Debbie! Look at you, sleeping on the floor in Caitlin's room! You've been avoiding him like the plague! And now you're playing right into his hands! What's the matter with you?'

Deborah's shoulders slumped and she looked slightly uncomfortable, smoothing her tights, and tweaking her hair. 'What choice have I got though, sis? How else am I going to get a start in life? If he's fool enough to try and impress me, why shouldn't I take advantage of it?'

Christina was appalled. 'Because you should have principles! Some self-respect! You don't need to prostitute yourself for the likes of people like him! You've got more talent in your little finger than he's — '

'Principles?' scoffed Deborah. 'Self-respect? Come off it, Chris! I can't afford to have principles! The only respect I've ever earned for myself is through my dancing. My pupils respect me, admire me even, bless them. I owe it to them, don't I, to make something of myself? I ought to have proper premises for them by now, a dancing-school of my own!'

Christina looked at her sister's face: her make-up was smudged around her eyes, the traces of last night's mascara spilling down her cheeks. The pathos of it all took her breath away.

'Where would you have your own dancing-school, Debbie?'

'Oh, around here somewhere. All my pupils live around St. Ives,' she replied, brightening.

'Where's René getting the money from? Properties aren't cheap around here.'

'How do I know?' she replied impatiently. 'That's his business. He's a very successful businessman in London, you know.'

'Yes, but I can't see a couple of wine bars in London making him a fortune exactly.'

'He's pretty clever! You've got to hand it to him. I know he's not your favourite person in the world but he's got connections in high places, he *knows* people,' cooed Deborah, fluttering her eyelashes.

Christina tried another approach. 'What about Caitlin? He hardly spends any time with her — in fact, he barely speaks to her these days.'

'He's a busy man! I know he's very fond of her, he said so. You know — ' Deborah regarded her older sister for a moment — 'I'm beginning to wonder whether you might be a tiny bit jealous.'

'Jealous? What of? A jumped-up chauvinist pig who thinks he's God's gift to women?'

'I mean, of opportunities coming my way; René's ambitious plans for me, and my new premises — and what he wants for Caitlin.'

'Oh? So he has got plans for his daughter then? What are they exactly?'

Deborah couldn't conceal her pride. 'He's promised her a pony! That's not to be sniffed at, is it? He knows someone with a riding school in Hayle, where she can have lessons and keep it stabled,' said Deborah. 'Caitlin's always wanted a pony of her own.'

'It's the first I've heard of it,' replied Christina, wondering what was going to spring next from Pandora's box of tricks. If it wasn't so tragic, so predictable, she could have laughed. Christina looked at her sister, her eyes shining with excitement, and she felt the cold hand of fate on her shoulder. Swallowing hard, she made an excuse and left the room.

★ ★ ★

The Wreckers' Bar was almost complete. Tall, red-leather and chrome stools were grouped around high tables and on the veranda these were topped with red parasols. It looked quite smart, Christina had to admit, when she called in one morning to make last minute arrangements with her future employer — René. It was sophisticated, totally unlike the Sea Café, and — she thought — completely out of character with the gentle seaside atmosphere of the beach at Crystal Barr. That afternoon finishing touches were being made to the exterior and workmen were busy putting up the new neon sign which would be displayed above the entrance. René was talking to a young man when she arrived. The mirrors sparkled and spot-lights suggested to her more of a night-club atmosphere. There was the heady scent of alcohol, which was, she quickly realized, because both men were already drinking.

'Ah!' exclaimed René, straightening up. 'Max, this is my sister-in-law; she's helping with bar snacks.' The man nodded and stared at her without speaking.

'Hello, I'm Christina,' she said and was about to extend her hand when he looked away and spoke to René. 'You want me to clear that stuff, boss?' he asked, and disappeared out of the back door.

She shrugged, hardly surprised by the rebuff. Any acquaintance of René's was unlikely to be amenable. 'It's nearly ready then,' she said, looking around. 'You've certainly changed the place. I don't recognize it at all.' René seemed pleased at this remark and smiled congenially. 'Can we talk about a few things?' she asked. 'We need to finalize my pay, and what I should wear. It all seems a bit disorganized considering everything else is sorted.'

'Yes, well as you can see, the decor is basically black and red. My boys have red

185

waistcoats, and black trousers; you get the picture? Think you can come up with something along those lines?' His mouth gave a twitch which served as a full-stop to the discussion.

'And wages?' she prompted.

He felt in his pockets for his cheroots and put one between his lips. 'My boys are experienced of course. They're used to London rates. Obviously you won't be expecting the same. What were you taking in wages before?'

'I'm surprised you haven't discussed this with my mother,' she said. 'It seems a bit late in the day to be deciding this now. Mum usually sees to the accounts.' She was embarrassed how low her wage packet had been and didn't want to say. The Sea Café had been like her second home; she hadn't been able to draw much out of the takings for herself.

'Well, since I've never worked with you before and haven't seen you in action I'd like to see what you're made of first. My chef's sorted out the menu — he'll see to ordering the stuff, show you what's what.' He looked absent-mindedly across her shoulder. 'You'll be paid something, don't fret. I'm a reasonable man. Now, if you'll excuse me, I've got a meeting with the local press.'

'When exactly do you want me to start?'

'The first night of course. Our opening night! Festivities start at six — see that you're here at five o'clock prompt. We want to make the night a huge success. Oh, by the way, can you do something with that hair of yours? We're trying to give the place a bit of class if possible.'

Christina looked at him. He just couldn't sustain even a degree of politeness for more than a few minutes. That fact had become obvious. Her stare took in the puffy conceited face, the sensual lips, the unfocussed eyes; she saw a man who really didn't care about her at all. 'René,' she said, 'unless you can start treating me with a bit more respect I don't see how I can work for you. I'm doing my best to be civil, which isn't easy in the circumstances.'

'Don't be so childish,' he spat. 'It's a tough business, the catering trade. You have to be prepared to take a bit of criticism. We're all going to have to smarten up; even my wife knows that much about running a business. Take a leaf out of her book. Your sister always looks smart and presentable. Ask her, she might let you borrow some of her pretty things.'

Christina stepped away and pushing the French-doors open felt the sea breeze on her face. Something was dreadfully wrong with all this. With a surge of indignation she made a decision and swung round. 'Actually, in the circumstances I think you'd better find someone else to take my place,' she said. 'Find someone who won't mind if you stamp their face into the dirt every time you speak to them.'

His eyes bulged. 'Don't be so bloody sensitive, girl!' he said. 'I can't work with drivelling idiots, never could.'

'Oh, don't worry; you won't have to. Get yourself another idiot, René, because I'm out of here. I'm not sure your *boys*, as you call them, do put up with it, but I'm not sticking around to find out.'

Flinging wide the French-doors she let the full force of the Atlantic Ocean burst into the premises, sending menus and napkins flying everywhere. She fled down the steps, and hobbled away across the sand shedding tears as she went. It was over. His attitude had confirmed what she had felt all along — there was no way she was ever going to work for that man.

★ ★ ★

That evening, when Christina and her mother were in the kitchen, Deborah and René arrived home together in the middle of a full-scale row.

Josie and Christina looked at each other. 'Here we go again,' said Christina, 'I wonder what's set them off this time.'

'Do you think I'm stupid or something?' Deborah yelled. 'I bet everyone's been laughing their heads off!' Slamming the front door, they heard her tearing up the stairs where she continued shouting obscenities from the bedroom.

René mumbled to himself as he went by the kitchen door. 'What I need is a drink.' They heard him go into the sitting room and the inevitable clink of glasses. Putting down the tea-towel, Christina went in pursuit of her sister but, hearing a cry, she peeked into Caitlin's room. She found the little girl wide awake and frightened. 'Poor little door-mouse!' she whispered, hugging her close. 'Don't worry, your mummy and daddy are a bit upset, that's all. It's nothing to worry about.' Caitlin gave a shuddering sigh.

'Why?' she piped up, half-asleep. 'What's happened?'

'Nothing important; you try and go back to sleep,' she replied, stroking her forehead. Caitlin lay back on the pillow, but reluctant to leave her, Christina sat with her, listening to her sister crying through the bedroom wall.

Within a few minutes, however, Deborah came shuffling into Caitlin's room carrying her duvet under her arm. She put the bedding down, before realizing her sister was there in the dark. 'Oh, so you're here,' she whispered. 'Did I wake her up? Sorry.'

'Caitlin's OK, aren't you little one,' murmured Christina, giving the child a kiss. 'Your Mummy's here now, so I'm going downstairs; all right?'

Caitlin nodded, sleepily. 'Mummy?' she whispered. 'Will you tuck me in?'

'Yes, darling, of course, pet,' replied Deborah sniffing. She unfolded herself again from the duvet, a bare shoulder revealing a glittery strap which picked up the light. 'He's so damn thoughtless, sis,' she mumbled softly.

Christina looked back at her. 'Are you OK?'

'Have to be, won't I,' she replied, sniffing. 'The rotten pig!'

'We'll talk about it tomorrow, Debs, don't worry,' whispered Christina. 'Goodnight, Caitlin,' she called softly before closing the bedroom door.

8

The night of the grand-opening arrived. Christina stood with Peter watching from far off on the headland. Loud rock music was pounding; and people could be seen moving about on the beach drinking and dancing. The Wreckers' Bar was in full swing.

'So the place is finally open again!' said Christina, sighing. It was a cold December evening, and pitch-black on the coastal path overlooking the beach at Crystal Barr. It wasn't a good time to be out, least of all up on the cliffs, but they had wanted to see the spectacle from a distance. Looking across the bay, Christmas lights in the houses served to accentuate their isolation. They stood together — two lonely people fighting an unknown future.

Suddenly there was a flash as rockets roared up into the night sky. Christina leant back against Peter, and her heart leapt as his strong arms came around her. 'It's the end of that place for me,' she said. 'I'll start looking for a job in the New Year.'

'There's not much going round here in the winter,' he replied. 'Where would you look?'

'In a restaurant or something, I know it's the wrong time of year but still.'

'You could come and work for me,' Peter suggested, breathing into her hair.

'Oh yeah?' she laughed. 'As a plumber's mate you mean?'

'I'm serious; I could probably find you something to do part-time — do my books or hold a hammer or something; couldn't pay you much though.'

'It's OK. I heard you were having enough trouble trying to keep yourself at the moment.' As soon as she had said this, she knew it had been the wrong thing to say.

'So Teagan's been talking behind my back, has she?' he said, withdrawing his arms and stepping away from her. With his hands in his pockets, he stood in silhouette against the night sky.

'No, of course not!' she protested. But he stooped and picked up a stone, throwing it angrily over the edge of the cliff. Ginger, ears pricked, rushed forward after it. 'No Ginger!' she shouted, frantically clapping her hands. The dog stopped just short of the steep drop, peering over into the abyss and wagging his tail.

'Sorry,' he said. 'Stupid thing to do. Here, boy!' he called, flinging another behind them into the undergrowth to distract him and draw him away from the edge.

'No harm done.' She took a deep breath. 'Peter, I didn't mean . . . ' She was stuck for an explanation. 'Teagan's worried about you, with the divorce and everything — and she just said you were struggling a bit, that's all.'

'If Nicola wants her pound of flesh, she can have it,' he growled bitterly. 'She'd have the clothes off my back if she could, Chris.'

'Here am I worrying about the café when you've seen your whole world being torn to pieces. I am sorry, really.' She stepped forward and gave him a hug.

A volley of firecrackers shot up from the cove and produced a shower of cascading light. She glanced at him and saw that he wasn't looking up at the sky at all, he was looking at her.

'You are beautiful, Chris,' he whispered. She laughed and kissed him. 'No I'm not but it's lovely of you to say so!' The tension had evaporated.

'You're beautiful to me — come here! How good are you with a fret-saw?'

'About as good as I am with a spanner,' she replied smiling. He took her in his warm arms again and kissed her tenderly. As more rockets shot into the night sky, they turned back to watch just in time to see the new neon lights come on: A garish sign announcing

'The Wreckers' Bar' lit up, flickered and burned steadily. They heard the distant cheer of a celebratory crowd down on the beach.

Peter stood behind her so they could both face the spectacle; he folded his arms about her shoulders and his breath tickled the back of her neck. Taking off his jacket, he laid it down on the grass and pulled her down next to him. It seemed strange, she thought, sitting in the cold night air, in the dark at the top of a cliff and she said so. But he merely chuckled and lay back, staring up at the stars. When she allowed herself to be drawn into his arms, he kissed her neck, her ear, and her lips and suddenly she wasn't thinking about the Wreckers' Bar anymore. Her mind was as silent as the night and her heart was quivering like a wild animal.

'I think I'm in love with you, Peter,' she whispered.

'You only think you are?' he chuckled, kissing her again. 'Christina! I love you too,' he whispered. 'I've known for some time.'

A firecracker broke in the sky almost over their heads and they both looked up and laughed and then he came onto her like a surging tide. He enveloped her in wave after wave of passion, his mouth devouring her. She dissolved into him and, pulling aside her clothes, she felt the warmth and heaviness of his weight on her, letting him mould her body to his own. At last she felt as supple, and agile and graceful as a dolphin diving in an arc of tingling salt spray. In his arms she felt beautiful. Over his shoulder, she could see the full blonde face of the moon. How close it was! It seemed to speak to her of a new life, as his caresses led her down a path she had never been before. His touch spoke of a different joy, as his urgency took her and she yielded to him with a tiny gasp of surprise.

★ ★ ★

Life at home grew more difficult for Christina in the days following the opening of The Wreckers' Bar. She occupied herself seeking a job. One advertisement, published in the Western Morning News, was for a waitress/receptionist in Truro. When she had phoned for an application form they had asked her to come straight over. Christina had gone straight away, relieved to be out of the house. René and Deborah's relationship seemed to have reached breaking point. They no longer went out to dine together, in fact they hardly spoke and communicated with each other only occasionally through their daughter, with Deborah saying such things as: 'Tell Daddy you'll need some new shoes for school,' or René saying, 'Ask your Mummy if she's put my cheque book away anywhere, will you darling?' Christina thought it was almost like a game they enjoyed playing.

★   ★   ★

When Christina got home from her interview, she found Ginger collapsed on the kitchen floor. He was lying on his side; his legs twitching rhythmically almost as though he was dreaming and his breathing was fast. Although wide open, his eyes were glazed over and as he panted, his tongue made a rapid clicking sound.

'Ginger? What's up, boy?' She stroked his stomach, his flank, and he flinched. He attempted to get up and fell back. His nose felt hot and dry. Then, coming from the corner of his mouth, she noticed a stream of blood. She rushed through to the sitting room where René was sitting.

'What's the matter with Ginger?' she yelled.

'No need to shout,' he replied, not taking his eyes from the newspaper. 'I don't know — you tell me.'

'He's been hurt! What's happened?' Returning to the kitchen, she saw a bubble of foam had gathered around his mouth. Panic-stricken, she rushed to her mother. 'Mum! It's Ginger, there's something dreadfully wrong with him!'

'What did you say?' said Josie, without stopping the machine.

'Mum, please!' she shouted. The machine stopped abruptly. 'What the hell's the matter now?'

'It's Ginger — he's in the kitchen!' and rushing to the foot of the stairs, she called: 'Debbie! Come down, quickly!'

'What's going on for God's sake?' complained her sister, stomping down the stairs in her dressing-gown with her hair wrapped up in a towel.

'Look at him!' Stroking him gently she coaxed, 'Come on boy!' and a flicker of recognition rippled across the dog's body. Then a long slow whine emitted from the back of his throat.

Kneeling down, Josie said: 'It's no use trying to move him. I'll phone for the vet to come out.' Deborah was on her knees too, tears welling from her eyes. The towel had slipped from her head and her wet hair hung down, dripping steadily onto the dog's flank.

'Mummy?' Caitlin's voice sounded sleepy, and her small pale face appeared round the kitchen door.

'It's OK, go back to bed, darling, I'm coming,' said Deborah, and turning back she added. 'Chris, ask René about it. I knew that would happen.'

Christina looked up at her in astonishment. 'You thought what would happen?'

'Oh, nothing, ask him that's all,' replied Deborah. She picked up her wet towel and taking Caitlin's hand, led her towards the stairs. But stopping by the sitting room door, Christina heard the first words she had spoken to her husband in days. 'See, now look what you've done.'

★ ★ ★

It was after midnight. Christina sat on her window-seat looking down at the street below. She held Ginger's collar in her hand and kept turning it over and over on her wrist, twisting it into a bangle and pulling it straight. A courting couple wandered past, their arms entwined, and the girl's stilettoes ringing on the cobbles. The man laughed at some private joke and they hugged each other. A taxi came, its headlights bearing down the street.

But the stragglers became fewer until the street was deserted. Christina hardly moved. A shudder travelled from her head to her knees. She raised the leather collar to her face, caught the musky scent of her dog, and broke down and wept.

The vet had told her there was nothing he

could do; several broken ribs had ruptured his spleen. Within minutes of examining him, the vet had made his decision. Moving him, he had said, would only prolong his agony. So he had put him to sleep there and then on the kitchen floor. Losing the café, and now her beloved dog, was more than she could bear.

9

A few months later

Reports that the Wreckers' Bar was making a name for itself began to spread. In the field of business, René excelled. Posters of the venue were a common sight around the town. With advertisements on Radio Cornwall, and leaflets distributed in the street, people were attracted to the new 'club' on the beach. The new tourist season promised a surge of customers at the Wreckers'. Local youths were quick to realize the attraction of 'club life' too, which offered late nights, and the novelty of cocktails. As its popularity grew, a manager was installed, enabling René to return to London.

Deborah, however, hoped it would give René more time to devote to her. Christina couldn't help feeling uncomfortable with her sister's undisguised pursuit of her husband's wealth. Using René's apparent indiscretions as a lever, and flattered by his attention, however brief, Deborah's lifestyle became ever more glamorous. She began to flash money around, impressing her protégés' parents with talk of long term plans for a new dancing-school premises. René, she assured them, had agreed to fund everything just as soon as they could find the right building and obtain planning permission. At a distance, Christina observed her sister riding around in a glass coach, and wondered how long it would be before it turned back into a pumpkin.

One morning Christina was sitting with Maudie Peacock in John Madison's kitchen.

'You 'eard about your caffy, lately dearie?' Maudie asked, sipping her tea. John sat apart from them, reading, while upstairs the girls' playful antics could be heard thundering through the ceiling. 'Folk's say it's harbourin' all manner of hoodlums!' Pleased with her introduction, Maudie prepared herself to relinquish the next juicy bit of gossip, glancing to her left and right as though to verify she was not being overheard. 'Mind you, it's not decent repeatin' what's goin' on there, so I'm told! And it ain't just inside the Wreckers' or whatever they call it. They've been out on the beach too — young girls and fellas prancin' about wi' nowt on! No shame these days! Don't know what their parents are doing lettin' them out all hours of the night anyway.'

'Maudie!' protested Christina. 'It's not like

you to be all prim and proper! You were in love once, weren't you?' At this, she glanced at John, but he was still reading. Just as well, she thought, as Maudie's comments had brought a blush to her cheeks. Nights on the cliff-top with Peter had sprung into her mind.

'In love?' laughed Maudie, her vast frame wobbling on the wooden chair. 'Them youngsters don't know the meanin' of the word, my flower! It's not love I'm talkin' about, it's all the drinkin' and cavortin' about. It's not right an' I don't mind sayin' so. If Sylvie an' Caitlin grow up to start dressin' an' behavin like some o' those, well!' She wobbled with indignation. Good old-fashioned tradition was Maudie's rudder and main-sail. 'It's not the girls so much anyway,' she continued undaunted. 'It's the fightin' and brawlin' that goes on down there! They've had to bring the police in twice already, so folks say. A lad got his face cut open with a broken bottle only last week. I'm tellin' you,' she put her cup down decisively, 'one o' these days there's gonna be someone murdered down there if I'm not mistaken.'

'Surely you're exaggerating, Maudie!' Christina exclaimed.

'No, I've heard about it too,' said John, putting down his book. 'Drugs and what-have-you. They ought to close it down and that would be an end to it.'

'Well, I hope somethin' gets done about it before our little ones come of age,' muttered Maudie.

'Don't fret yourself. I don't think our girls will be going out on the town at night just yet,' he said, smiling. 'More tea, anyone?'

'No thanks, I'd better be getting back,' replied Christina.

'Yes, I'd better make a move as well. Be a dear an' call the girls down for me, will you, my 'andsome?' asked Maudie. 'We'd best get young Caitlin back home before they think we've kidnapped her!'

★　★　★

One night, Christina and Peter entered the dark interior of the Old Ship Inn. Peter ducked to avoid the heavy wooden beams which sported a range of fishing-nets strung on old rusty nails. Candles flickered from wine bottles caked in volcanic sculptures of melted wax. A band of musicians had struck up a merry folk tune on guitars, banjos and penny whistles. She sat in the corner and soon Peter returned from the bar with their drinks.

'I've been thinking, Chris, I might be leaving here soon.'

She looked up in dismay. 'Why now?'

'My divorce will be through soon. I agreed that the marriage had broken down irretrievably. I didn't contest it; it's far simpler that way and it speeds up the whole procedure. I've got to sell the house and split the proceeds down the middle. All I'm hoping for is regular access to see the boys.' He coughed as though the subject had caught in his throat. 'But Chris, Teagan and Connor won't want me to keep hanging round their place much longer. I've stayed too long already. It's not fair on them.'

'I thought you were going to rent a flat and start your business down here though! You've done a few contracts already — there'll be more. I'll be your plumber's mate if you like, I'm OK with a bit of copper pipe when the mood takes me.' She was trying to raise a smile.

'I'd like to stick around here, but there's more work up country — well, more money anyway. There's plenty of work here, but not many able to pay for it. Paint's flaking off walls, boats left to rot in the harbour, but no money here to help things along. No, I'll find a flat in Devon or Somerset where there's plenty of holiday cottages to work on. I'll start a new life for myself there.'

'But I don't want you to go!' she cried

desperately, realizing how serious he was.

'That's what I was getting round to say, Chris. Will you come with me?'

His face looked so honest and appealing it almost hurt. 'Come with you?' she whispered.

'Why shouldn't you?' he asked. 'You've got nothing left here, you said so yourself. Why not start afresh and leave René to his sleazy wine bar and all the rest?'

'But this is my home!' she protested. 'I've got commitments here, family, friends,' and then she trailed off, thinking hard. What did she have left though? There was no more café; no job. Why *did* she want to stay? Did she really feel her mother needed her? Or her sister? And what about little Caitlin? Then she thought of John — quiet, steadfast, sober John.

She had legally agreed to be Sylvie's guardian if the necessity arose. In spite of her love for Peter, John's need seemed to have some kind of hold over her.

Peter put his bear-like head in his hands. His nails were broken and engrained with dirt; they were a worker's hands. She reached across and tugged gently at one finger.

'Let me help you,' she said. 'Stay a while longer and try?'

'I don't think anyone can help at the moment,' he replied, squeezing her hand before letting it go. 'I need to get myself sorted out. I've wasted too much of my life already.' He gazed at her, and she sensed he was falling away from her as though his bags were already packed.

'Don't go, Peter!' she cried 'You're the only person I really trust! There could be a future here for both of us!' She hadn't meant to mention it yet, but the urgency of the situation loosened her tongue. Since hearing about the Wreckers' Bar running into trouble, the germ of an idea had taken root in her mind. 'I'd love to come with you but I can't,' she said decisively and took a deep breath. 'The thing is, I want to fight to get the café back. I want to raise enough money to be able to buy it back off René. It's already in trouble; I could have guessed it wouldn't work. If there are enough of us, we could get together and raise the money somehow — I know we could!'

He smiled, genuinely amused. 'You and whose army? How are you going to do that? I've just been saying there's no cash about.'

'I know — but there's time yet. There must be something we can do!'

'If you're right and the Wreckers' does turn bottom up — you could try for a business loan. Why not forget the Wreckers' though and find a different premises? You could start up again somewhere new if you want your own café so much? We could do it together.'

'The Sea Café's the only place I want, Peter. I still think of it as my dad's place and I want to save it. Look at what's happening to it now! You know my dad worked so hard trying to keep it going. Anyway, even if I did try for a loan — I've got no security — the bank manager would laugh at me.'

'There are ways and means,' replied Peter, serious at last. 'If you don't want to give up without a fight, you could start looking for people to come in with you to share the costs. What about friends or some of the customers?'

'None of my friends have got any money.'

'OK, don't rub it in!' he chuckled, his old sense of humour returning. 'Drink up, plumber's mate, we both need another drink. I might have to start earning some real money if you're set on this idea. Why don't you just leave René to his own fate? Your sister seems to put up with his seedy life-style all right.'

'She's not quite as tolerant as you'd like to think. She'll keep René dangling for what she can get out of him, money-wise, I'm afraid. But once she's got what she wants, it's likely he'll be out on his heel. I would have argued with her not so long ago — but not now. He deserves everything he gets, that man.' She sighed. 'Poor Debbie, she always had stars in her eyes, even when she was a little girl.'

'So you're getting bitter too, in your old age?' teased Peter. 'I can't say I blame you. Life is hard. I'm finding that out for myself all right.'

'It does make me sound a bit cynical, sorry!' She reached across and kissed him. 'You'll be OK, won't you? I'll still see you, won't I?'

'Just the odd weekend probably. I can't promise I'll be able to come down that often.'

'Then I might catch the train and come to find you,' she replied. Placing her small hand over his, she noticed how small her hand looked, almost like a child's hand.

'You're young yet, Chris. There might be a sailor come along one day who'll take your mind off saving the café and sweep you off your feet. What would you want with a big oaf like me anyway? A second-hand plumber with not a lot goin' for him and a divorce and two kids in tow?'

'Hey! You're not much older than me! You remind me of my dad. He was never quite sure of himself. And my mum didn't help, always putting him down.' She shrugged. 'When I was working in the café in my teens, she'd come in from the Cash 'n' Carry and just keep moaning at him all the time. He never answered her back but he used to catch my eye sometimes and just give me a wink! Poor Dad!'

'Some women! I'll never understand 'em,' chuckled Peter. 'What happened to make him leave in the end?'

'It was the way she shut him out, I suppose. She was working all hours of the day and night. The noise of the sewing-machine drove him mad. She wouldn't eat meals with us; sometimes she hardly spoke to him.' Christina paused. 'Her earnings kept us going, still do. Poor Mum! It was my fault he left home though,' she said.

Peter was incredulous. 'How do you figure that one out?'

'If I hadn't fallen and half crippled myself when I was little, she wouldn't have blamed him and turned against him in the first place.'

'She might have,' he replied seriously. 'You don't know that.'

'I do. Theo said that whatever he did, she'd never forgive him for letting me fall off the harbour wall.'

'But that was what — twenty years ago or more? I wish I'd been there to catch you, Chris,' he whispered, taking hold of her hand.

'So do I,' she said, smiling sadly. 'Don't go, Peter,' she said. 'Stay here with me, please?'

However, in spite of her pleading, two weeks later Peter left St. Ives to start a new contract in Bristol. Christina was devastated. They hardly had time to say goodbye. She saw him off on the platform, but there was an unusual silence between them. Too much had been left unsaid, too much left undone, and now there was no time. He wished her luck and promised to phone and she told him things would work out for him and not to worry. But it had all sounded so hollow. Both of them knew life wouldn't be the same.

At the last minute, his physical departure ripped her raw. 'Ring me when you get there?' she shouted, as the sound of the train approaching threatened to snatch him away. She couldn't bear to think of the days ahead without him. Within minutes she knew his body against hers and the sweet aroma of his breath would be gone. He kissed her passionately, pressing his mouth onto hers and holding her close.

'I'll be back soon, don't fret, my little plumber's mate,' he said. 'Take care of yourself.'

The stinging sensation on her lips was all that remained as she stood alone on the platform watching his train pull away until it was out of sight. As the cold morning ahead wrapped its arms around her, she longed to whistle her dog, or to feel Peter take her hand. Walking back along the platform, she had never felt so lonely in all her life.

10

Caitlin was sitting on the floor watching television in the sitting room. Christina was there with her, reading a book when René, on one of his brief visits from London, sat down and attempted to draw his little daughter into a conversation.

'What would you like for your birthday then, sweetie?' he asked. It was her sixth birthday the following week.

Caitlin shrugged. 'Dunno. My friend Sylvie wants a TV in her bedroom for her birthday so we can watch films, but her dad said she can't have one till she's much older.' She spoke without turning to look at him, keeping her eyes firmly fixed on the screen.

'That's a shame. Is that what you'd like then?' he asked. 'I'll see what I can do, shall I, poppet?' Taking a slurp of Scotch and resting it on the table beside him, he sighed contentedly as though to suggest these things were so easily remedied.

She was wrinkling her nose. 'No Daddy, I don't want that!'

Christina corrected her. 'Say 'no thank you', Caitlin. Don't forget your manners.'

'What would you like then, darling?' He reached forward, patting her affectionately on the top of her head. She tossed her hair indignantly. 'Nothing!'

This time Christina left it to him — Caitlin was his daughter after all — and went back to her book. A few minutes later he accidentally knocked his drink sideways off of the table and for the first time Caitlin looked round at him, saw what he had done and giggled.

René swore under his breath before resuming in a nonchalant tone, 'Your daddy's so clumsy, isn't he!' he chuckled pleasantly, mopping the spill with his handkerchief. While doing this, he looked fascinated by her sudden attention to him. 'You love your clumsy old dad, don't you, Caitlin?' he asked, almost earnestly. He was gazing at her as though seeing her for the first time. 'You're growing into quite a young lady now, aren't you!' he said. Caitlin turned back to the television. 'Let's hope you don't carry too many of your mother's genes, mmm?' he trailed off, mumbling quietly to himself, 'or in ten years from now, some poor chap will end up . . . ' Without finishing his sentence, he rose and went to re-fill his glass. Caitlin had already forgotten him.

'What was that you were going to say, René?' asked Christina but he didn't seem to hear.

Deborah's loyalties had shifted. Christina noticed that her sister's bedding had disappeared from Caitlin's bedroom floor and she was again sleeping in the marital bed. Long after René had left for work, Deborah would stay in the bedroom pampering herself with the expensive toiletries he had bought her.

Making her appearance soon after ten o'clock in the morning, she made no attempt to hide the fact that she shared his bed. 'Oh I wish he wouldn't toss and turn so, he keeps snorting like a horse on a bed of straw! I don't know how I manage to get any sleep at all!' she complained. 'Men! They all rummage around like animals in their sleep, as you'll discover one of these days perhaps.' She was looking at Christina curiously. 'So your Peter's up and gone then? Why don't you go into the town tonight and let your hair down a bit?'

'I'm not in the mood OK? Anyway, he's not gone for good — he's working that's all. He'll be back before long.'

'Oh honestly! I don't see why you encourage him; he's not even divorced yet!'

'How do you know so much all of a sudden? Come off it, Debbie! He's Teagan's brother and she's been my friend for years.

He's not just anyone I've picked up off the street.'

'Well I don't like him — he's so . . . ugh! So physical! What about John Madison? He seems much more your sort.'

'John's a good friend but — Peter! He's so genuine and honest and caring. We seem to balance each other.'

'Oh!' cried Deborah impatiently, 'like me and René you mean? We balance each other all right!'

Christina regarded her sister for a moment, seeing the sadness behind her artificial façade. Her hair had lost its natural colour under the onslaught of bleach and dyes. The character in her eyes was hidden behind purple eye-shadow and thick mascara. Of course she wouldn't be able to understand. Hadn't she been treated like a commodity all her life? Hadn't she been picked up and put down again like a performing doll? She was a clock-work toy, wound up and set to dance on the stage: Dance! Sing! Look pretty! Glamour and glitz would always mask her true feelings, and wash off like make-up after the show. No wonder she never seemed to be able to demonstrate any real affection for Caitlin. When had any love been shown to her? Life must be like some sort of stage to her, where the bright lights are switched on and then, without warning, switched off again. Suddenly Christina could see how hard her sister's life was — just trying to keep up the glamour-puss image that her husband desired. Poor Debbie!

'A man should love you for yourself,' said Christina matter-of-factly. 'You shouldn't have to bow down to him all the time.'

'I don't! René won't get the better of me, don't worry! I won't let him,' said Deborah, pouting. 'I've worked too hard getting this dancing-school organized, I won't give up now. Whatever he wants me to do, or be, or look like, I don't care so long as he buys me my own dancing-school.'

'Do you need René to do that? Couldn't you get a business loan yourself? It's a feasible option surely?' Just for a moment Christina recalled that awful night, trying to reason with her when René first proposed to her — how their father had objected and it had caused such a rift in the family. As of that day, Deborah's future had been placed firmly at René's feet; she had agreed to marry him, run away with him and in doing so had virtually laid down her life for him. All her dreams and ambitions had been her dowry, handed over to him, and sadly, rendered worthless.

'Come off it, Chris! I couldn't raise that

sort of money. It'll take thousands to get it off the ground.'

'You could try, Debs! Why don't you work out just how much you would need and go to the bank? I'll help you if you like.'

'The income from my classes wouldn't even cover my pupils' tap shoes! I'm not stupid! Half of them can't afford to buy the right shoes because their parents are out of work. This is Cornwall remember!'

'Does René realize the financial risk he's taking then?'

'He likes making me happy,' she replied with a satisfied self-assurance. 'Anyway, once I've got my own premises it will be different. I won't have to rent village halls and those stupid scout huts anymore. Renting premises is a waste of money. No, I can put up my fees and make it more up-market — attract the rich kids in Truro who go to private schools. Some of their parents are loaded!'

Christina was tiring of this conversation. She could still visualize her sister years ago, spellbound by René's glamorous world, marching down the stairs carrying her pink suitcase and leaving a trail of sequins, taffeta and glitter behind her. She remembered seeing her climb into René's car and take off that day, a vulnerable petite girl of nineteen huddled beside a rather large toad.

* * *

One evening after dinner, as Christina sat alone in the sitting room mending a tear in her jeans, she noticed the unusual sight of René moving around outside in the backyard. Menial outdoor tasks, such as putting out the dustbin, sweeping the yard, and cleaning the windows, were as remote to René as any other chores indoors. It apparently never occurred to him who maintained the house. It was already dark so seeing him out there intrigued Christina. Knowing Josie was back at her machine and Deborah was upstairs bathing Caitlin, she went to the kitchen and picked up the bin, intending to empty it outside as an excuse.

'Burning the evidence, René?' she said. He was no more than a few feet from her.

Her attempt at a joke failed. He turned around looking startled. 'As a matter of fact, yes,' he said, throwing a crumpled ball of paper into the oil-drum which had stood in the yard for years. 'What the eyes don't see, the heart can't grieve over, isn't that right?' Taking another wad of papers drawn from a briefcase on the ground, he peered at them short-sightedly. The light from the bonfire revealed the sweat on his forehead. He took a sheet, screwed it up and cast it into the fire.

'That depends,' she replied guardedly, watching the flames lick around the pages. They looked to her like sheets of accounts. 'When some things are concealed and you don't know what's going to happen, you tend to fear the worst. It helps to face the facts sometimes,' she replied, 'have it out in the open and see things in black and white, however bad they are.'

'Not in this case,' he said. 'Fire is a wonderful thing.' He held a sheaf of paper in both hands and tore it in half before sending the pieces tumbling into the flames. 'Yes, fire is a wonderful tool,' he added with satisfaction. Turning to her, he continued: 'Not going to tell me to stop then? Where's this self-righteous, dignified, law-abiding sister-in-law of mine got to, mmm?' he asked, tipping the whole briefcase upside down now and letting the remaining scraps and receipts fall into the inferno which rose crackling into the night sky.

'You really think I'm that interested in your wheeling and dealing, René? How you manage your affairs is up to you. If you choose to go about things in an underhand way, do you think it surprises me? No, it doesn't.'

'Thank you. I always knew I could rely on your vote of confidence. Close the door when you go back in, will you?' he said, dismissing her. 'We don't want certain people complaining about the smoke blowing into the house now, do we?' He gave her a sly look.

'I hate your world, René,' she said.

'My world? What is my world, mmm?' He poked at the fire with a stick thoughtfully.

'A world all based around money, business and contacts. It's all so under hand, so seedy, so — '

'So corrupt and materialistic, you mean? Yes, I hate it too. I loathe it, as a matter of fact. But I'm only a puppet. *My world* as you call it has got no real power or wealth outside its own ugly game. What my business amounts to is nothing short of blackmail at the end of the day.'

'Is that what holds you to it, makes you stay a part of it all? Are you afraid to break away? You could take Debbie and Caitlin away from all this, cut off your contacts with London and all that dodgy stuff — start again somewhere else.'

'Start again? And what would my dear wife say to that I wonder, mmm? Oh, sorry! No dancing-school, dear! No more new clothes; no meals in expensive restaurants!' He reeled these things off bitterly. 'Don't make me laugh! I'm up to my neck in it all, and she doesn't give a shit!'

He gave another savage stab at the flames. 'Take away *my world*, as you call it, and what are you left with, mmm? A bundle of rather large-sized clothes and an empty man, a poor man actually — a rather pathetic puppet.' He turned and smiled at her; for once in her life she saw the real face of René; a tragic, frightened, lonely face. 'Be a good girl and don't mention this conversation to your dear sister, will you? She might just choke herself to death laughing at me.'

Christina was shocked by his sudden humility. It was all so surreal, and yet she found herself understanding him. 'Do you love Debbie, René?' she asked.

'I can't afford to have feelings,' he replied, off-handedly. 'Love her? Of course I don't love her! I wouldn't be so stupid. Let her under my skin? No dear, too dangerous.' He smiled again. 'Much safer to play the part, then at least when I'm not on duty, I've still got a bit of myself left intact.'

'On duty?' she queried, scrutinising him now in the half-light. 'Is that how you see it?' Strange, she thought, how the flames lit up the contours of his face, making him look haggard, like an old man. 'Is that really how you view your married life?'

'Yes,' he replied abruptly. 'It's easier that way. She knows no different — and if she did she wouldn't care anyway.' He snorted, clearing catarrh from the back of his throat.

'You make my sister sound so hard! So insensitive!' she protested.

'She's not hard, she's just shallow. She can't help it. Pretty, ambitious, and shallow. So!' He turned to her, 'What's the verdict, Sister-in-law, guilty as charged, mmm?'

Christina turned away, immediately feeling the coldness of the night air as she stepped away from the fire. 'I wouldn't like to say, René. It all seems a bit sad to me, that's all. I'll see you later,' she added, stepping towards the back-door.

'Sad? Oh, it's sad all right, bloody sad.'

She stopped. 'I could almost feel sorry for you, if I didn't know you better.' A vision of her dog's body twitching on the kitchen floor sprang before her eyes. 'If I didn't know what you're capable of, I mean. Look at my poor Ginger and what you did to him.'

'Oh, that!'

'Was it to get back at me?'

'Nothing so dramatic I'm afraid. I was pissed that's all; the bloody dog got in my way.'

Something inside her welled up. The pain of a scream clambered in her throat.

'I didn't intend to kick him quite so hard actually, but the bugger went for me. I'd apologize but . . . '

'But what René?' she managed to say.

'It was an accident — shit happens, you know. It was no one's fault.'

'How can you just excuse yourself like that? You were blind drunk and my poor Ginger had to suffer for it. How can you be so cruel? Don't you care about anything or anyone? You could at least try saying sorry.'

'What for? To be polite?' He paused. 'Oh, yes, sorry. I forgot, one has to apologize, be civil — try and make amends. Yes, well, what do you say to me buying you a new dog? I've heard Rhodesian Ridgebacks make good companions; ever thought of getting one of those? I'll buy you a nice one if you like, a pedigree. I know a chap who breeds them. They look the part, big, muscular dogs — good guard dogs.'

'No thanks.' Unable to bear any more, she turned again to go indoors.

'Why am I so damned obnoxious, you might ask?' he said suddenly.

'You said it, René. I didn't.'

'Come back here a moment. I suppose you expect me to make excuses, tell you I had a bastard childhood, beaten up by my father, locked in a dark cellar, starved, that sort of thing? That would make you happy would it? Make it all add up nicely.' He stopped, perhaps waiting for a response. 'Well, it wasn't like that at all. I was the only son of a middle-class couple. My father was a lawyer, my mother a respectable business woman in property. As a boy I wanted for nothing, except to get away from them both as fast as I could. Does that make any sense?' He challenged her to answer. 'Well, does it?'

'No. And why are you telling me all this?'

He resumed poking the burnt paper, prodding the flames into life. 'Actually, Sister-in-law, I'm fonder of you than I care to admit to myself. It's laughable. You're much more like me, you see.'

She could hardly believe her ears. 'How can I possibly be like you, René?' she asked.

'Well, look at Debbie, she's so superficial — so much tinsel and tripe, all legs and bottom.'

'How can you say that about your own wife!' she protested. 'How dare you say that about my sister? You whisked her off and married her before she was barely old enough. I think you underestimate her. She's a brilliant dancer and all the children love her. You never give her a chance, you never listen to her!'

'Listen to her? Good God girl, most of the time I hear nothing else!' He sighed, and taking a deep breath put his stick aside and faced her. 'I've got a kind of disability too, you see.

224

I've got a limp, like you, but it's in here.' He thumped his chest dramatically. 'No-one can see it — but I feel it, deep in here.' He swallowed hard, 'And it's killing me.'

'René, you must be ill or something; you ought to see a doctor.'

'No dear; it's not an illness, not even demons, nothing so logical. It's just me. It's a pain of the spirit. I've always had it, born with it probably — not the result of an accident, like yours.'

'Have you told Debbie about this feeling you have?'

He gave a sudden raw laugh. 'You really think for one minute she would understand? Do me a favour!'

'I'm going back indoors.'

'Yes, back to civilization, whatever that is! If life wasn't so bloody complicated, we could have been friends, you and I, lovers even.'

She stared at him. She couldn't speak. He was looking at her so honestly, so open and vulnerable she could simply find no response. Turning away, she left him and went inside, numb with shock.

★　★　★

Back in her bedroom, Christina lay on her bed staring at the ceiling. All that had passed between herself and René was like a dream. Going to her windowseat, she looked down at the street below, trying to capture a sense of reality. What had René meant about his feelings for her? Was he going mad? She began to wonder what the papers were that he had been destroying. How had Debbie convinced herself that her husband was rich and powerful yet failed to notice the artificial glint of those riches, the hollowness of his promises? What could save her from a man so blatantly false he was even prepared to admit it and still keep up the pretence? Why had he told her all this? It frightened her and yet somehow she couldn't help feeling sorry for him, the stupid propped-up lump that he was. Something in those few honest words he had spoken had got under her skin.

11

Christina enjoyed sharing the task of collecting Caitlin from school with Maudie and taking her to play up at John's cottage. Sylvie was a bossy girl for a child of seven, even scolding her father sometimes for being untidy. Once they found her standing on a chair at the kitchen sink, washing up. A year older and twice as confident as Caitlin, Sylvie led the way in what games they would play and what programmes they watched on television. Caitlin accepted her friend's superior role without question, unspoken admiration and acceptance of her authority written all over her little face. But then one day the two girls fell out.

When Christina knocked on the back door with Caitlin at her side, John told them Sylvie wouldn't be playing. Caitlin looked up expectantly.

'Is she sick?' she asked. 'We had chocolate cake at school today, for Miss Riley's birthday, and Robert was sick.'

John looked awkward. 'No, she's not ill.' He came out and closing the door behind him, suggested Caitlin ran to play in the

227

garden. They watched her skip down the path chasing a butterfly and when she was out of earshot, John explained, 'She says Caitlin's been telling lies and she's not her friend any more. I don't know what's brought that on.'

'Telling lies? I've never known her to tell a lie! She's so innocent. She wouldn't know how to, poor thing! She worships your Sylvie, you know!' They watched Caitlin practising her ballet steps down the end of the garden as though she was in a world of her own.

'Don't worry, it'll blow over I expect,' said John. 'I don't know what's got into Sylvie's head, too much imagination that's her trouble.' He gave Christina a wistful smile. 'I'll make you a coffee, shall I? Caitlin?' he shouted, 'Would you like some lemonade?' She stopped dancing and nodded energetically before seeing a butterfly and trying to catch it in her cupped hands. John went inside leaving the door ajar and Christina followed him.

'Where's Sylvie now?' she asked.

'Upstairs in her room, sulking probably.'

'What was Caitlin supposed to have said?'

John chuckled. 'She told her that her daddy was going to buy her a real pony,' he said, glancing at Christina with playful blue eyes. 'A pure white one apparently, with a flowing mane and a long silver tail.'

'Oh no!' exclaimed Christina.

He raised his eyebrows questioningly, 'So it's true?' he whispered. 'Lucky little princess!'

'No it's not true! Of course it's not! René must be putting ideas into her head. Oh, that man!' she sighed impatiently. 'Of course she can't have a pony! We've got no means of looking after one for a start,' she added, peering through the half-closed door to make sure Caitlin was still outside.

'He might mean it. I gather he's very wealthy.'

'I expect he's trying to impress her, that's all, win her over to his side. He's promised to buy Debbie a dancing-school premises as well. I'm sure he can't really afford it.'

'He must have some money! It can't be that bad if he's offering to be so generous.'

Christina looked at him. Too many times she had seen John worrying about his finances as one disappointing fishing trip after another threatened to destroy his livelihood. Rising fuel costs and more and more regulations pouring out of Europe were making his life increasingly difficult. Money! She thought to herself. Why did everything have to revolve around money all the time?

'Let's sit outside, shall we?' she suggested and taking their drinks, they went to sit in the sun.

Later, walking home holding Caitlin's hand, Christina wished she had Peter to talk to. His common sense so often put her mind at rest. She resolved to phone him once the house was quiet and she could get some privacy. How she longed to have him back, have his reassurance and strength; how she missed his sense of fun and the way he teased her! But Caitlin's voice piped up, interrupting her thoughts.

'I won't have to walk all this way when I've got my pony, will I! Will you lead him for me?'

Christina hesitated. Perhaps she had better go along with it for now, until she could speak to René. 'You will have to learn how to ride before you can think about getting a pony,' she said. 'Perhaps your mummy will take you for riding-lessons if you ask her nicely?'

She shook her head. 'No! Daddy said I can learn on my *own* pony. He said all little girls can ride — it's just like riding a bicycle, that's what Daddy said.'

'Sylvie doesn't go riding though,' reasoned Christina.

'When I've got my pony, I said she can have a go everyday if she wants to, and she said . . . ' Caitlin's face fell. She pouted her lips and put her hands on her hips in a gesture Christina recognized as Sylvie's own. 'She said I was telling fibs, and I'm not going to have one *really*. But I am, aren't I!'

'We'll talk about it with your daddy later, shall we?' she suggested gently. In fact she had every intention of asking René as soon as Caitlin was safely tucked up in bed.

★ ★ ★

As it turned out, the discussion about the pony, and her phone call to Peter, had to be postponed. When they got home there was a full-scale row going on. Josie was shouting from the top of the stairs with a dry cracked voice.

'No-one takes any notice of me; I might as well be invisible! Who pays for the electric and gas? I do! Who stays up half the night working while you're zonked out in a drunken stupor? How many bills are there with your name on, René?' She was waving a bundle of letters as she came down the stairs. 'When are you going to pay them? That's what I want to know!'

'What's going on?' Christina called, helping Caitlin with her coat. 'Go on upstairs, love, and I'll bring you up some supper.'

Josie stormed past her, saying through gritted teeth: 'If I don't get out of this house

231

soon, Chris, I shall go stark raving mad!'

'What's happened, Mum?' Christina asked, following her into the sitting room. Deborah was sitting on the sofa, legs crossed, flicking through a fashion magazine irritably. Beside her, staring out of the window stood René holding a glass of Scotch.

'Perhaps you ought to explain to your mother, Debs, there's been a bit of a hiccup in the City. I've got to leave for London first thing in the morning.'

Josie looked shocked. 'Are you telling me you're going away again when all these bills need sorting? Our suppliers have put in a final demand and the re-fitters haven't been paid yet! Write me some cheques before you go, René, I can't stall them any longer. We'll have the electric cut off at this rate.'

'Yes, yes, yes,' muttered René, in a pacifying sing-song voice. 'Yes, dearest Mother-in-law, I shall write you some nice little cheques right now! Debbie, fetch my cheque book,' he commanded.

'Fetch it yourself,' she hissed, flinging the magazine across the sofa.

Christina had intended to make Caitlin's supper. It was only toast and hot milk and it wouldn't take long, but she felt rooted to the spot.

'Mother-in law? Perhaps you wouldn't

mind getting it? It's on the bedside table.' He sat down waiting to be obeyed like a king with his arms folded across his belly.

Surprisingly, Josie left the room without a word and she could be heard mounting the stairs. No-one spoke while she was gone. Several minutes later she returned, carrying the business cheque book, her face strained with anxiety.

'Thank you kindly!' said René, with a smile, reaching out his hand to receive it. A number of bills were spread out before him. With his pen poised, he began writing — signing cheque after cheque with a flourish and ripping them out of the cheque book systematically. Finally, he handed the bunch of bills and cheques back to Josie. 'There you are, sorted! Happy now, mmm?' This settled, he stood up, stuffed the cheque book into his back pocket and lumbered out of the room.

★   ★   ★

Christina usually avoided going near the Wreckers' Bar. The gaudy sign outside was enough to turn her stomach. Maudie's gossip about the place had proved to be true. It had become a meeting-place for the rougher elements of today's youth. Drunken loud-mouthed yobs hung around outside drinking and leering at passers-by. Excitable girls with short skirts and purple hair stayed flirting late into the night. It affected the whole stretch of the beach; litter and broken glass began to accumulate along the top straight of the cove where the tide didn't reach. For Christina, the Wreckers' reputation had become an embarrassment.

'It can't be the kind of establishment René intended to run!' Christina told her mother one day while they were washing up. 'Have you seen it lately? It's getting so rough down there — all you hear about are fights and stories about drug trafficking and goodness knows what. I thought he was supposed to be creating a sophisticated wine bar, not some awful — '

'It'll take time,' interrupted Josie, somewhat guardedly Christina thought.

'Poor Dad, he wouldn't recognize the place now!' Christina let the words slip without thinking.

Josie stopped what she was doing and held a soapy plate in mid-air. 'He'll find out soon enough,' she said. 'Since you've mentioned him I might as well tell you. I was going to tell you this sometime anyway.'

'Tell me what?'

'I've heard from him again — another of his rambling letters. Seems he's got to hear about the Wreckers', it's in the papers up in

Plymouth. Don't know why that man can't just say a few words and has to write a flipping autobiography every time.'

'What did he say?' asked Christina impatiently.

'Oh, that he's surprised, or shocked I suppose, to hear about the café falling into the wrong hands. He asked if we were all right and had we had any trouble. And then the other — the usual stuff . . . '

'What other stuff?'

'Well!' She emptied the bowl, upturned it and dried her hands. 'He's always going on about what a flipping failure he's been and how he should've done this or he should have done that. I've heard it so many times I get fed up with hearing it.'

'Did he say anything else?' replied Christina. She was eager to hear more and couldn't believe she was actually talking about hearing from her father at last.

'No, but surprise, surprise, he's sent some money for you and your sister. He said he's making a bit of money now in the bakery. He's had promotion or something.' She clicked her tongue, as though it was worthless. Nothing he could do, it seemed, would ever impress her.

'Money? But I don't want his money, Mum! I'd rather see him, and talk to him!'

Josie was unmoved. 'You might be interested when you hear how much it is. He's sent each of you two thousand pounds. It's more than he's ever given me.' She folded her arms and faced her daughter. 'Christina, if I was you I'd take the money and say thank you very kindly — it's the first good thing he's ever done for you that I can see. I bet Debbie accepts it. She knows a good thing when she sees it.'

Christina replied, more earnestly than before: 'But that's incredible! I ought to thank him, Mum. Can I go and see him?'

'What for? It's all right for him, up there in Plymouth, blowing his trumpet about earning a lot of money. I'm the one who was left to raise you girls, working my fingers to the bone to bring you up. What good has he ever been? When he had the café he was next to useless. It didn't make a profit and he couldn't bring himself to admit it. Then he goes and blames me for neglecting the place when I was run off my feet doing the out-work to pay the rotten bills. It's a bit late now isn't it, sending me long sloppy letters saying how sorry he is.' Josie turned her back and Christina didn't need to ask, she knew by her voice that her mother was crying.

'Would it help to see him and tell him how

you feel?' she asked gently.

She didn't reply and putting a hand on her shoulder, Christina prompted: 'Mum? It might help.'

Josie had never been a physical person; a hug was out of the question. But suddenly she turned round and said, 'Chris, love, it was years ago he upped and left us. We've managed together without him all this time, haven't we?'

'I want to see him again, Mum. Theo was telling me he'd met him in Plymouth only a short while ago. I couldn't believe it! You never talked about him; it was like he didn't exist anymore, almost like he was dead.'

'I know I shouldn't say it, but I wish he was dead,' Josie replied, regaining her self-control and straightening her back. 'Life would be a lot simpler. I should have divorced him then; I've just let it drift. He'd never get round to anything like that.'

Christina felt a chill. 'Do you want a divorce then, Mum?' she asked.

'There doesn't seem much point. It's not as if I want to marry again.' Surprisingly, a new thought seemed to occur to her and her hard face crumpled into a smile. 'Poor old Charlie! I am a bit hard on him I suppose. Still, it's too late now. Come on, girl: let's get these dishes put away.'

12

A few days later, Josie was again fretting over some papers spread out on the kitchen table.

'Goodness knows what Debbie's going to say about this lot,' she said as Christina came into the room.

'Trouble?' asked Christina, pouring herself some coffee and pushing a slice of bread into the toaster. It was unusual, she thought, that her mother wasn't at her sewing machine.

'Remember those cheques René wrote to pay all those bills? A letter's come from the bank this morning. Most of them have bounced and been returned unpaid — there's a charge of forty pounds on each one! What's he playing at, Chris?'

'You mean he hasn't got the money to cover them? You're kidding?'

Josie looked up, her face revealing that she was far from joking. 'Remember how he just reeled them off? He must have known there was no money in the bank to pay them. He was just bluffing! How could I have been so stupid not to see through it?'

'Let's go down to the Wreckers' and see

what his manager says,' suggested Christina. 'He must know how the business is doing.'

Josie shook her head. 'I've just done that — and he said René does the books and banks all the takings himself so he couldn't help us. It's worse though — none of the staff have been paid for two months.'

'Oh my goodness!' she exclaimed, realizing the seriousness of the situation. 'Have you tried phoning René?'

'Yes, several times. His phone's switched off and there's no answer-phone on.'

Christina was leaning against the sink watching the toaster, but when the toast sprang up she ignored it.

'Oh, Chris!' exclaimed Josie putting her head in her hands. 'The day I signed the café over to René, that was a bad move! This is all my fault! I wish I'd helped you with the Sea Café; we might have saved it between us. I've let you down, haven't I,' she admitted. 'We've both let you down, your father and I. We never meant you to struggle like this! Right from when you were little — it was our carelessness that caused you to run off and fall over the harbour wall. If it wasn't for that — and your leg — you might have found yourself a nice young man by now and be happily married.'

'Mum!' she protested. 'Why would I want a

man who only married me for my legs? I'm all right as I am, honestly! You can't blame yourself for everything that happens in life! Or Dad, I don't blame either of you anyway.' She relaxed as her mother's anxious face surrendered a smile. 'Now, come on, let's see if we can sort out this bank before any more cheques bounce. Make an appointment with the bank manager and we'll go together. Meanwhile, we'll ask Debbie to get hold of René for us.'

Contacting René was proving impossible, even for Deborah. By the evening, she had still been unable to speak to him, but her excuses began to irritate them. While she sat on the sofa apparently oblivious of their crisis, and dismissing their questions, she kept flicking through the pages of an estate agent's portfolio.

'So you say he's still at a meeting?' Christina challenged her. 'He can't be after all this time.'

'That's what his secretary told me,' replied Deborah dismissively, turning another page. 'Ooh, I like the sound of this one. Listen to this: 'Situated in a quiet part of the City of Truro, this former art gallery offers spacious premises comprising main hall with annexe, inner lobby, and kitchen.' That sounds ideal.'

'What's happening exactly about this new

dancing-school then, Debbie?' asked Christina, unable to hide her impatience.

Deborah sighed dreamily. 'When René gets back from London, he said it's the first thing he'll do. That's why I've got lots of property details!' She waved the wad of papers with shining eyes. 'I'm going to look at this one tomorrow actually!'

'But Debs!' Christina exclaimed in exasperation. 'How can you be so relaxed about it? There are so many bills to settle here. We can't stall the bank manager much longer!'

'I know! Do you think I'm stupid or something? He'll see to them when he gets back. He's a busy man, I keep telling you!'

Christina sighed, trying to remain calm. 'So when is he coming back then?'

'Soon, he promised me,' she replied. A trace of doubt flickered on her soft cheek and she bit her lip. 'He'd better not let me down. I've told all the parents my school will be up and running by this time next year.'

'Up and running? Debs! You haven't even found any premises yet!'

Her sister's enthusiasm faded visibly and her shoulders slumped. 'It won't take long to convert it,' she added miserably, 'once we've found the right place. René said so.' Her voice rang hollow and she glanced up at her sister nervously.

'Just try and be realistic, Debs. He might want to — but he might not have the financial means to buy you a place.' She tried to be gentle. 'Consider an alternative, just in case, eh?' she whispered, stepping forward to give her a hug.

But Deborah pushed her off. 'Why should I?' she retaliated. 'It's all I've ever wanted. He knows that!'

Christina couldn't reason with her anymore. All too soon, she feared, her sister's dreams would all come to nothing. That pink glittery world she inhabited was as much a reality to her as stage lighting, make-up and music. She wondered how Deborah would cope when the whole thing came tumbling down.

★ ★ ★

The next morning, returning from the café and throwing a bunch of keys down on the kitchen table, Josie announced: 'Well, that's it. The manager's shut up shop and gone.'

Christina was eating her breakfast. 'What do you mean, 'Gone'?'

'He's closed it and put a notice on the door. I just caught him leaving. He handed me the keys and said 'That's it! I'm finished.' He hasn't been paid and he said he's not

242

working for nothing anymore. The electric's been disconnected and all the food in the freezer's ruined. I can't say I blame the chap, it's not his fault.'

Christina couldn't believe it. 'But what about the rest of the staff?'

'They've been gone a day or two already apparently,' Josie replied. 'I don't know what game René thinks he's playing at, I'm sure. I'm going to go straight back now, to see what it's like in there and what's there we can salvage — do you want to come?'

'Yes, but Mum, I never thought it would come to this. So much for René bragging about how good he is at running a business!' In spite of the crisis, a thrill was quietly working its way up in her mind. Like a rising tide, her care and responsibility for the place was flooding back to her. Her love for the old building instantly re-kindled. If René had messed up and the business was in deep trouble, she was going to claim it back. The Sea Café needed her.

★   ★   ★

It was the middle of the night when something woke Christina. She had no idea of the time when she heard what turned out to be a loud hammering on the front-door.

243

Caitlin began shrieking, 'Mummy! Mummy!'

Leaping out of bed, she stumbled to the window to look out. There were some men below and a car parked with its head-lights full on. Was it the police? Was there terrible news about René? She peered at her watch. It was 3.25 a.m. — perhaps he had been in car accident or been arrested for drink-driving or something. Peering out, she listened intently.

Someone must have opened the front door because she heard a man's voice: 'Mr St. James, please. We need to speak to him as a matter of urgency.' Christina left the window and putting on her dressing-gown, opened her bedroom door a crack.

'He's not here!' she heard her mother say. The first man must have pushed his way in because the voices became clearer. 'Who are you?' came her mother's voice again. 'Are you the police? Show me some identification please.'

Without hesitating, Christina pulled on her boots and began to descend the stairs. She saw, at the open door, a man in silhouette standing against the dazzling headlights. The car was revving-up outside.

'What's going on, Mum?' she shouted.

Eyeing her furtively, the man took a card out of his pocket. 'Bryan Griffin,' he said. 'I'm a debt collector by trade, ma'am. Where

244

is René St. James, may I ask?' Another man, so tall he stooped awkwardly, was leaning against the door-frame. He had black hair and a pin-striped suit. He looked up at Christina and scowled.

'He's in London; he has business there,' said Josie, with a quiver in her voice. 'What do you want with him?'

'It's confidential, ma'am. We're acting on behalf of our client. Do you have his London address to hand?'

'Yes, probably,' she replied. 'I'll look upstairs.' She withdrew, leaving Christina to face the men alone.

'Was your business so urgent you had to wake everyone up at this unearthly hour?' asked Christina.

'That's confidential too I'm afraid, Miss. He's in trouble with the law, that's all I can tell you. Friend of yours, is he?'

'Not exactly,' she replied.

'He's got business premises in these parts I believe,' he continued, 'name of The Wreckers'. Is that right? Where is it exactly, this Wreckers' Bar?'

Christina looked away, imagining them putting a boot through the patio doors. She could visualize the glasses and bottles flying, the mirrors behind the bar shattering, as surely as if it was happening before her eyes.

She didn't reply. Within seconds, Josie reappeared.

'Do you normally call on people in the middle of the night?' she asked as she descended the stairs again clutching a piece of paper. 'There's no excuse for such aggressive behaviour you know. I could report you to the police for this intrusion.'

'Report away, ma'am!' replied the man. 'I'm only doing my job. If folks paid their bills I could quite comfortably stay in bed of a morning instead of driving around the country half the night.' Jerking his head to his colleague, he turned to go. 'If we don't find him, ma'am,' he said, waving the scrap of paper carelessly, 'we'll be back here with a search warrant. Nothing personal like.'

'You won't be so lucky next time,' shouted Josie. 'I'll know not to open the door.'

The man paused and stared at her. 'If we have to get in, ma'am, we'll get in,' he said. 'Day or night, makes no difference to us. Don't wait up.' And they were gone. Closing the front door, they heard the car rev up loudly and take off at speed.

'Who was that?' Deborah's sleepy voice came from the top of the stairs.

'Friends of your husband's,' shouted Josie. 'Didn't you recognize the tone?'

13

The months passed. Vacant now, the Wreckers' Bar lay shut-up and abandoned. Christina often walked past, looking sadly at its ancient granite walls, and the peeling paint on its wooden veranda. The windows were boarded up and were starting to accumulate graffiti. She didn't think of it as the Wreckers' anymore. She thought of it as her Sea Café again and the face it bore now was just an ugly mask.

The news that Teagan's baby was born safe and well took Christina down to the beach one day in a light-hearted mood. A turquoise light washed over the old harbour in St. Ives, driving away the mist and picking out the diamond sparkles in the granite. Seagulls left off their whining sadness and began their raucous calling urgently in their search for food to feed their young. She thought to herself: the two thousand pounds that her father had sent her, with what she had managed to save herself, could go a small way towards buying the café back. What if others could help too? She thought this new idea over with a kind of curious excitement. It might be a hopeless idea, but then again, there might be a chance. If she could accumulate enough people prepared to invest, they could buy out René's share and save the Sea Café from falling into ruins. Wandering along the water's edge she began to dream.

The soft sea breeze played around the open doors, her pots of scarlet geraniums danced in the sunshine, and her dear dog Ginger lay stretched out contentedly in the hot sun. She could imagine her old customers sitting at the tables and she almost caught sight of her father wiping down the tables, taking a few minutes away from the hot kitchen to breathe in the cool Atlantic air. With flushed cheeks and shirt sleeves rolled up, he was waiting for her with a tea-towel tied around his waist and a mug of coffee cupped in his hands. His tired eyes scanned the horizon looking for her. She walked towards him, limping along the beach. He waved to her, beckoning her to hurry up, welcoming her with a broad grin.

'Come on, my girl!' he shouted as soon as she was within earshot. 'Don't hurry yerself on my account, will yer!' he laughed, greeting her with a big bony hug. 'How was school today, Chrissy?'

'Boring!'

'Boring? Of course it's boring! Wouldn't be

school if it weren't boring, would it?'

A seagull swooped down, skimming the surface of the sea with pink eyes, its powerful wings beating the air. Somewhere in the distance, the plaintive sound of an ice-cream van chimed and turning, Christina was suddenly plunged back into reality as she saw the pitiful sight that had once been her beloved café.

The fact that René had managed to escape bankruptcy had astounded not only Christina, but everyone. He boasted of 'pulling strings' and having 'influential connections', and managed to pass off the humiliation of the Wreckers' skimming close to bankruptcy with his usual bravado. His career in London, as far as he was concerned, was apparently back on track. By whatever means that had become available to him, resources beyond the knowledge of his wife and family it seemed, René had apparently settled his affairs and was financially buoyant once more. However, the Wreckers' Bar no longer amused him and he made no secret of the fact. One night, Christina raised the subject with Josie.

'Do you think René would consider selling his share of the Wreckers', Mum?' she asked.

'He's already suggested it to me, Chris. I wish I could afford to buy it back, but the truth is, and I'm ashamed to admit it, a lot of the money he paid me has gone. It's kept us going at least. Maintaining this house and keeping us fed and clothed isn't easy without a regular wage coming in.'

'But if we all got together and somehow raised the money, then he would sell?'

'If he could get his greedy hands on any more money he'd snatch it back just like that, I'm sure. He's considering putting it on the market anyway but he still needs my co-operation for that.'

Christina was thoughtful. A lot depended on her wording the next question carefully.

'What about,' she began, 'if I could get a group of our friends together, and we all put in a fair share, you think René would agree on a reasonable price?'

Josie looked at her over the top of her reading glasses. 'Have you ever known René to be reasonable? What's going on in that little head of yours, Chris? To raise enough to pay him back wouldn't be easy to say the least. I could make up some of it, but I haven't got enough to pay it all. I can't see the bank manager being over-enthusiastic either, with the poor history the place has got and the state it's in now.'

Christina's face brightened. 'But you could afford some of it, Mum?'

'I could put a little towards it, yes.' Josie continued to look at her daughter and then shook her head with a sad smile. 'You are your father's daughter, aren't you!' she said. 'Head full of dreams!'

★   ★   ★

When Deborah found what she considered to be the perfect premises for her dancing-school, René amazed them by immediately making an offer and having it accepted. From there, things started happening. However, finalizing the deal was another matter. The solicitor needed questions answering. Deborah was under pressure from the vendors to come up with the deposit, but René was back in London, and true to character, unobtainable.

'It's all right for him!' she complained. 'He's not down here having to stall people all the time!' Deborah was sitting on the sofa with an array of papers in front of her.

'Why don't you try ringing him again?' ventured Christina.

'You think I haven't tried! I'm sick of calling him. All I seem to get is some stupid girl saying, 'Mr St. James is out of the office right now, please leave a message after the tone'.' She sang this response in a mocking

American accent as Christina retreated upstairs before her sister's frustrations built up any further.

Josie's sewing machine was trundling away as Christina passed by. The harsh spotlight fixed to the machine seemed to accentuate Josie's hunched profile as she bent over, her glasses balanced on the end of her nose. She stuck her head round the door and called: 'Do you want any tea, Mum?' Josie shook her head, acknowledged her offer with a quick glance of thanks. She often interrupted her machining now to give a deep rumbling cough, something which caused Christina concern. On her way upstairs, she passed the heaped bundles of out-work which were stacked there for the factory man. It seemed endless.

A letter on the hall table caught her eye. To her delight, it was addressed to her, and had a Bristol postmark. It was Peter's handwriting! Taking it upstairs, she sat on the window-seat in her room to read it.

'My dear Chris,' she read. 'I'm not much of a letter writer as you can see. Fact is, Teagan's agreed to have me back to stay for a month or two, even tho' baby's come. Like to meet you if poss. at noon by the old Sea Café on Saturday next. Will wait for you there.

Love you. Miss you. Peter.'

Christina saw him straight away, standing on the steps of the veranda like a sea captain at the helm of a ship. His long hair was blowing in the wind.

'Peter!' she shouted, hobbling slightly in her haste to greet him. Soon she found herself engulfed in his arms, his rough jersey smothering her and his strong arms lifting her clear off the ground.

'You came!' he growled, hugging her. 'I wasn't sure you would. Useless I am at writin' letters.'

'I'm glad you chose to meet me here,' she cried, 'where it all began!'

'In a poor way now, isn't it!' he said, looking over his shoulder at the boarded-up windows. 'The state it's in!' And turning back to her, he scrutinized her face. 'How have you been then, my little plumber's mate?' he asked, gazing at her curiously and leaning his back against the wall.

'I'm OK really considering everything that's happened. How about you?'

'I stayed in Bristol to get the two contracts finished, but then the competition got a bit much so rather than start any others I thought I might try my luck down here again. With the winter coming there'll be a few 'summer lets' needing some repair; at least I'm hoping so.' He winked at her. 'That's my excuse out the way,' he smiled mischievously. 'I wanted to see you, Chris. I've thought of nothing else but seein' you again.'

She gasped. How soon she'd forgotten his directness — his honesty. 'Me too,' she replied. 'I can't tell you how strange it's been without you.'

'What's new then? Where's bully boy gone?'

'I'll tell you all about that later. What happened about — you know?'

'It's all over and done with.' He shrugged. 'Nicola got custody of the boys. I get to see them once a month if I'm lucky.' He winced, but recovered himself almost immediately and continued: 'I think Nicola bit off a bit more than she could chew with that man from what I can tell. Still, that's all in the past now. She doesn't tell me anything.' He jerked his head towards the building. 'What's happenin' to that place?'

'Oh!' she exclaimed. 'That's a question everyone's asking! I wish I knew. René's not interested in it anymore and he's just left it. He's supposed to be in the process of buying Deborah a new dance studio in Truro. She's all ready to exchange contracts, but he's done a disappearing act again!'

Peter suddenly took her in his arms. 'I've missed you so!' He breathed the words down the back of her neck, causing her to shiver with excitement. And then he kissed her. She felt again the storm of love rising up inside her like a hunger and she clung to him as they kissed again, lingering as their lips remembered. Finally, as he held her close he stared over her head, far out to sea, his kind rugged face creasing up against the light. 'What would you say to me stopping down here for good, Chris, and renting somewhere permanently? I'll have to get out of my sister's way — she's up to her eyes in nappies.'

'Oh I'd love you to stay! I hoped you would,' she said. 'I certainly need a friend right now.'

'Ah! And there's me thinking I might be a bit more than just a friend.' He gave her a teasing smile. 'You know how to kick a man when he's down, don't you!'

Christina punched him playfully.

★ ★ ★

Later, Peter hired a car and as they drove up to Bent Cross, Christina couldn't wait to tell him about her idea. 'I've been thinking,' she began. 'René's in the mood for selling his share of the Wreckers' now. My mother's prepared to contribute some of the money — do you think there's a chance we could raise the rest between ourselves somehow, to buy it back from him?' She watched his face break into a brilliant smile.

'I didn't think a plumber's mate earned enough to go into property speculation!' he chuckled.

'I'm serious! What if we asked Teagan and Connor, John Madison and perhaps a few others, to come in with us? And you too of course — what do you think? Is there even a remote chance we could do it?'

Peter was quiet for several moments and a frown creased his brow. 'It sounds a great idea Chris,' he said, 'but I'm sorry, there's not much I could put in — the divorce has left me skint.'

'No I understand that, but if we all pulled together we might raise enough. Mum said the bank might help if we had enough to make it sound convincing.'

Still he was quiet and thoughtful and finally he asked, in a hushed tone, 'Haven't you had enough of that place though, Chris?'

'No! It still feels like my café. Somewhere under all that black paint and rubbish the old place is still there! I can't wait to get rid of those sleazy bar stools and mirrors, and clear it all out. Ugh! It's so horrible! If I could get it back and make a success of it, it would mean so much to me and all the customers who used to come. Actually, I've thought of going to see my dad and asking him if he might put something towards it too.'

'I can't see it meant that much to him, the way he walked out on it — and you.'

'He didn't mean it, I'm sure of it. Things between him and Mum were so difficult, that's all. He just couldn't take any more.'

Peter pulled up suddenly, parked and turned off the engine. 'You're a bit of a dreamer, aren't you? You're seriously thinking we could all club together and raise enough to get the café back on its feet?'

'Yes, I do! I can just imagine it. We could clear it all out, hot soapy water and a bit of white paint; we could all work together!'

'It needs more than a coat of paint, Chris!' he chuckled, 'but I get your point. We could put our backs into it and see what we could do; I can't help much financially, but I'm not afraid of hard work. If I could rent a place to live and secure a few contracts down here then it might just be possible. I'll think about it. No harm in askin' the others though. They can always say 'no'.'

She hugged him and smiling, he started the engine. 'We'll be there in a minute. There's a baby fisherman to welcome into this crazy world of ours first. Have you got our presents ready?' Pulling up outside the cottage, they were walking towards the door when he said: 'I'm looking at a couple of flats later. Fancy comin' with me?'

'I'd love to, but I'm sorry I can't. I promised to collect Caitlin from John Madison's, good luck though.' She knocked and Connor answered the door. He stood with arms outstretched, beaming broadly as though to embrace them both.

'Aah 'tis our babby's Uncle Peter! And Chris too! Welcome! Welcome!'

Teagan was nursing the baby on the rocking chair, her full breast luminous in the half-light. She smiled, not attempting to cover herself. A perfect peace surrounded her and the tiny infant, causing them to speak in hushed tones.

'Why are you whispering?' Teagan giggled, looking up from the baby.

'How are you then, sis? We've brought some presents for little sonny here.' Teagan thanked them and said, 'He's sleepy now. Would you like to hold your little nephew?' she asked, buttoning up her blouse.

Peter took the infant from her; his big face gazing at the child with a kind of rapture. 'Little man,' he said. 'You've come to take charge o' these two I hope; no slackin' mind! Hurry up and grow into a good strong boy, eh?' Christina saw the fullness of tears cloud his eyes; he was thinking of his own boys she realized, and when he turned and held the baby towards her, she stretched out her arms willingly.

'He's a grand little babby eh!' said Connor. 'See, he's got a good head of hair on him, just like his dad. We're calling him Shaun. Shaun Andrew Mulligan — son of Connor Mulligan, fisherman and skipper of good fortune!' he boomed. 'He'll grow up to be a fine fisherman just like his father. I can be thankful, now I have a boy to follow in my footsteps!'

'He's a grand lookin' little chap,' said Peter, passing him to Christina. 'Congratulations to you both.'

'Come on then, little one!' coaxed Christina holding out her arms. As the warm bundle was placed in her arms, she was enveloped by the aura of sweetness that came with him. He gazed around and took hold of her finger tightly. His eyes were crystal clear and blue, sharp and curious. Without meaning to, Christina remembered what John had said all that time ago — how he had wished Sylvie had been a boy — how he longed for a boy to follow in his footsteps. How proud these fishermen are of their heritage, she thought, how passionately they feel a need to father a son. Gently she kissed the soft top of the baby's head and curiously, it tasted salty. 'Shaun,' she whispered. 'You've got the best mummy and daddy in the whole world taking care of you. Did you know that?' Hearing what Christina said, Teagan smiled a grateful, wistful smile.

Connor was still talking: 'I was just telling Tig here, I'm going to train him up as soon as he's out o' nappies. We'll take to the open sea together, him an' me, and find that young fella's sea-legs! He'll be a grand sailor. He's got it in his veins, you see. My, I bet he can't wait to be out there with the wind in his face and the rising tide under his feet. Oh boy!' Connor rubbed his hands together in glee.

Christina saw a flicker of anxiety cross Teagan's face. Poor girl. Would she be left to wait for both the men in her life to come safely home from sea? Her thoughts were confirmed when Teagan protested:

'Shaun might not want to be a fisherman!'

'Not want to be a fisherman? Who's his daddy then but a fisherman through an' through! Don't talk such rubbish, eh?' Connor laughed, planting a kiss on his wife's cheek.

She could see, the new arrival filled his parents' hearts with joy. His little life was all they cared about for the time being. Christina passed the baby to Connor and Teagan began to unwrap some of the presents they had brought. For now, Christina knew putting her idea to them about saving the Sea Café would have to wait.

★   ★   ★

Returning to town, Peter dropped Christina outside John Madison's cottage. She walked round the back and heard the girls' voices through the open windows. John was smiling when he opened the door. 'Come in, they're driving me mad!'

The disagreement between the two girls had long been overcome. When the idea of Caitlin having a pony was discovered to be pure speculation, Caitlin had quickly learned that not all her father promised her was true. She was growing up quickly and had picked up some of Sylvie's discerning ways; a quality Christina considered useful. She found the girls sitting on the floor beside a large cardboard box, giggling excitedly. Caitlin was cradling something in her arms.

'Look, it's a kithen,' she lisped, having lost a milk tooth the day before. 'We've got three kithens!'

'Aren't they sweet? Where did you find

these then?' asked Christina.

'Mithus Peacock gave them to us,' said Caitlin.

'She gave them to me actually,' Sylvie said importantly. 'I've got to feed them. Their mother died in childbirth.'

'Oh dear, I see,' replied Christina, pulling a face and catching John's eye.

'Can we have thith one?' Caitlin asked, cradling a skinny kitten the size of a mouse.

'Misses Peacock said they've all got to stay together, Caitlin, I told you, until they're weaned,' said Sylvie.

John raised an eyebrow. 'Here's your coffee, Chris,' he said, holding out a mug to her.

'Thanks.' She went to sit on the sofa. 'Looks like you've got your hands full.'

'Not me,' he said, winking at her. 'Maudie's given the girls strict instructions. Anyway, she's coming back for them tonight. I put my foot down — definitely no night duty!'

'We're having them again tomorrow, Daddy,' Sylvie reminded him. 'We've got to feed them every day.'

'John?' said Christina. 'Can I have a word?'

'Sure,' he replied and led her into the kitchen.

'I know it's a lot to ask and I don't stand much chance, but . . . '

He looked at her curiously. 'I don't think

Maudie's exactly short of cats,' he said, 'if you *really* want one, I'm sure . . . '

'No!' she laughed, her smile disappearing instantly. She looked serious and took a deep breath. 'I want to try and buy back the Wreckers'.'

'You what!' he exclaimed loudly. 'What do you want it back for? It was just a load of trouble! Best thing that happened to it, being shut down.'

'No, you don't understand! I want to clean it up and turn it back to how it used to be — have the Sea Café back again — only more profitably of course, I hope!' she added.

'But that's impossible! Where will you get the money, for goodness sake?'

'I'll need lots of help, John. I've just talked to Peter about my idea — he's moving from Bristol to work down here again. My mum said she can raise some of it. Finding the rest will mean a few of us clubbing together, and have a share in the profits depending on what percentage they put in. It'll need a solicitor to work it out properly, but the thing is, I'll need you, and Peter, and Teagan and Connor too, and perhaps my father as well if possible. I haven't asked anyone yet except Peter, and my mum.' Charged with excitement she grabbed hold of his arms. 'Please, John!' she cried. 'Will you think about it? I know it's a lot to ask but . . . Would you be able to help?'

He looked absolutely astonished. His pale complexion took on an almost ghost-like fragility as he drew away from her awkwardly. 'How can I possibly do anything?' he asked.

'Your boat . . . ? If you do sell her, and get the decommissioning grant come through, I wondered if you might . . . ' She was floundering. She felt she had made a terrible mistake and quickly tried to make amends. 'No it's OK, it was only an idea. It doesn't matter. Forget I said it, sorry!' Her cheeks were burning with embarrassment and she turned away in confusion. How stupid to have suggested it! While she scolded herself inwardly for not having thought it through, there was a long silence. Squeals of delight came from the other room as the girls tended the kittens.

John took a deep breath. 'Even if I had the money, I couldn't run a café to save my life. I've been at sea too long; I'm too used to the freedom and rough weather. Fishing's in my blood. Work indoors in a hot kitchen? I'd go mad!'

Hearing this, she swung round. 'I'm sorry. I didn't mean you'd have to work in there. I just meant you could have a part share, put some money in and hopefully get some income out of it — I would do the work or some of us would . . . '

'A part share? Me and whose army? How much do you need anyway? It must be way over anything I could afford! Actually, since you ask, the *Coral Princess* has already gone.'

'Gone? What d'you mean? You mean she's sold?'

'Not exactly. She's gone for scrap. I watched her go. I've never felt so bad in all my life, not since Kate died. They'd stripped the wheelhouse and structure out of her before I even got there; a massive crane came down and gripped her. Inch by inch she was hoisted up creaking and groaning and shuddering as though she was reluctant to leave her moorings. Poor girl! They let her fall down into the yard like an old tin can. She came down alongside five or six others. I recognized some of them: none of them old boats, years of work left in them yet. I know the lads who worked on them; they've got dependants, families . . . and no jobs now. Yeah, so my *Coral Princess* has gone to the scrap-yard. It's sickening. It fair broke my heart it did, to see her like that.'

'John, I'm sorry. Why? You didn't have to do it, did you?' she cried.

'Didn't have to do it? Ha!' His face hardened. 'It wasn't my choice in the end. The bank decided. I couldn't keep up the payments on the loan they'd given me for the new equipment. I only borrowed it to keep within the EU regulations, and it was a loan on top of what I already owed. They wanted their money back.'

'I'm sorry, really I am,' she whispered.

He shrugged. 'You weren't to know. I can't see the point myself in scrapping decent boats. There's fish out there but we're not allowed to catch them — it makes no difference to Brussels. Save the fish stocks?' He exclaimed bitterly, 'Yes, save the bloody fish and damn the rest of us!'

There was a shuffle of feet behind them. 'Daddy, it's time to warm the kittens' milk,' said Sylvie coming into the kitchen.

'Yes, I'll do it in a minute.'

'But they're hungry, Daddy, they need to be fed now!' insisted Sylvie. John took a small saucepan and began pouring milk into it. 'Go back in the other room. I'll bring it through in a minute,' he told her sharply. As soon as she had gone, he turned to Christina and said: 'When I get the compensation cheque through, and if I manage to sell my quota for a good sum, I'll think about what you've said. I'm not saying I won't do it — but I'll think about it. I'm sorry; it came as a bit of shock, that's all, on top of everything else.'

Christina laid a hand on his arm and gave

it a squeeze. 'Thanks, John,' she said. 'I'm sorry about your boat. Things aren't ever going to be the same again, are they?'

'No, if only we could turn the clock back,' he murmured, staring at the saucepan of milk heating on the gas ring. 'What was it you said once: 'You can't change history'? Well, you were right. Have you stopped to consider that perhaps the Sea Café would be better left in the past?'

'Yes, I have, but it's just abandoned there on the beach, like an old wreck. I can't bear to see it like that.'

'Like the *Coral Princess* you mean, just waiting for the breakers to finish the job. Forty-eight hours and all that was left of her was a mountain of scrap metal. It goes to Germany apparently, to be melted down for the car industry,' he said, before pouring the warm milk into a saucer, and taking it through to the kittens. She turned to gaze out of the window at the quiet garden, where birds on the bird-table were spilling crumbs on the path.

When he returned his eyes had softened and the anger was gone. He touched her cheek sympathetically and gave her a sad smile. 'I'm sorry, Christina; I didn't mean to bite your head off. I'll see what I can do about your little café — no promises, mind!' he said.

14

Christina found Plymouth unsettling. Although the harbour beckoned, she was there for a purpose; she had waited years for this moment. With her father's address running through her mind, she turned into a narrow alley-way and climbed a flight of concrete steps up to a raised Victorian terrace.

It was Sunday morning and the shops before her were closed — apart from a newsagent and tobacconist. Here, litter circled in the draughty street. Clifton Bakery was situated about halfway along this row; it was painted brown. The façade had seen better days but Christina, looking through the slats in the blind saw a clean and tidy shop. To the side was a door marked: Private. A doorbell with a tiny Perspex box underneath contained a scrap of paper showing the name: Charlie L. Tobermory Esq. Top Flat.

With a sense of apprehension, Christina almost turned away. Somewhere in the distance a peal of church bells rang out and simultaneously a woman came down the street shouting to her children. 'Not so fast! Steady on!'

Christina rang the bell. A sudden gust of wind threw a drift of dust in her face and as she raised her hand to her eyes, she heard the sound of bolts being drawn back. Blinking, she found herself face-to-face with her father after seven years. His open honest expression at once seemed familiar to her: freshly shaved, pink and well-scrubbed, he wore a white vest tucked into corduroy trousers. He looked vulnerable, like a small boy.

'Chrissy?'

'Hello,' she said simply. The word 'dad' just wouldn't come.

'You've caught me gettin' dressed, girl!' he said, smiling impishly. 'Come on in!'

She followed him up the steep worn staircase, trying to ignore the smell reminiscent of her school-days, of boiled cabbage and disinfectant. He was breathless when they reached the top.

'Just through here,' he said and led her into a small sitting room. The furniture was dull, old-fashioned and brown. There was a hard wooden table with a single chair. His attempt to smarten the room amounted to a vase of daffodils on the table, but little else made it in any way homely. There wasn't even a newspaper.

'Going to sit down? I'll put the kettle on, shall I?'

'Thanks. Mum sends her regards.'

'That's nice of her,' he said. 'Give 'er my love, will yer?'

She nodded and she began to wonder if her visit would be no more than this; a few words exchanged without meaning or emotion.

Suddenly her mind raced back years to when the man from the textile factory had just arrived to collect her mother's outwork. He had taken the pencil from behind his ear, and was scribbling figures in his grubby notebook, when her father had confronted him:

'*How about you payin' a bit more for this work my wife's doing?*' *Charlie said, rather too loudly.* '*She's wearin' her fingers to the bone! £1.50 you're payin' her for makin' a whole skirt? You're havin' a laugh, aren't you? How much is your company sellin' these for, I'd like to know! It's a pittance you're paying her, a flamin' pittance!*'

'*It's the goin' rate, mate,*' *he replied.* '*You can take it or leave it, it's up to you — or up to your missus rather,*' *he said, turning to Josie. She had left her machine and had been waiting with her arms folded defiantly. She looked at Fred's tired face, his worn-out clothes and his shabby shoes.*

'*Charlie! Be quiet, will you!*' *she said.* '*He's only doing his job, for goodness sake!*'

270

But Charlie wouldn't be quiet. 'What are you payin' the others?' he demanded. Fred mumbled his reply, his expression failing to disguise the fact that he knew it wasn't the first or the last time he would have this argument.

'I can't believe they'd settle for that!' exclaimed Charlie. 'Do you know how many hours my dear wife slogs away at that machine? Well, do you?'

'Leave it out, Charlie,' Josie said. 'Stop showing me up in front of everyone. Here, Fred, give me what I'm owed and let's have the next lot in.' She began fetching in the fresh bundles of work off the step herself and stacking them beside the sewing-machine. 'Come back for them tomorrow, love, they'll be ready, and take no notice of my husband here, he doesn't recognize hard work when it's staring him in the face.'

Christina heard the sound of him filling the kettle. After a few moments he returned, this time wearing a clean shirt. A small shaving nick on his chin bled slightly. She worried about the blood staining his white shirt, but said nothing.

'Bit quiet here,' she said.

He nodded. 'Does me all right. Your sister's OK, is she? And your mother?'

'Debbie's hoping to get her own dancing-school, if René keeps his promise. Mum's all right — well, y'know . . . ' She shrugged as though it was self-explanatory.

'I know,' he sighed, sitting down beside her. 'She blames me, you know, for all of it.'

She looked at him. Regretfully she remembered how her sister's love of the stage used to bring such a light to his eyes. He had seen a glimpse of its magic through Deborah's talent, a world he would never be a part of — he was like a ragged boy, standing on tip-toe and peering in through the window of a grand house, in awe of the crystal chandeliers, and the gold lacquered mirrors, knowing he could never enter — but lost in wonderment. Now, alone with her father at last, she found talking more awkward than she had imagined. His world was mysterious to her now. She asked about his job.

'I've been bakin' bread for years now. Tell you what, girl, it fills yer belly but makin' it an' bakin' it in that heat, it just drains the weight off of yer,' he said. 'Well, you can see that.' A short silence ensued during which she cast around for something else to say.

'I didn't know you were a baker,' she remarked. It felt strange; she couldn't bring herself to call him *Dad*. 'I was talking to Theo. He told me where you were.'

'Bakin' stopped me goin' mad, I guess,' he said. 'Reckon I kneaded an' folded more worries into that dough than air. It's a wonder it never came out of the oven as flat as a flippin' pancake.'

'Why didn't you write to us, at least tell us where you were?'

'I did, Chrissy! I wrote to your mother every week at first, then at least once a month. I sends 'er money regular, for the bills too. She never told you?'

Christina shook her head. 'Not until recently. Thanks for the money you sent me and Debs.'

'That's all right, duck. I wanted to give you both summat. Not much else your old dad can do for you now, is there, eh? Your mother's had to hold the fort all these years. She's had a lot to put up with. Don't know if you'll ever prise her away from that sewin' machine now. I tried long enough, God knows!' He chuckled and waggled his big ears. 'Don't judge your mother too hard, Chrissy, eh?'

'Mum doesn't seem well, though, I'm worried about her. She coughs so much with the dust, and works such long hours over that machine. She's always so tired.'

'It's all my fault,' he said, looking troubled. 'If I could have made the café work, brought enough money in, she could've stopped that sewing for good. It seemed to get a hold of her, but you know your mother — you won't change her mind unless she changes it herself. She's a single-minded woman, always has been — always will be.'

There was a lull in the conversation, both of them alone with their thoughts. 'What do you do when you're not at work, Dad?' This time she had called him Dad without even thinking about it. 'Do you go out in the evenings?' The things she really wanted to say were buried deep inside her, but aware that she had such little time, she just took a deep breath and came out with it. 'Is there a new lady in your life?' she asked and immediately blushed.

To her surprise he chuckled in delight. 'You think a handsome dashin' young man like me must have a pretty new woman tucked away, eh? You thought I lived in a semi-detached house with two clever kids, an estate car and a satellite dish eh?' He laughed good-humouredly.

'No!' she said, protesting. He was suddenly so like the father she knew.

'I've rented this place above the bakery for near-on five years now, Chrissy, love. My boss was the one who got the pretty wife an' the semi.' He looked at her, serious now. 'To tell you the truth, I suppose I live in the past a bit. I spend my time thinkin' about the life I left behind me. I go up the pub of a weekend, play a bit o' pool perhaps. Don't go out much; have to be up early, see?'

She paused. To ask him about the money now, without any build up, just didn't seem fair. To talk about making an investment while sitting in this poor room suddenly seemed ridiculous. She stood and went to look out of the window. In the street below she saw a group of youths, talking and smoking. One was kicking a can.

'It's good to see you, good you came,' he said. 'So, since the Wreckers' closed down I suppose you've got some time on your hands?'

'I haven't worked there since René took it over, Dad. I couldn't face working for him. Did you hear about it from Theo? It's all gone to pot now, with boards across the windows and paint peeling. It's in a right state.'

'I saw it in the paper a few months ago, the scandal about all the fights and stuff — right mess that René made of it then. I knew he was bad news from the start. I told your mother what a — '

'I'm going to try to buy the café back from him.'

Charlie's eyes bulged in surprise. 'What? You don't say! Have you won the lottery or what, girl?' A cheeky smile spread across his face.

'No,' she replied, stepping away from the window, and flinging down any reservations she had about bringing up her idea. 'I'm trying to get a group of people together to buy his share back. Mum said she can raise some of it, and if enough people club together we could raise the money between us — well, there's a chance anyway. It might be a crazy idea but . . . What do you think?'

'What do I think? I think it's a brilliant idea — if it's possible. I'm surprised at your mother being so keen.'

'There're a few people interested, Dad. I've saved up a little, including what you sent me. There's Peter, that's Teagan's brother of course, Teagan and Connor and John Madison. Then there's Mum — she said she'll put in what she can. We'd have to convince a bank manager it would work and we'd need security.' Christina was looking at his face keenly, seeing the curiosity stirring his complexion as a rash of excitement began to creep up his neck.

'Who would have believed it?' He scratched his head. 'They're all prepared to have a go you say?' He looked flabbergasted. 'Well I'll be jiggered!' He pinched his nose between finger and thumb and blew out his cheeks in astonishment.

Christina thought to herself: If I don't ask

him now, I might never have the chance again. 'Dad?' she said. 'If you weren't stuck with the bakery and everything, I'd ask you to come in with us too. It's asking a lot at the moment I know, but if you could put in a little bit . . . I mean, between us, we could all make it work, and make a success of it. Open it up again, just like the old days.'

'The old Sea Café! Have her back again eh? Ha!' He shouted in glee. Standing up he thrust his hands into his pockets and paced around the room, his face bursting with excitement. 'The Sea Café — open again — ha!' he exclaimed again loudly.

Christina watched him curiously. 'You think it might work?' she asked. 'I'd hate my friends to risk losing their money . . . '

'Work? It would if I was in on it! I'd make sure it did if I had that chance again!' He continued to pace the room thinking, sometimes aloud, sometimes screwing his face up into complicated knots. 'Go and put the kettle on again, girl, we've got some calculations to do. Now let's see . . . I've saved up a bit while I've been on my own. I could ask a few of my old mates — see how much we can come up with . . . your mother's keen on it too, is she? Ha!'

'Dad! It's just an idea at the moment. We need to think about it a bit — '

'Think about it? I've thought about nothin' else ever since I walked out that door. To get the old Sea Café back — make it a family business. Ha! Fetch that wad of paper from under the sofa there, Chrissy love, and I'll get a pen.'

Rolling-up his sleeves, he set to work while she went to make some more tea. As she rinsed out their mugs, she realized the sound coming from the other room was her father whistling.

★ ★ ★

When Christina got home from Plymouth the BMW parked outside set her pulse racing. She let herself in quietly and made a cup of coffee before going into the sitting room to fetch her book. René was sitting in the armchair watching the Six O' Clock News on the BBC. A slight tremor caused his hand to shake as he held his Scotch, but he appeared oblivious to the repetitive sound of his gold bracelet clinking against the glass. Christina had already decided that whatever it was René had been burning in the backyard that night, it was of little consequence now. What he had said about his feelings had mystified her, but she put it down to his drinking and had given little thought to it since.

278

'Evening René,' she said.

He grunted, 'Yes, evening Sister-in-law.' She decided against going straight upstairs and sat down to read. If she had been in a different frame of mind she might have begun to feel sorry for him as he sat there blunting his perception of life with alcohol. She felt like telling him whisky was never intended to be a pain-killer, but she knew he wouldn't take any notice. Anyway, what did it matter? What did she care?

In Debbie's selfish world, control over her husband's cheque-book seemed to have become her marital rite. What had her sister done with the money their father had sent them, she wondered? Quite likely it was already squandered on clothes and accessories. Would her sister worry over René's state of mind? Probably not. Sadly, she knew the state of René's wallet was of more interest to her sister than his health. But as these thoughts went through her mind, she watched René and feared he was letting his life ebb away. He often had the flush of fever on his cheek, and while he sat sprawled in the chair, he seemed to drift in and out of consciousness, muttering to himself without any due concern as to who might be listening. Reason and sanity seemed to pass him by. It began to worry her.

'Are you all right?' she asked.

'Mmmm?' he replied, half turning to her. 'Yes, yes, never better,' he said sleepily.

'René?' Suddenly Deborah's shrill voice called from the other room; it made him jump. 'René, have you signed that contract yet?' He looked around in a daze as though waking from a deep sleep and attempting to focus, he partly gained his composure.

'Yes dear, anything you say dear,' he mumbled to himself, with no intention of letting his wife hear. Looking in Christina's direction, he said, 'Pass me those wretched papers across here, would you?'

'You don't have to sign them, you know,' said Christina coolly, picking up what appeared to be a contract and holding it out to him. 'If Debbie wants a dance premises you can't afford, just tell her so. Try saying 'No' for a change.'

René looked up as though he was hearing voices.

'You think that would work, do you, mmmm? You think that would pacify that pretty little dumb sister of yours? Don't make me laugh!'

Deborah appeared at the door, dressed in a shocking-pink jump-suit.

'Well?' she demanded, hands on hips. 'Have you signed it? Honestly! Why does everything have to take so long?'

'Actually, I can't sign without a witness to my signature darling.'

'Is that all?' she said. 'Chris, you're here.'

'The answer's no, so don't even ask,' said Christina, standing up. She was ready to leave the room. 'Calm down a bit, Debs, can't you? Read the small print, see if it's really what you both want. René, wouldn't you rather think about it a bit more first?'

Turning round he stared at her, his eyeballs bulging. Deliberately, with a fat chubby hand he took the pen. 'Think about it?' he said. 'I don't think any more, girl. Thinking is a luxury I can't afford.'

He looked up into the face of his wife like a calf about to be slaughtered and said, 'Like it or not — you're a witness Sister-in-law,' and he signed the papers savagely. 'There! It's done. You've got your dancing-school, Debbie, now get lost both of you and leave me alone.'

15

In Truro, Pigeons flocked to peck among the cobbles. Tourists and shoppers rested in the shade of Truro Cathedral as the bells rang out across the busy streets. Months had passed since Christina first ventured into the idea of trying to buy back the Wreckers'. René, travelling back from London by train, was expected to arrive at any moment for a meeting with the solicitors — he was about to sign another contract. This time he was selling his sixty per cent ownership of the Wreckers to a syndicate of buyers.

To mark the occasion, a lunch had been arranged by Josie in a quiet Italian restaurant where they had all arranged to meet before going on to the solicitor's office to finalize the transaction. Christina and Josie, with the help of Connor and Teagan, Peter, Charlie and John, plus a small business loan from the bank, had managed to raise the funds between them. Christina's anxiety caused her eyes to keep flitting towards the door in search of her brother-in-law who had still not appeared. In hindsight, she thought to herself, it would have been much better to have arranged the meal after the business had been done. But it was too late now.

To her relief René arrived. He swaggered into the restaurant wearing a formal dinner suit with a pink carnation and carrying a cane which he twirled once in greeting as though he was Frank Sinatra. Christina thought he was looking unusually pleased with himself. As he came to their table, he tore the carnation from his button-hole and held it out to his wife in a melodramatic gesture.

'There you are, my sweet!'

Deborah wrinkled her nose slightly. 'Thank you, René,' she said, taking the flower and rising from her seat to give him a dutiful peck on the cheek. 'Lovely to see you again, darling.'

'Mmmm, you too lovey,' he replied. 'Good afternoon, Mother-in-law, Sister-in-law.' He nodded to the others around the table — Charlie, John, Peter, Connor and Teagan. Throwing his briefcase onto a nearby chair, and sitting down, he turned to his wife.

'Well, how are you, my sweet?' he asked and began squinting at the menu.

'Oh, you can't imagine how busy I've been, René,' she began in her sing-song voice. 'You were right about the floor, darling. Once the sanding was done it looked fantastic.'

'Terrific. My, haven't we been busy,' he said

flatly. His eyes roamed across the restaurant restlessly.

'Yes, I'm exhausted!'

'Poor you,' he muttered. 'Over here please!' he added sharply to a passing waiter.

'One moment, sir!'

Christina shot him a quick glance. Was he mocking her so openly? But Deborah was trying to capture his attention again, she looked every inch a glamorous dancing-school proprietor. The waiter arrived and with brisk formality took their order. He left them briefly and returned with a bottle of champagne. As the bubbly was poured, René rose from his seat ceremoniously and held up his glass:

'This is a momentous day, all things considered, mmm?' he said, gazing around at those present. 'Shall we propose a toast? To the future of . . . whatever it's called.'

'To the New Sea Café!' broke in Christina defiantly, standing up and raising her glass.

They all rose to their feet. 'The New Sea Café!' they all chorused.

'What about a toast to my new dancing-school too?' said Deborah indignantly.

'Yes, that too,' added René under his breath, immediately downing his champagne and re-filling his glass. 'I'm surprised you could spare the time to meet us for lunch, my pet,' he said, rolling champagne around in his mouth. His manner disarmed her slightly.

'I . . . I wouldn't have missed this; I know how important it is to our family.'

'Do you? Mmm, that's nice.'

To Christina's relief, the starters arrived. She looked at her scallops, and immediately they stared back at her like René's eyeballs, opaque and yellowing, with thread veins running through them. Charlie launched into a discussion with Peter and Connor about the décor of the café, and Teagan sat quietly picking at her bit of salad and smoked salmon.

'Is the little girl all right?' René asked amicably.

'She has a name you know, or have you forgotten it?' snapped Deborah. Her tone didn't make the meal any more appetizing. Everyone fell silent again and Christina stabbed one of the scallops with her fork.

'Caitlin's doing very well at school, isn't she, Debs?' offered Christina helpfully. 'She might be going up into the top group next term.'

'Good, good,' muttered René. 'Must get her brains from her father then.' He was dipping bread in his soup.

'Will you . . . ' began Deborah. 'After you've been to the solicitors, will you come home with us? Caitlin would like to see her daddy again.'

'And I'd like to see her too of course, but I've got to get straight back to London, my pet. Meetings in the morning, you know what it's like,' he replied, gulping and wiping his mouth. He looked to his left and right as though, somewhere nearby, he had mislaid his napkin. 'Well, Mother-in-law!' he declared suddenly. 'I hope there aren't going to be any awkward clauses in this contract? I don't intend to hang about all afternoon. Damn solicitors, they've wasted more than enough of my time already.'

'It should be a simple procedure,' Josie replied. 'One way or another, the café will be open again by next summer.'

'I'm not interested in seeing that place again, open or otherwise — bloody waste of time if you ask me.'

'You will come down for my opening-night, won't you, René?' pleaded Deborah in her best little-girl's voice. 'I've invited the local press. My pupils have been working ever so hard on their new routine. You'll love it, René. I'm sure you'll be impressed!'

'Waiter!' he clicked his fingers, ignoring her. 'How long until the main course? We haven't got all day you know.'

'I'll see what I can do, sir,' replied the waiter nervously, eyeing him like a startled rabbit and beginning to clear away their plates.

286

Christina couldn't bear it much longer. Why René's mood had changed so dramatically from when he first came swinging through the door she couldn't imagine. Exchanging glances with her mother, she tried to preserve the peace. One hasty remark on their part might cause him to up and leave at any moment causing the whole thing to fall though. More than once, Christina noticed her father catch her mother's eye uneasily and she could detect something between them — a fleeting amusement perhaps, or embarrassment or even sympathy. It made her eyes return to them again and again in curiosity. Did they understand each other at last, after all these years?

The waiter removed the last of their starter plates and almost immediately the main course descended on them, issued by a flurry of waiters and waitresses. Christina had ordered a salad and the sight of the fresh green leaves revived her. She tried not to look at René who, with his linen napkin tucked into the collar of his shirt, proceeded to gnaw his rack of ribs, ripping the flesh with his wet lips. A line of gravy began to trickle from the corner of his mouth causing her to look away in disgust.

'Who are these new punters anyway?' he asked suddenly. 'This so-called *syndicate* as they call themselves — remind me who they are, will you? I presume you've approved them, Mother-in-law? You've sussed them all out, as it were, made sure they're not weirdoes, have you?' Christina's heart turned over. He already knew the identity of the group; what was he playing at?

Josie was pushing her food around the plate. 'You're not too bothered who they are exactly, are you, so long as you get your money?' she replied.

'Fine! If you don't want me interfering . . . ' he tore his napkin from his collar. 'Let's get it over with,' he exclaimed, rising from his chair irritably and standing up. 'Load of amateurs who don't know what the hell they're doing.'

Taking her jacket, Christina also started for the door. 'We'll walk down to the solicitors' then,' she said. Josie stopped to pay the bill but the others were already trooping out into the breezy air. Half their meals were untouched.

Deborah made an excuse. 'I'm not going to the solicitors', René, if that's all right?' she said. 'I've got so much to do before the glaziers come tomorrow.'

He didn't look at all surprised, but stood adjusting his tie and attempting to hail a taxi. 'When is your opening night again, my sweet?' he asked, not looking at her.

'I've told you a thousand times!'

'Right, I'll get on then,' he said, giving her a peck on the cheek. 'Let's get this business out the way shall we?' he added and set off, swinging his cane and snatching a glance at his reflection in the shop window. Lifting a hand to correct a wayward hair, he strutted off down the street.

★　★　★

After a few moments, Josie and Charlie found themselves alone. It was Josie who broke the silence. 'So, has Chris said much to you about what the renovation plans are? There's a lot to do.'

'Yeh, an' I'd like to help get the place back on track a bit, that is, if you don't mind,' he said, looking at her curiously.

'You do what you like Charlie. If you can help at all, we'd appreciate it.'

'Josie, love, you know — I never meant to . . . ' He appeared to search the sky for the right words. Pigeons were cooing peacefully on the gutters above them, reflecting nothing of the tension that now sprang up between them.

'There's no need to start explaining yourself,' said Josie. 'That was then, and this is now. I'm not one to pick over old bones.'

It isn't the time, she thought to herself, to start talking about what had happened. Whatever tears she had shed for him had long since run dry. There were faults on both sides, but she hadn't helped, she knew that, by burying her head in the outwork and neglecting everything else — including him — she realized that now.

'Right!' He scratched his head and held out his hand to shake hers and then she saw the tears colouring his eyes to a moist pink.

'No hard feelings then, eh, Josie, love?' he said.

She took his hand, giving it a squeeze and held on to it for several moments. 'Thank you for helping us out, Charlie,' she said. 'You needn't have done. I do appreciate it, really I do.'

'Oh, I needed to, Josie, believe me, I needed to!' he said, and when he turned away, she saw the tears stream down his face.

He stopped a little way off to wait for her. 'Best get on to the solicitor's office then, Josie love. Are you comin'?' he called. 'Can't keep good people waiting can we?'

'No Charlie,' she replied, catching him up. 'Can't keep good people waiting.'

16

A biting sand-laden wind stung Christina's face as she and Josie walked along the beach at Crystal Barr. The keys were safely in her pocket once more. Gone was the mournful feeling of being banished from the place she loved. In the distance they spotted Peter, John and what looked like Teagan and Connor. To their surprise, a loud cheer went up as they came near.

'Three cheers for Christina!' shouted Peter, 'Hip Hip, Hurray!' they all cried as she put the keys in the lock.

'It's not just me!' she protested. 'I couldn't have done it without all you lot.'

'But it was all your idea, Chris!' said John. 'Without you getting us all motivated we wouldn't have even thought of it.' There were several cries of agreement and with her heart bursting she turned the key. Opening the patio doors, they all trooped inside.

There was no light, daylight or otherwise, because the windows were boarded up. It smelt musty, of mildew, stale beer and cigarettes.

'Right! Let's get some light into this place!' shouted Peter, going outside again and ripping the boards off the windows with the edge of his hammer. Once they could see the interior, the sight was shocking. Papers and other rubbish littered the floor. Shards of broken mirror, beer cans, and broken bottles presented quite a danger. Where someone had removed the fruit machines, gaping holes sprang from the walls and the carpets were ruined. As Peter released more windows, darkness gave way to dust laden air, cobwebs and smelly damp patches.

'First thing that's going is that sign!' announced John and with a fierce determination he set about removing the one thing everyone loathed: the large neon sign on the outside of the premises saying: 'The Wreckers' Bar'. With a ripping sound and a warning shout from the men it came crashing down. Strings of lights and wires tumbled down onto the veranda.

Work was soon well underway. A skip was delivered and they all began clearing away the ghosts of an unhappy past. Connor was up a ladder disconnecting a light-fitting when Peter shouted to him: 'You've not put to sea today then?'

'No, the forecast's rough. They say it's getting up to Force Six,' he replied. 'If it settles down I'll be away tomorrow. It's good for the catch anyway, a bit of bad weather.'

Peter looked impressed. 'You're keepin'

goin' all right then? John here, he's jacked it in — ain't that right, John?'

'No, not exactly,' he replied. 'I've decommissioned my boat, yes, but I've bought a smaller boat. I'm catching brown crab and lobster close to shore off the Lizard — there's plenty out there and not so much hassle. There's money to be made in shellfish — I can keep this here café supplied with fresh crab for a start.'

They wrenched a heavy piece of board away from the main window and sent it crashing to the ground. John dusted his hands together with satisfaction and continued: 'The French beam trawlers are coming so close to the six-mile limit now. They've got much bigger vessels; they can catch in an hour what we used to land in a week. They've quotas for plaice and cod much bigger than we could ever afford. So I thought, if I can't compete with them I'll go for shellfish instead — it demands a good price. So long as it keeps the wolf from the door anyway, eh? We've all got mouths to feed.'

Christina and her mother began investigating the storeroom to see what René's staff had left behind. However, as they might have guessed, there was nothing of any real value.

'How could they let it get into such a state!' Josie exclaimed.

A shout of greeting was heard and Charlie popped his head round the door.

'You all right, you two?' He took in the devastated scene with one sweep of his eyes. 'I'm not too late to help out then! Blimey! Made a right mess in here haven't they!'

'Hello Dad!' said Christina, smiling. Her happiness was complete.

He greeted her warmly, but his attention strayed to Josie who was looking about her anxiously. 'Going to make a start on the stock-take then, love?' he asked nervously. 'I'll help if you like.'

'No Charlie, see for yourself: they've only left us the rubbish.'

'Oh, don't say that, Josie love. There's bound to be something here we can salvage.'

Josie responded with a shake of her head. 'The eternal optimist, your father, Chris. Here, let's go and get some of that coffee Teagan's brought shall we?' Back in the main part of the café, Teagan cleared a space on the counter and took out the vacuum flasks.

'Well,' said Charlie as he stood sipping from his mug. 'I should be up bakin' at four on Monday mornin' but I could ring the boss an' ask for a week or two off though. I'm owed a few days holiday.' He looked at Josie for a reaction, but his smile wavered. 'If you want me, that is,' he added quietly, but she was busy picking up shards of glass from the dust and putting them into a cardboard box.

Eventually, she glanced up, 'Take longer than a few days to put this lot right,' she said bluntly.

Christina saw her father's eager expression crumple at Josie's response. 'That would be great, Dad,' she said quickly. 'I'll book you a room over at the pub in town, if that'd be easier . . . '

'Thanks, Chris, I'd like that.' Putting down his mug, he stooped to take the cardboard box from Josie and said gently, 'Careful of that glass, love. Come on, I'll do that. It could give you a nasty cut. We need to find you some gloves before you do anything like — '

'OK, Charlie,' she said, 'you do it then. Reckon your skin's tougher than mine.'

'I wouldn't bank on it,' he replied meaningfully, holding her gaze for a moment. 'Folks say I'm too used to kneadin' dough to be any good for much else. My skin's as soft as a baby's bottom.'

'That's not what I meant,' she replied. Her words were snatched away to fill the empty void between them. Charlie's eyes moistened. He made no further comment and it was only Christina who witnessed his pain.

They began pulling down sheets of mouldy plaster-board noisily, heaving bar stools and tables outside. Soon the atmosphere became even thicker with dust. Work continued for an hour or more and gradually they began to see a real difference. As Charlie was removing the mirror tiles, he was surprised when Josie came and laid a hand on his arm.

'When you've got time,' she said quietly, 'perhaps you and I could have a talk?'

'I was hoping you'd ask that,' he replied. 'It's good we've got the café back, isn't it? It'll help all of us in a way, and give Chrissy her life back again, eh?'

'Yes — a second chance, Charlie. Sometimes it's all any of us needs.'

'So it is, Josie love, so it is,' he replied.

★   ★   ★

As it turned out, they didn't have to wait long for their discussion. Later that afternoon, Christina and Peter left with the others to fetch the children from Maudie. Charlie and Josie stood alone together — the place was now almost stripped bare.

'So, Charlie, here we are,' said Josie, surveying the bare scene with her hands on her hips.

'Yes,' he replied, 'here we are, love. It takes some getting used to, being back here, seein' as how it's all changed so much.'

'We're putting it right though, slowly,' she replied, 'and we've changed a bit too.' There was so much she wanted to say and now she had the chance to say it she couldn't think how to put her feelings into words. Instead she stood looking slightly bewildered and tiredness crept over her. 'I feel exhausted,' she said.

'Come and sit down, love, take the weight off your feet for a minute,' said Charlie, sweeping a hand across a chair to dust it off.

Even his kind voice, instead of helping her to relax, had the effect of making her feel more anxious. Her face took on the shadow of years. Her eyes sunk into their hollows, her shoulders sagged and her cheekbones looked skeletal. She took a deep breath as he sat down near her. She suddenly felt she had nothing to lose and plunged in with the first thing that came into her head. 'Charlie,' she said. 'I'm so sorry! I was wrong! I was wrong all along, I admit it. I made a mistake.'

'Wrong about what, love?' Charlie's honest face was as cheerful and curious as ever. None of life's problems seemed to make a permanent mark on his good nature.

'Years ago, I shouldn't have blamed you like I did for Chris's accident — for being careless and not watching her when she was a baby.' She steeled herself to carry on

— forcing herself to say the words. 'I couldn't forgive and forget — I just couldn't! Something was eating away at me and I couldn't get over it.'

His eyes were wide and shining, 'It were my fault,' he said. 'I should've been keepin' an eye on little Chrissy, I know I should've an' I can't — '

'What I'm saying is, Charlie, you didn't mean it. We all make mistakes — let me finish. I've been rotten to you, blaming you for Chris being disabled, and I shouldn't have argued with you about Debs marrying René either. He's a bad lot, we know that now. You saw through him, you saw that from the start.'

'It's all right. You only wanted what you thought was best for her. It ain't your fault he's turned out like he is. Anyway, like René said himself at the time: we weren't in any position to stop her going off with him. She was old enough to make up her own mind.'

'Oh Charlie! It's what I felt inside that was so wrong! I blamed you for everything. Right from when our Chris fell off the harbour — I,' she sighed. 'I was a stupid woman full of self pity. I was always thinking I could have done better for myself than — '

'Than being married to a fool like me, you mean? Well, you weren't far wrong there, Josie love. I ain't been able to give you the nice things you deserve. To see you working away at that sewin'-machine for hour after hour — it fair broke my heart it did. If it weren't for you earnin' summat we would've gone under sooner, I reckon.'

'No Charlie,' she admitted. 'If I'd done what you said and we'd all pulled our weight together with the café we might have got back on our feet.' She stood up wearily and, in response, he rose too.

'Josie!' His voice was almost a whisper as she leant forward into his arms. It was strange, to breathe in his familiar manly scent, to feel his body against hers again after all those years. She knew she was a mere ghost of the woman he once knew. 'Josie,' he breathed again, and instinctively wrapped his long gangly arms around her. She relented, and he enfolded her thin bony body against him. And perhaps because she felt not so much like a woman, but more like a wooden clothes-horse, what escaped from his throat was more like a sob of disappointment and anguish. He held her tenderly, resting his chin lightly on the top of her head and they stayed like that for a long time, both drawing comfort from the other. It grew dark when they finally released each other. There was nothing more to say, nothing could describe what healing they had found in each other, or whether from this moment on their lives would change. But an understanding had passed between them which went beyond words. Simply holding each other had washed away all the hurts of the past.

★ ★ ★

In the months that followed, Josie's anxious face softened, her skin took on warmth and a sparkle lit up her eyes. Christina noticed glances were often exchanged between her mother and father which suggested they were more than friends. The old hostility had evaporated and with renewed vigour, work on the café premises continued. They were aiming to be open again for the summer. Peter and Charlie both donned boiler suits and, splashed with paint, worked tirelessly; gradually the black and chrome gave way to white and aquamarine blue. Teagan painted fish and sea-horses along the dado rail. Josie stitched new table-cloths and blinds, and together with Christina, searched the flea-markets for second-hand tables and chairs. These the men painted white, while John renewed the wiring, the kitchen appliances and put up shelves to display crafts, sea-shells and pottery.

As the winter turned to spring, at last it was seen to be taking shape. With a sense of excitement Christina stood beside Peter one day and watched their new blue sign being erected over the patio doors: 'The New Sea Café'.

'Look!' she whispered, 'I can hardly believe it's happening!' He put his arms round her and kissed her. 'But there it is, girl!' he said. 'Bet you never thought you'd see the day! Come on, we've got to get the openin' posters put up. Not long to go now! I've got them back at my place — fancy a walk?'

When they came to Peter's apartment on the upstairs floor, Christina looked out over a rather drab scene. There was a tarmac grey car park almost full of cars, traffic cones and recycling bins. If it hadn't been for the call of gulls, and the odd boat parked there, it could have been the car park in any suburban town.

'Coffee?' called Peter from the small galley kitchen where sounds of rattling cutlery suggested coffee was already on its way. When she didn't reply Peter came to the doorway.

'Are you all right?' he asked.

'Yes, I was just thinking about my dad, that's all. It's a shame things got as bad as they did.'

'What, with the café you mean?'

'Yes, and between him and mum. The café

was losing so much money — and she was so hostile all the time. It's no wonder he couldn't cope.'

He went and stood behind her as she gazed out of the window. Looking out over the top of her head to the car park below, he said, 'What do you think of my garden? Beautiful, eh?' he chuckled, kissing her neck.

'Peter, I wonder what we'll be doing in ten years' time? Do you think we'll still be here, with the Sea Café up and running and you and me together?'

He drew her close and folding his arms around her face, she could feel his forearms against her lips and his body pressing warm against her back. 'We might be an old married couple by then, don't you think?' he mused, rocking her slightly as he spoke. 'You an' me could be livin' right here together. When we've finished work in the café, we can come home here and have a bit o' dinner and watch the T.V. or do a spot of gardening.'

'You haven't got a garden!' laughed Christina, swivelling round to face him and inviting him to kiss her.

'No,' he murmured, kissing her on the mouth gently, 'but I've got you, haven't I, and nothing else matters.'

Two days before the New Sea Café was due to open, a luxury hamper was delivered to the house. 'I know what this means,' said Christina, carrying it through to the kitchen where her mother was cooking. 'It's addressed to René so I suppose he's bound to turn up again shortly. He's the only one who buys this sort of stuff.' She poked through the contents to find crackers, select cheeses, caviar, and a small bottle of port. 'Huh! No chocolate either, damn!'

Josie clicked her tongue. 'He's the only one able to afford such luxuries.'

Christina put the box down on top of the fridge. 'Especially now he's got all our money as well.'

'At least we've no need to worry about him interfering with the café anymore,' said Josie, turning the cake mixture into a tin and levelling it with a spoon. 'And thank goodness for that!'

Christina sighed. 'Yes, and everything's coming together so well for our opening on Saturday. We couldn't wish for a nicer bunch of people to be working with either, could we, Mum?'

'One of them is certainly a surprise. I'd never have guessed your father would be back helping us out like he is.'

Christina looked at her quickly, afraid to see the barrier return. But Josie's face looked almost girlish and she was smiling.

'It's great though isn't it, Mum,' she said,

'to have Dad helping out again.'

'He's trying his hardest, Chris, I'll give him that.'

★ ★ ★

René drew up in his open-top BMW sports car that afternoon. Josie was on her own at the time, cleaning all the dust and oil out of her sewing-machine. Because she had finally given up her out-work, she was waiting for it to be collected by the factory. Hearing the door-bell, Josie left her machine to open the frontdoor muttering to herself: 'It can't be them for it already, surely?'

'So it's you!' she said, as René brushed past her. 'We were expecting you.'

'Good, good,' he muttered. 'Get the hamper all right, did we?' he asked amiably. 'Some nice things for you in there.'

'Yes, thank you,' said Josie, knowing the delicacies were not really intended for her. 'Debbie's at work, in fact, everyone's out at the moment.'

'That's all right. I didn't come to see everyone,' he declared matter-of-factly. 'So you're all busy with the little 'what's-its-name' I presume?'

'The New Sea Café? Yes, we've been working at it round the clock to get it ready in

304

time for Saturday.'

'Mmm,' replied René. 'And it's on schedule? Good, good. I don't recall receiving an invitation to the celebrations . . . I presume there are going to be some celebrations, mmm?' He was seated by this time, his fat thighs sprawled out and his thick neck supporting an unusually cheerful-looking face. He gazed at her innocently. 'I suppose I don't qualify for an invitation; still, little tea-parties aren't quite my thing.' He gave one of his quick twitches of a smile. 'When will my dear wife be back, did you say?'

'It's only 3.30,' replied Josie. 'These days, she doesn't get back until 7 or so — she's a busy girl you know, with her new dancing-school. It's very successful.'

'Right!' he declared. 'I'll just get my suit-case in then!' Heaving himself up out of the chair, he disappeared out of the front-door. When he came back, he asked, 'Where's my daughter, at school?'

'She'll be finished and on her way to John Madison's by now. Mrs Peacock usually takes both the girls back to his house. They play there together after school. I'll go up and fetch her later, if Chris doesn't get back in time.'

'Nope, that's all right, I'll go. Where is this John's place?' he asked offhandedly.

Taken aback, Josie had no time to think.

'There's no need, René, really. Caitlin will be quite happy there until someone collects her.'

He stood there smiling. There was no question of him changing his mind. 'It's no trouble, just give me the address,' he sang lightly. 'I promise I won't lose her, or feed her to the sea-lions or anything.' Josie wrote the address down for him and murmured a few words of direction.

'Right!' he exclaimed good-humouredly. 'Toodle-oo!' She followed him to the door and watched him climb into his car. He donned some designer sunglasses, started the ignition, and drove off at speed with the wheels screeching. As she watched him go, she muttered to herself, 'Oh God, what's he up to now?'

★ ★ ★

A long while later, when Deborah arrived home, her entrance caused a commotion. As she set down numerous packages, shopping bags, shoes, papers and folders, she shouted, 'Any calls for me?'

'No,' answered Josie, 'but René's here.'

'Yes, I saw his car outside.' A shadow crossed her brow. 'Where is His Majesty?' she asked, rolling her eyes.

'Upstairs, having a shower. He's been up and collected Caitlin from John's himself.'

'Oh?' she said, pulling a face before going to greet her daughter. As she kissed the top of Caitlin's head, heavy footsteps sounded on the stairs. 'Talk of the devil,' she muttered catching Christina's eye before retreating to the kitchen saying, 'I need a coffee, my throat's parched.' As she did so she brushed past René in the hall. 'So you're back then,' she said casually.

'Yes, delighted to see you too, my sweet,' he said.

'Hello, poppet, still here?' said René, ignoring Christina who was reading. 'What's that you're watching, mmm?' he asked, not looking at the screen at all, but gazing blankly round the room with a short-sighted stare.

'It's Blue Peter, Daddy!'

'Are we here for dinner, René? Mother wants to know,' shouted Deborah from the kitchen.

'Is that supposed to be an invitation?' he asked himself. 'Yes,' he replied, louder. 'I would like to stay for dinner, dear, thank you. I would have preferred to be asked nicely, but I suppose that's too much to expect. No one thinks to include me in anything it appears.'

'Was that an answer?' demanded Deborah, as her face came round the door. He didn't reply. She waited, raised her eyebrows at Christina and finally slammed out of the room again. Caitlin's eyelashes flickered.

307

'Tell Daddy what you've been doing at school today,' remarked René amicably.

'Numbers and Projects,' she announced.

'That's nice.' Clearing his throat, he looked across to the sideboard where the drinks were kept. His hand visibly shook, and a slight sweat stood on his brow as he stared in the direction of the drinks cabinet for several minutes. 'Mmmm,' he murmured to himself. And then he whispered something, causing Caitlin to glance round at Christina curiously. In response, Christina merely shrugged.

'My friend Sylvie's going to come and play with me after school,' volunteered Caitlin suddenly, still not taking her eyes from the television. 'Her daddy's going to be helping at our new café.'

René's eyeballs became enlarged. He tugged his glasses off of the top of his head and shoved them firmly in place. 'What's he going to be doing in your new café then, washing-up? Any more of your friends' daddies doing their bit?' he asked, muttering to himself.

'There's Peter,' volunteered Caitlin proudly. 'He's Chris's proper boyfriend now, isn't he Chris?'

'Proper boyfriend is he?' he emphasized.

'Shut-up, René,' hissed Christina, glaring at him.

'So it's going to open soon then, is it, your

little café?' he asked. 'Pretty little café,' he mumbled under his breath. 'Have a nice little tea party — nice little cakes.' Caitlin looked round at Christina with a frown and in return, Christina shook her head and gave her a reassuring smile. While he said this, René was staring at the drinks cabinet. Finally he stood up, and selecting a bottle poured himself a drink. Without noticing, he spilt some on the sideboard and went ambling across to the window spilling more as he went. There he stood for some time, glass in hand, with his back to them, and deep in thought.

'Daddy?' asked Caitlin. 'Will you play snakes with me?' But he didn't respond. Instead he seemed to be holding a conversation with the fly that was buzzing against the window-pane. After a few minutes, both Caitlin and Christina ignored him.

★ ★ ★

The night before the official opening of the New Sea Café the quietness of the cottage was shattered when the phone rang.

Teagan, jolted awake, grabbed the receiver. 'I'm about two miles off Godrevy Lighthouse!' came Connor's voice shouting above the noise of the engine. 'We can see a fire, Tig!' Forcing her eyes open she was straining to look at the clock. It was 3.10 a.m.

'It could be a bonfire on the beach, but I don't think so.' His voice kept breaking up. 'I'm too far out, but — it looks like the café's on fire! Call the fire brigade, quickly!' he shouted. 'And tell the others. I'll tell the coastguards and head straight back into harbour — be there as soon as I can! Be careful! You stay there and look after babby!'

The fear hit her like cold water. She dialled 999 and then phoned Peter. Shaun awoke in his cot and began to cry. Struggling into her clothes, she picked the baby up, longing to hear her brother's reassuring voice. When he finally answered, her message was punctuated by gasps of anxiety. 'The café's . . . the café's burning!' And she tried to explain what Connor had told her.

'Take a deep breath, sis,' said Peter. 'Don't worry! I'll drive straight down an' see what I can do. Can you phone Chris and tell the others? Tell them I'll see them down there.'

★ ★ ★

When the phone rang in the hall, it was an unfamiliar sound ringing in the dead of night. It took several rings to penetrate Christina's consciousness, forcing her awake. She heard her mother answer the phone and exclaim,

'Surely not!' But what she heard next caused her to jump out of bed and make her way down the stairs shouting:

'What's happened, Mum?'

'That was Teagan on the phone — the café's on fire!' Josie shouted. 'Connor spotted it from sea — he phoned her from offshore and he's on his way in.'

'No!' cried Christina. 'It can't be true!'

'The fire-brigade's on its way,' said Josie. 'I don't think René's home yet so tell Debbie what's happened and tell her to stay here with Caitlin. Teagan said she'd phoned Peter and he's already gone down there to see if he can help put it out. I'll go and start the car.' Within minutes they were on their way.

As they approached, a plume of smoke rose above the rooftops.

'I can't believe it!' cried Christina, flinging open the car door the moment they arrived. But the air was thick with smoke. Lights from the fire-engine flashed across the scene, throwing eerie shadows. She heard the searing smack of water as hoses skimmed onto the flames and the next minute a window exploded in a frenzy of glass, showering sparks like a Roman candle.

'All that work we did, just look at it!' cried Josie. 'We're ruined! All that money and time and effort we've all put in. What are we going to do? Oh, Chris! Just when I thought everything was going to be all right again.'

'Perhaps it's not as bad as it looks, Mum,' said Christina, trying to reassure her, but even as she said it, she felt she was having a horrible nightmare. One minute being safely asleep in bed, the next cast out into the cold night watching helplessly while everything they had lived for over the last few months destroyed itself before their eyes.

Josie began to look round. 'I wonder where Peter is,' she said. 'Didn't Teagan say he'd come down first?'

'He must be here somewhere,' said Christina. 'It's hard to see anything in this smoke.' She peered through the smoke at the people huddled to watch, but there was no sign of him. A thought suddenly occurred to her and she said, 'He wouldn't have gone inside, would he?'

'I don't know, it looks bad — I don't see how he could have.'

A fireman appeared, searching the faces of the crowd. 'Who's in charge here?' he asked. 'Are you the owners?'

'Yes, we are. How did it start?' asked Josie.

'Too early to tell, ma'am. There was no-one in there was there? It was all locked up for the night I suppose? Just checking.'

'It was locked, yes,' said Christina, 'but we

can't see our friend Peter. Someone said he came down to try and put it out — he would have got here first.'

'Not to worry, Miss,' the fireman replied. 'We'll go in now and check right through — just make sure no-one's in there.' The flames were being fanned by the breeze drifting from across the cove. Christina and Josie watched as, having broken the door down, two firemen entered wearing breathing apparatus. The minutes dragged by as they waited for them to reappear.

Charlie came and stood beside them craning his neck to try and see. 'Can you make out what's happenin' in there?' he asked. 'What's taking them so flippin' long?' Among the crowd were Quinn and Olga. Also, Maudie stood watching with Theo and several other familiar faces. They were all silent, their eyes fixed on the mouth of the fire. Connor arrived.

'Have you seen Teagan?' he asked and hearing that she hadn't been seen there he went off to look for her.

John appeared. 'I'm here, Christina,' he said simply, and she felt his strong arms come around her shoulders.

'What a thing to happen!' she said. 'We don't know where Peter is. I hope he's not in there!'

Suddenly there was a burst of activity and the firemen emerged shouting: 'Keep back! Keep back!' They were bearing a stretcher. The scale of the tragedy was only beginning to reveal itself.

'Please, please don't let that be him,' Christina cried. But as the procession came slowly towards them, light shone on the face of the man they had saved: it was him. Christina rushed forward crying: 'Peter! Oh no, why did you go in there?' she implored him.

'Stand back, Miss!' commanded a fireman. 'Sorry, love. Let's see to him, please. Come on lads, one . . . two . . . three . . . Up!' They heaved the stretcher into the ambulance and within seconds the doors were closed and it drove off with its siren blaring.

Christina collapsed. John called out to the fire crew, 'I think she's fainted!' Seconds later, she was laid gently on a blanket and they placed an oxygen mask over her face. Only semi-conscious, she stirred in his arms.

'John!' she protested. 'Let me get up, I must go to him!'

'Later, later,' he murmured.

When she had recovered a little and struggled to her feet, she went to speak to the fire crew.

'The man you brought out?' she asked.

'Will he be all right?'

'He's been taken to Truro, Miss. It's best you enquire there. We got him out as soon as we could. Seems he went in to try and put out the fire. A brave man!'

'I must go to him!' she insisted.

'No, wait, Christina! Give yourself more time!' John protested, but she pushed him away. 'No, I'm going. Leave me alone!'

'Then I'll take you. Come on, we'll go together.' At that moment Teagan rushed towards them out of the darkness.

'Where's my brother? Has anyone seen Peter?' She sounded desperate and it was John who had to explain where he was.

Josie was being comforted by Charlie. 'Anything I try to do to help our family,' she cried, 'is always spoilt!'

He put his arms around her. 'No Josie love, don't say that. You've always done your best.'

The hiss of water ceased, and the whole scene seemed darker once the flames were extinguished. All at once they were enveloped in a fog of steam and smoke. They held each other close, each with their own thoughts. Moonlight appeared on the horizon of the sea. The sky turned from black to silver to grey. The waves tinkled softly on the shingle and it grew colder.

17

In the intensive Care Burns Unit, Christina finally found herself alone at Peter's bedside. Olga and Quinn, his parents, had kept vigil for hours, huddled together wrapped in blankets like two forlorn refugees. Teagan was exhausted and had been coaxed away by Josie to buy a cup of tea. They had all been waiting while Peter was in theatre. Now, barely recognizable and covered with dressings and tubes, he lay motionless in the hospital bed surrounded by machines that were keeping him alive. The regular bleep of electronic instruments was all that accompanied his strenuous breathing.

'Peter?' whispered Christina, holding one of his big bandaged hands. Little of his face was showing. His eyes were puffy and blood-shot; the skin which wasn't covered by bandages was a mass of blisters and red raw patches. He opened his eyes and tried to speak.

'I . . . I can't talk,' he croaked and his cracked lips quivered. She had only a fleeting reminder of what his loving brown eyes used to be like and she choked back her tears.

'Don't try, Peter,' she said. 'I'm here. All you need to do is rest. I'll stay with you, I won't leave you.'

'Chris, listen . . . please! It's important . . . you must know. I saw René in there, I . . . ' His voice broke into a cruel hacking cough. 'You must tell someone . . . ' She moved closer, to hear what he was trying to say, but he gasped for breath.

'It doesn't matter!' she cried. 'Don't try to talk. Nothing matters, Peter, except for you to get better. Don't worry about anything. You've got to save your strength. I love you. I do love you so!' Unable to stop herself, her tears flowed freely.

'Listen to me!' Peter hissed impatiently, almost attempting to sit up. 'It was René, I tell you!' he said. 'Chris, listen! You must understand. René torched the café! I caught him in there — I tried to stop him! We fought . . . but I couldn't . . . ' Peter's strength failed him. Immediately a nurse appeared, checking the monitors, and shaking her head at Christina.

'Don't tire him,' she advised. 'Please, dear, give him some rest for now,' she said, beckoning her to come away.

Christina followed her into the corridor and there the nurse took something from her pocket and whispered:

'Can I give you this? We had a job removing it I'm afraid, it was burnt into his hand.' She passed it to Christina adding, 'I thought it was probably yours, my dear.'

'Thank you,' she replied. Taking it, she went and sat down on a nearby row of seats. There, she found herself looking at René's gold bracelet in her hand.

★ ★ ★

When Josie and Charlie left to take Teagan home, and Olga and Quinn had also left, promising to return in the morning, Christina sat alone in the corridor. John came and sat down beside her. He put his arm around her and she rested her head on his shoulder. But suddenly a cacophony of alarms brought doctors and nurses hurrying. Christina fled back to Peter's bedside, but she couldn't get near him. The medical staff were working frantically. She could only stand helplessly and watch. John was beside her, but when they looked at each other neither of them could speak.

The urgent voices receded, the bleeping of the machines faded and Christina stood watching Peter's life ebb away. All the vibrant times they had shared were dissolving away like a sand-castle slipping into the waves. As she watched, he became still and perfectly pale, like the pure sand on the beach at Crystal Barr. She gazed at him for the last time, and when a nurse whispered a word in her ear, she stepped forward as though in a dream, kissed his kind rugged face and held his dying hand. The tide turns, she seemed to hear the wind sigh, the waves come and wash everything away and nothing matters any more, nothing matters. The next minute she was falling — falling from a great height. But this time John was there to catch her.

★ ★ ★

It was early morning, just beginning to get light. Christina found herself in her bed fully clothed. How did she get home? How could she still be alive? She detested feeling her own breath, wondered how her chest could keep rising and taking in air. She pulled the sheet up over her face and lay with her eyes open, her eyelashes brushing the rough cotton surface. How she longed for some comfort; she recalled the musty scent and warmth of her dog Ginger — he would have been such a comfort now.

'I don't want to feel. Don't let me feel!' she whimpered quietly. 'I don't want to think about anything.' Tears overwhelmed her.

Stifling her cries she turned over and buried her face in the pillow. But on doing this, she became aware of the curious, pungent smell of smoke. It permeated her breathing space and brought before her a vision of the café burning. She could taste the smoke and her tongue felt like a dry cloth. She began to choke, throwing back the covers and gasping for breath.

Birds began to sing outside her window and it grew sunny in her bedroom. How could life go on? She tried to make herself believe everything was normal. She told herself the café was still there. It was freshly painted, with new tables and chairs and flowers on the tables and they were ready to open up. The tide would be out, leaving the beach glistening where sand gives way to pebbles, where shells collect on that sandbank ridged and scattered with debris thrown up by the sea. It was easier to think of familiar things: the litter on the beach, a plastic bottle, a child's broken spade, a piece of fishing net. The gulls would be there, chattering on the roof, squabbling over morsels of fish.

Christina got up from her bed and flung open the sash window. She could join the gulls now, she thought, she could leap from the windowsill and fly away to skim the surface of the silver sea and cry their poignant, melancholy cry: '*It's too late! It's too late!*'

The morning air was cold. It swept into her room with restless hungry fingers, scattering papers and sending the curtain blowing. It knocked the bedside lamp over and it went crashing to the floor. Closing the window, she sat on the edge of her bed, put her head in her hands and cried. What would she do without Peter? Their love had only just begun and it was now stolen away. Peter! How she longed for him now! How desperately she loved him and yearned for his physical closeness, for his laughter and kindness. How could he be gone?

Suddenly the reality of Peter's dying words shot back into Christina's mind. 'René torched the café!' Had he really said that? Everything was so confused. She couldn't think. She pictured the hospital ward and all the machines and tubes and saw the nurse coming towards her. It was only then she remembered; she felt in the pocket of her jeans, brought out René's gold bracelet and read the inscription on it in absolute terror.

★   ★   ★

She left her bedroom, went downstairs and slipping out of the front-door, walked through the streets. Once they were so familiar, but now everywhere seemed hostile and strange. These were the streets she had walked hand in hand with Peter, streets she had known and loved since she was a small child. There wasn't a soul about. Shops and houses were closed and still sleeping. The chill morning gave a hollow ring to the cobbles now. The plaintive call of herring-gulls, mewing softly, offered no consolation besides their watchful presence as they circled mournfully and witnessed her walk. The air retained a tang of smoke from the café fire. It took her back to the days when she used to walk down to the harbour on the morning after Guy Fawkes' Night with her father. He would hold her hand so tightly, whistling quietly to himself.

It's funny how the body keeps going even in the face of tragedy, she thought, realizing with a twinge of guilt that she was hungry. But she walked on, finding comfort in places of familiarity; there was one last thing she could do for Peter. And this she must do no matter what. The police station loomed in front of her with such formality that she instantly felt self-conscious. It was as if the building could see right through her, and peer into her pockets. Mounting the steps, René's voice came back to her from all that time ago when he had been burning papers in the backyard. 'What's the verdict, Sister-in-law, guilty as charged, mmm?' Steeling herself, she opened the door and went inside. The police officer at the desk looked up in surprise.

'Morning Miss, you're an early bird!'

'I've come to make a statement,' she said. 'The fire last night — I know who did it and I can prove it.'

★   ★   ★

An hour later, having left the police station and all their questions behind, Christina was again down by the harbour. She stood watching the fishing boats landing their catch and the men's activity and banter helped her forget. It would be better, she felt, if she were a seagull, then she could just fly off screaming. Was that all Peter's life amounted to? Here and alive and laughing one minute — and the next stone-cold and dead. What was the point of it all, if it was to end like this? All that warmth and energy! All that loveable clumsiness! All that restlessness and passion! What love he gave her! Such love! She remembered him as the boy she'd known at school, a tough, strong boy, funny and clever. She remembered him as the brother Teagan loved and fretted over, and as the man who married Nicola and fathered two little boys; the man who Nicola no longer wanted. If Nicola hadn't thrown him out, he wouldn't have been in Cornwall at all and if she hadn't met him, and fallen in love with him. If she hadn't encouraged him to become involved in the café, he would still be alive.

She turned away from the working fishermen, desperate and blinded by tears. The tragic injustice of it all was enough to make her feel like throwing herself off the harbour wall. At that moment, one of the men recognized her and waved. He took off his cap and waved again, unable to see the ghosts standing around her it seemed. She wasn't Christina Tobermory any longer — she wanted to tell him — she was only a shadow left over from someone's dream. Ignoring his greeting, she walked on.

It was after nine in the morning when she returned home. The house was quiet. Before going to her room, she knocked on her mother's door, but receiving no response she opened it to find her sitting by the window. She looked paper-thin, like a husk of wheat in the dim light.

'Mum?' She touched her mother's hands; they were ice-cold. 'Does Debbie know?'

'Yes, I told her when I came in.'

'Is René here? Has she told him what

happened to Peter?'

'I doubt it,' replied Josie, sniffing and reaching for a tissue. 'He's still snoring like a pig, can't you hear him? Debbie's been in with Caitlin all night.'

'Mum, listen!' She drew herself closer to whisper, 'There's something I've got to tell you.'

'Yes, Chris, it's all right, you needn't explain — I understand about you and Peter. I saw you together. You loved each other very much, didn't you?' As Josie spoke she didn't look at her, but stared straight ahead.

'Yes, Mum, much more than I ever knew.' She choked back new tears. 'Mum, listen, look at me! About the fire: I know how the fire started.'

Josie turned her face. She was like a ghost herself. 'You left something switched on, you mean? You mustn't worry about that now, Chris, we all make mistakes.' She patted her daughter's arm. It was the gesture of a frail old lady; all the fight had gone out of her.

'No, Mum, listen! Peter told me something, in the hospital just before he died. He went in to try and put out the fire. He met René in there and he tried to stop him! He fought with him. Mum? He told me René torched the café!'

Josie sprang from her chair crying, 'Don't

be ridiculous! René's a bit mean, but he wouldn't have done that, Chris! You shouldn't even hint at an accusation like that! How could you?'

'Ssshh!' Christina grabbed her mother, imploring her to be quiet. 'Ssh! Sit down, be careful! He'll hear you! Please, Mum, just listen to what I've got to say.'

Josie sat down again, staring at her in horror. Christina continued in a whisper, her voice so quiet now that Josie had to lean forward to hear. 'One of the nurses told me Peter was holding something when he was admitted. Mum, it was burnt into his hand; they had a job to remove it. The nurse assumed it must be mine and she gave it to me.'

'What? Gave what to you? What are you talking about?'

'René's bracelet! He must have lost it in the fight!'

Hearing this, her mother sank back into her chair. Christina put an arm round her shoulders and waited. Her burden was lifting slightly. She could feel it and she sighed. The silence was tangible.

'What are we going to do?' she asked. 'If that's true, what on earth are we going to do, Chris?'

'There's nothing more we can do, Mum,'

she replied. 'I've just come from the police station. I handed René's bracelet in and made a statement. The rest is up to them. The police will come for him soon,' she said. 'Do you feel up to brewing us some tea?'

Josie straightened up. 'Yes, let's go downstairs together and I'll put the kettle on.'

★ ★ ★

In the kitchen twenty minutes later, they were both drinking tea when Deborah, having just got up, flounced into the kitchen. She eyed them both uncertainly. Her T-shirt hung off one shoulder and her eyes bore the shadows of mascara from the night before.

'Sorry to hear about . . . you know.' She bit her lip. 'Wasn't there anything they could do for him?'

Christina shook her head and looked away. 'I'll be better talking about it a bit later, Debs.'

'Are you all right, Mother?' she asked.

'I'm OK. Make us some more tea, will you love?' she asked. 'Suppose you haven't told René about it yet?'

'No, he's still asleep. I don't know where he was half the night. I heard him turn up in the early hours falling about like a drunken idiot.' At that moment a thumping was heard upstairs. 'Oh, sounds as though he's up and about.' They soon realized René was making his way downstairs. Josie caught Christina's eye.

'Do you feel like going back to bed, Chris?' she asked.

'No, I want to go and see how Teagan's managing — see if there's anything I can do.' Her voice broke and she made an effort to steady herself. 'There's the baby you see and she might not — ' She stopped speaking abruptly as the door opened.

'Well, what a cosy little gathering,' said René as he ambled into the kitchen. He was half-dressed, and, to their surprise, he had a purplish black eye.

They all stared at him in amazement, but only Deborah dared mention it: 'That's a shiner you've got there! What've you been doing to yourself for goodness sake?'

'Oh, that!' René shrugged. 'Yes, I walked into the wardrobe last night. Not pretty, is it. That'll teach me to drink too much, won't it, silly old fool.'

'You haven't heard the news, I suppose?' ventured Deborah. 'Being knocked out in a drunken stupor as usual.'

'What news would that be, dearest? he asked. 'Something devastating happened to the economy while I've been asleep?'

Deborah looked up to the heavens and caught her mother's eye.

'Surely you heard all the commotion during the night?' Josie asked.

'What commotion? If I was here, I guess I was . . . how shall I put it? A bit the worse for wear?'

'René! I don't care what state you were in,' said Josie. 'You might be interested to know the café caught fire last night!'

He gave an uncomprehending blink. 'Pardon?' he said, 'Are you sure?'

'That's right, pretend you didn't hear a thing!' exclaimed Deborah. 'The house could burn down around your ears and you'd still be snoring your head off, you lazy pig!'

'That's probably true, dearest, but you could express yourself more eloquently,' he replied, giving a sour chuckle. 'Was it bad then?' he enquired, staring at Josie. She looked at him, but didn't reply.

'Peter was rescued from the fire and rushed to hospital — but he didn't make it,' said Christina.

René looked at her steadily. 'You shouldn't make jokes like that, Sister-in-law, you might turn round and find out they're true.'

'It is true,' she said. 'Although, I can't believe it.'

'Oh, I do apologize.' His face looked

genuinely downcast for a moment. 'That's very unfortunate. I've always had respect for the dead, you know me.' He sat down heavily, and taking a handkerchief from his trouser pocket, began mopping his brow. 'Well, that is a shock. What was he doing in there anyway? Saving a damsel in distress?'

No-one answered. He gaped around, his eyes finally coming to rest on Josie. 'What happened to the man then, Mother-in-law? Out with it!'

'He went in to try and put out the fire,' said Josie as calmly as she could. 'It was a heart attack that killed him, so the doctors said — the effects of burns and trauma.'

'Oh, well that is sad; I am sorry.' He seemed at a genuine loss for words and stared at the floor, but after a few moments he stood up and opened the fridge. 'Any yoghurt left?' he said.

Josie quickly slammed the fridge door, almost catching his hand. 'Can't you show a bit of respect?'

'I said I'm sorry. But it was an accident waiting to happen, frankly; the place was rotten, as dry as a tinder box. Now, I know we've all had some bad news but we still need to eat and I for one intend to have some breakfast.' Again he went to open the fridge, took out a carton of yoghurt, removed the lid, and fetched a spoon.

'Where's your bracelet, René?' asked Christina suddenly.

'Upstairs, why? What's my bracelet got to do with anything?' he asked, spooning the creamy contents of the carton into his mouth.

'I want to see it, that's all.'

René stared at her for a moment. 'Debs, you'd better see to your sister, it must be the shock or something.' Taking two slices of bread he rammed them into the toaster, turned and saw she was still staring at him. 'Why do you want to see my bracelet all of a sudden? Go for a walk or something, girl, get some fresh air to your head.'

'It's not up there is it?' she said.

He stopped eating. 'This obsession of yours is starting to get on my nerves.'

'Someone found it last night in the café. They gave it to me.'

'Don't be so idiotic! I haven't even been up there for months,' he retorted. 'If this is some kind of sick joke, Sister-in-law, it's in very bad taste, if I might say so. If you've got it, hand it over and stop wasting my time.'

'Hang on, René,' said Josie. 'Calm down a bit. Chris has had more than enough upset already and she's been up all night. It's only a piece of jewellery!'

'Tell her to give it back then,' he said, 'and

stop being so childish.'

The front-door bell sounded.

'Hadn't you better answer that?' said René. 'It'll be your little man with the white van I presume.'

As soon as Josie was out of the room, he grabbed Christina round the throat and thrust her against the wall. 'I'm warning you,' he said, his ugly face almost touching hers. 'Always acting so bloody high and mighty. Give me my bracelet now before I — '

'Before you what, René?' she asked. She wasn't afraid of him any longer. 'I haven't got it actually,' she said. 'I handed it into the police station this morning, when I made my statement.'

'Christina!' he hissed. 'What have you done?'

It was then, when he called her by name, she knew she had beaten him. He broke away from her and in his haste, almost knocked Josie over as she came back into the room. But in the hall he walked straight into two police officers. Before he had even finished eating his breakfast, René was sitting in a police car, staring in disbelief at a pair of handcuffs on his wrists. They weren't the bracelets he was used to.

18

In the six weeks following the final court hearing, Christina often sought refuge at John Madison's cottage. For months after Peter's funeral, once the police enquiry into the fire had led to René being charged and held in custody, they had all been called as witnesses. The case was heard at Truro County Court; it was only a few streets away from where they had all attended the solicitor's office and signed the contracts.

Having stood trial for arson and manslaughter, René was found 'Not Guilty' and released as a free man. Christina had agreed with the verdict. René's description of the events leading up to the fire had been so typical of his usual behaviour she had had little difficulty in believing his explanation. Endless questions also lead to the insurance claim being settled in their favour. True to character, Josie had kept the premiums paid up-to-date and, therefore, all the syndicate's investments in the café were secure. Charlie had given up his job in Plymouth and was throwing himself into starting again.

Christina was sitting out in John's garden

this chill autumn afternoon, watching him repair a fence. The girls were playing indoors. As she watched the birds feeding, her thoughts went back to the previous day when she had been to visit René.

René was being nursed in a rehabilitation centre in London, undergoing treatment for alcoholism. Yesterday he had seemed depressed — she reflected — not a fragment of his old self-assurance remained. She had found him sitting in the conservatory of the nursing-home wrapped in a blanket. There was no sign that he bore her any grudge. He appeared to accept it all philosophically, and she — in her loyalty to Peter — knew she couldn't have acted in any other way.

'*So what actually happened then?*' *she asked him.*

'*Thought I'd go down and take a look around — never got an invitation, no one thought to ask me I suppose. I'd had a tankful as usual,*' *he said. His voice was slightly slurred.* '*Drink — that's been my downfall, Sister-in-law. Debs will tell you that. I felt a bit woozy — thought I'd make myself a coffee, blundered about in the dark for a bit, couldn't find the bloody light switches, couldn't find the damn coffee filters. I sat down and lit a cigarette. Next thing I knew I woke up — couldn't breathe! I went down on my hands and knees,* crawling around the floor like a bloody dog. Then that idiot Peter came out of nowhere and got me by the throat — yelling at me, he was, like a maniac. Somehow I got away from him, got to the car. Didn't know he never came out after me. Couldn't see anything with all the smoke anyway . . . '

A lump came in Christina's throat. It was all so pathetically logical. 'I must go now,' she said. 'I'll ask Debs if she'll come with me next time. When you're better she might bring Caitlin to see you too.'

'No, don't bother,' he replied, sounding tired. 'Who cares about me anyway? Not my wife, not my daughter, nor Josie or the others. No-one gives a damn, Christina, believe me.'

'I do, René,' she said.

She meant it. She did care about him in a funny sort of way.

★   ★   ★

'Penny for your thoughts?' said John as he came and sat down beside her.

'Oh, I was just thinking about poor old René,' she replied. 'He told me once that I was lucky, at least I didn't have to hide my injured leg. He said that he was crippled too — hurting on the inside where no-one could see it. I felt sorry for him then, and I still do in a way.'

'You're a softie,' said John, smiling. 'If anyone can feel sorry for René after all he's done, well!'

'That's just it — he hasn't done anything. He's his own worst enemy that's all,' she replied.

'Are you OK here? I'll just go and make the girls a snack,' he said. 'I'll be back in a minute. Shall I bring you a glass of cider?'

'Lovely,' she replied, and watched him disappear into the cottage. And, as she turned back to gaze at the garden created in Kate's memory, she gradually became aware of a sense of her own destiny. There were bridges to be built, wounds to be healed, and sins to be forgiven. All these things mend themselves in time — just as the tide surges to cover sand scarred by spades and children's sandcastles. Doesn't the sea also wash over the imperfections of our lives? Doesn't it bathe away the jagged lines and furrows, and leave the sand as smooth and pure as it once was?

In her mind's eye, she was walking along the beach at Crystal Barr again. Far out at sea, a gannet hovered in mid-air. Then it made a sweeping dive, cutting into the surface of the ocean like a sword. Ghosts of the past flew over her head. She could hear the crying of the gulls and a splash as the gannet broke the surface with a fresh herring in its beak. It was like the days of the old Sea Café, when the ships of history passed by, leaving snatches of people's lives scattered on the beach. Some were collected by beach-combers and cherished, others discarded and forgotten. Those fragments of memory she knew would be washed up again, as the sea follows its rhythm and the tide turns. They would be picked up by people who might stop by the Sea Café for some cake and a cup of tea on their way home. The pain of those lonely days was long gone now, washed away like footprints in the sand. Peter was a part of that rugged landscape and he would always be a part of her. Yet she could feel a process of healing taking place in all their lives. The Sea Café would re-open again one day. There had been closure on the old wounds between her mother and father. And René? She would visit him again soon. She had no desire for retribution. There would be no more ghosts.

John reappeared carrying two glasses. 'So, what are you looking so serious about this afternoon?' he asked.

'We ought to start planning for the future soon,' she replied. 'My dad's coming down next week. He said now the legal side's over he's going to get some friends to help start clearing up the café, plastering and re-decorating again.'

'For ever the optimist isn't he, your dad.'

'He wasn't always,' she replied, studying his face for a moment. 'You know, life's not easy, but you just have to keep going. You've always had courage, John. You didn't give up when Kate died and Sylvie was crying for her feed — you just kept going, didn't you?'

He sat up and looked her straight in the eye. 'I had to, yes. I've worried about Sylvie's future ever since. Remember the time I asked you to become her legal guardian in case anything happened to me? I fought with myself for days before I could find the courage to ask you that.'

She blushed; she wasn't prepared to admit how clearly she could recall that evening too and how often she had thought of it. 'Am I really that frightening?' she asked and smiled because he looked so earnest.

'It's just that when Peter . . . ' He stopped and then seemed to decide what he had to say was more important than the nervousness which hampered him. 'When you and Peter got together, I was — how shall I put it? Devastated, I suppose. My thoughts, they were only dreams really, but my long term plans were for you and me to be . . . '

'It's OK — I understand what you're trying

338

to say. I think I always knew. There's no need to say it, honestly.' She reached out and took hold of his hand. 'John, it's just that — it'll take me a while to get over Peter. He was so full of life! Sometimes he reminded me of a bear, like a big shaggy dog full of bouncing energy and affection!' Saying this, a sense of Peter's presence bounded up to her as she described him so vividly and her words caught in her throat. She squeezed John's hand tightly.

'It's hard for me to explain, John. Sorry!' Tears flooded into her eyes.

'I could never even pretend to replace Peter,' he said. 'I wish I could. I wish I could impress you with wild gestures and love you how he used to, but Chris!' He reached forward and took her in his arms. 'I'd like to think that at the end of the day, when you're tired and all you want to do is go home, you'd be happy to come home here to me. I know I'm quiet and boring and I don't hope for much out of life, but — '

'John Madison! You're not such a quiet boring old thing as you make out!' she cried. 'You're sensitive and thoughtful, and I love the way you always worry about everything, honestly! It shows you care!'

At that moment Sylvie and Caitlin came running into the garden and the spell was broken. But as they chattered away to them about what they had been doing, her thoughts drifted back to what John had been trying to say. He needed her, she understood that now, and perhaps she had known it for some time.

When the girls ran off indoors, John put his arm around her shoulders and looked at her in earnest. 'I love you,' he said. 'I just love you so much! I want to look after you, but I want you to look after me too, and Sylvie. You'll need time, I understand that and I know I'll have to wait but . . . Christina, will you marry me one day?' He looked so serious, and his eyes so piercingly blue, all thoughts and regrets about the past, about Peter and René and the café drifted away as carefree as a seagull on the wing.

'I'd love to,' she whispered. 'Time's flying already; I can feel the tide turning.'

John smiled and kissed her. 'How do you know that?' he asked. 'We're not on the beach now.'

'I thought a fisherman knew about these things,' she said, and before he could reply she closed her eyes and kissed him gently on the lips. They sat together in perfect peace, their arms entwined, the girls playing in the background, and the sparrows pecking seeds on the path.

We do hope that you have enjoyed reading this large print book.

Did you know that all of our titles are available for purchase?

We publish a wide range of high quality large print books including:
Romances, Mysteries, Classics
General Fiction
Non Fiction and Westerns

Special interest titles available in large print are:
The Little Oxford Dictionary
Music Book
Song Book
Hymn Book
Service Book

Also available from us courtesy of Oxford University Press:
Young Readers' Dictionary
(large print edition)
Young Readers' Thesaurus
(large print edition)

For further information or a free brochure, please contact us at:
Ulverscroft Large Print Books Ltd.,
The Green, Bradgate Road, Anstey,
Leicester, LE7 7FU, England.
Tel: (00 44) 0116 236 4325
Fax: (00 44) 0116 234 0205

Other titles published by
The House of Ulverscroft:

SHADOWS OF CONFLICT

Jennifer Bohnet

When Katie accepts an offer to take over a shop in Dartmouth, A Good Yarn, she expects her life to be busy and unexciting. But with an American film crew in town intent on uncovering buried secrets from World War II, and a disgruntled relative amongst other problems, life is neither simple nor quiet. When Patrick, her ex-boss, offers Katie the chance of her dream media job, she must decide whether it is worth turning her back on everything and everyone in Dartmouth — including Leo, a friend from the past who plans to be a part of her future. Will Katie make the right decision?

EVERY SEVENTH WAVE

Daniel Glattauer

Emmi and Leo met, fell in love and broke up via e-mail. After nearly a year of silence, they find themselves in contact once more. Yet Emmi is still married to Bernhard, and Leo is just back from Boston with Pamela, his American girl-friend. As the e-mails grow increasingly passionate, Emmi and Leo are faced with a difficult decision: could their romance survive the transition from digital to actual, or is it the distance that is keeping them together?

Swansea Libraries

#		#		#		#	
1		25		49		73	
2		26	8/18	50	8/19	74	
3		27		51		75	
4		28	1/18	52		76	
5		29		53	7/23	77	
6		30		54		78	
7		31		55		79	
8		32		56		80	
9		33		57		81	
10		34		58		82	
11		35		59		83	
12		36		60		84	
13	3/19	37		61		85	
14		38		62	2/20	86	
15		39		63		87	
16		40		64	8/17	88	
17		41		65		89	
18		42		66		90	
19		43		67		91	
20		44		68		92	
21	1/29	45		69		Community Services	
22		46		70			
23		47		71			
24		48		72			

ART

in an
e US
:oots,
ancé,
ord, a
espite
to be
flies
it her
mess.
the
ently,
that
been